P9-EAJ-672

STILL LIFE

LAS VEGAS

STILL LIFE

LAS VEGAS

JAMES SIE

ILLUSTRATED BY
SUNGYOON CHOI

ST. MARTIN'S PRESS ≋ NEW YORK

This is a work of fiction. All of the characters, organizations, and events portrayed in this novel are either products of the author's imagination or are used fictitiously.

www.stmartins.com

Lyrics to "Never Say Goodbye, Say Ciao" by Liberace. Copyright by Liberace Foundation for the Creative & Performing Arts, www.liberace.org.

Designed by Anna Gorovoy

The Library of Congress Cataloging-in-Publication Data is available upon request.

ISBN 978-1-250-05566-8 (hardcover)
ISBN 978-1-4668-5926-5 (e-book)

St. Martin's Press books may be purchased for educational, business, or promotional use. For information on bulk purchases, please contact the Macmillan Corporate and Premium Sales Department at 1-800-221-7945, extension 5442, or write to specialmarkets@ macmillan.com.

First Edition: August 2015

10 9 8 7 6 5 4 3 2 1

TO MY PARENTS,
WITH GRATITUDE

AND TO DOUG AND BEN,
WHENCE ALL BLESSINGS,
AND DISTRACTIONS, FLOW

PREFACE

It always starts with a blue Volvo, driving away.

No, that's not right. It starts with graphite poised above a clean white page. Or fingers crouched over a keyboard. And then, a memory. One that often involves a blue Volvo, driving away.

The memories are not always mine. They come from varied sources, but over time, I've claimed them as my own. I have so many of these beginnings: bits and pieces of the past transcribed over the years, squirreled away in un-lined notebooks, virtual folders, and, of course, lining the twisted corridors of my most unreliable brain.

Time to lay them out, end to end, and see what manner of creature is being conjured to life.

About the Volvo. Did she hesitate behind the wheel—key in the ignition, hand on the key, ready to turn over the engine—Lock-Acc-On-Start—and split her life from the early-morning quiet of the known world into the inevi-table roar that followed?

I don't know. Yet. But I've got a new cup of quarters by my side, as they say, and I'm ready to start feeding.

Away to Las Vegas we go.

PART 1

EMILY

WISCONSIN

EARLIER

She drove the blue Volvo station wagon away from Vee's house with a sober determination, like it was a lame horse she was leading out of the barn. She was going to drive both the car and herself over the nearest cliff, or, rather, it being Wisconsin, the nearest steep embankment. But sailing south along I-94, in the early morning before rush hour, she found she couldn't let go of the Volvo and she couldn't let go of the road, and the highway racing before her seemed to offer a faster route to oblivion than sailing off into some moderately inclined culvert. All might still be lost, in time. There were other opportunities up ahead to smash into and through some guardrail on her journey. Colorado, now there were some cliffs worth driving over.

But she needed speed, more speed, and the ballast in the car was too heavy to let her fly down the highway, no matter what the speedometer was registering. So she twisted her upper body like a contortionist and managed to snake her right arm around and under the baby car seat behind her in order to unshackle it from the upholstery, and with a desperate, sudden yank which would cause her a good deal of shoulder pain later that night, she managed to hoist the seat over the gear shift and partly into her lap. Moments later it was pushed clumsily (understandable at ninety-five miles an hour) out the passenger-side window. It bounced twice along the highway like a skipping stone before skidding to rest on the side of the road.

Three minutes later the second car seat, toddler-size, followed.

(The two abandoned car seats were accounted for later that day; the second one landed in the middle of a lane, causing the rush-hour traffic delay that Owen heard on the clock radio as he was trying to will himself awake; the other was discovered and identified by Vee in her car, just outside Racine. Neither was saved.)

And for a time after, Emily did feel lighter, her mind clear, even excited, and her breathing deepened for the first time in almost five weeks. This continued until just past Madison. Approaching the slowdown that was inbound Chicago traffic, she began noticing through her rearview mirror the imprints of the car seats in the upholstery. Also, a small teething ring, a scattering of Cheerios, and a grimy diaper rag.

The backseat, the entire backseat, was gone by the time she hit Iowa.

WALTER

VIVA LAS VEGAS!

LATER

Those who do not learn from history are doomed to repeat it. That's what they say, but I'm not so sure. I've learned my history, and I go on repeating it. I repeat it, on average, eight times a day, five days a week. Time off for lunch.

It's not my own history. I'm a minion of Viva Las Vegas!—the historical-museum-slash-tourist-trap now in its twelfth shabby year on Fremont Street. I made the mistake of finishing my high school course-work a full seven months before the end of the year; I was in such a hurry to eject myself from that particular hell that I forgot there was nowhere for me to go once I got out. So now I'm waiting out my time before graduation here in my own little neon Purgatory. Not Hell, but close. Hell with a waxwork Elvis Presley.

Viva Las Vegas! is also Purgatory for most of the people who throw down their ten bucks to the King and enter, a good place to do penance until the hangover clears and they're ready for the slots. It's dark, quiet by Vegas standards. I think that's why this place has hung on as long as it has: it's hopelessly outdated, so lacking in any kind of glamour or excitement or even decent lighting that it feels innocent. It's so tacky it's virginal.

I've got the first shift of the day, and I'm late. The red digital readout in the lobby has been displaying TOUR IN 1 MINUTE! for about ten. I throw on my dreaded red vest, a striped polyester number that flaps around my skinny body like wings. There also used to be these tiny striped straw hats we had to wear that made me look like a giant anorexic Disney penguin, but luckily the tops of those have, mysteriously and simultaneously, all been punched out.

Yrma behind the ticket desk has corralled the first group. She sighs heavily when she sees me coming through the curtains and shifts her weight to the other side of the desk, where she can punch a button that changes the readout above her. The slack-jawed Yrma (pronounced EAR-ma) has the coloring and consistency of burnt caramel pudding, and she moves at the pace a burnt caramel pudding might move, were it mobile. The digital readout changes from TOUR IN 1 MINUTE! to TOUR STARTING NOW!!!—the red words blinking urgently, doing their best to justify the two additional exclamation points.

Usual crowd. Three seniors, a mom with a stroller looking to beat the heat, five Korean tourists, and a teenage couple—locals who, thank the gods, I don't recognize from school. They're wearing faded T's and torn jeans, and their arms hang limply over each other like they've both just been saved from drowning. The guy smirks at me. His eyes are dark and hard. The girl just pouts and nuzzles into Smirky Boy's collarbone.

I take my position by the turnstile. "Ladies and gentlemen, welcome to Viva Las Vegas. Right this way." We're supposed to draw out the "Vee" part of "Viva" so that it builds an excitement—"Veeeeva Las Vegas!"— and punctuate that with a big sweep of the arm up into the air. I can't bring myself to do it. None of the tour guides can, except for Kenny, who's new and operates at three exclamation points at all times. His rousing tours are known to cause fainting, mass suicides, and bleeding from the eyes. He'll be assistant manager in no time.

"Watch your step, please." The guests file past me into the first room, led by the three seniors, who are from Texas, I'm guessing. Their matching pastel I LOVE TEXAS T-shirts kind of give it away. The five Koreans turn out to be two couples together and one Asian woman by herself, who's got the kind of hair that's constantly flapping over the front of her face, and dark glasses. She stares down at the floor and looks away from me as she pushes through the metal bar. Could be thirty, could be sixty. Could be the right age. Could be . . . I get that old, reflexive urge to stare her down, catalog her face, but I brush it away. Childish habit, like biting your nails or wetting the bed.

"Nice vest," Smirky Boy cracks as he saunters through. Whatever. I'm not the one wasting twenty bucks. Just wait. He who smirks last, and all.

Once they've clicked past the turnstile it's the point of no return. Anyone who has bought a ticket because of Elvis beckoning in the window or the sound track of him singing "Viva Las Vegas" in the lobby is going to be sadly disappointed. Elvis is not part of this tour. Elvis would rather have puked up fried peanut-butter-and-banana sandwiches than be part of this sad, sad pilgrimage.

I'm part shepherd, part guide, leading my sheep to each display and making sure no one strays from the path. The first diorama starts us off in 1829. A mannequin with dark hair and a conquistador helmet stands, one hand resting on a plastic palm tree, the other shielding his eyes from the baby spotlight shining directly on his face. There's a dusty rubber snake hissing at his feet. Sand all around. Here I go. "On Christmas Day 1829, Rafael Rivera set foot on an oasis in what would be known as the Las Vegas Valley. He was a part of a party led by Antonio Armijo, looking for their way to Los Angeles. 'Las Vegas' means 'the Meadow' in Spanish. . . ."

Rafael's supposed to be scanning the horizon of this brave new world. This is the extent of his movement: his head turns thirty degrees to the left. His head turns thirty degrees to the right. His hand doesn't even move with his forehead, it just stays frozen in a permanent salute position.

But the sheep are still into him. Lots of murmuring, lots of "oh!"s and head nods. Cameras click away at Rafael, at the sand and the tree. Everyone's carried away by the emptiness because of the promise it holds. They can't wait to see the magic that turns all this sand into casinos. Everyone except for the teenagers, who hang in the shadows and snicker

to each other, and the Asian woman with the sunglasses, who's not looking at Rafael, either. What's she here for?

Next room: Mormonville. "In 1855, Mormons began settling in the
area to protect the mail route from Salt Lake City to Los Angeles. The
fort you see in front of you is a replica of one made by the Mormons out
of clay-and-grass bricks known as adobe. . . ." Mormonville gets a few dull
head nods. The Railroad Town display gets less. The sheep are getting
tired of all this dirt and dust. Where's the vice? they wonder. Mormon
life is not what you'd call electrifying. Or maybe it's my presentation. I'll
bet Kenny whips them into a frenzy. Adobe forts!!! Lead mining!!!

Still no questions, except one. As we pass out of 1905 into the next
room, one of the women in the Korean foursome hurries up to me. "Excuse
me," she whispers, already smiling in apology, "ehm, would you mind,
to tell me please, are you, ehm, Filipino? Japanese?"

This is not an uncommon question. Asians can't figure me out, and
it drives them nuts. I'm like Asian, but stretched tall. Long body, small
features. Curly dark hair. Like one of those long-necked aliens, with a
wig. I get Mongolian a lot, or Siberian; once I got albino Samoan. That
was creative. Sometimes, if they're rude, I'll tell them I'm Swedish, just
to watch their heads explode.

"Vietnamese," I tell her, because she's decent. "Half Vietnamese."

"Thank you!" the woman gasps, like I've handed her a present. She
scurries back to the group and sets off a flurry of Korean whispers. They
can't believe it. Vietnamese? Impossible! What must the other half be?
Giraffe? I'm worth the price of admission, right there.

And what about her, the one with the sunglasses? Is she wondering,
too? But when I glance back she's already passing me on her way to the
next room. She's small. Her hair's got some gray in it, I think. Hard to
tell in this light. She'd be the right age. She could be Vietnamese, too.
She could be. I shake my head, but the words "she could be" play over and
over again like a stupid nursery rhyme you can't get erased from your
mind.

A life-size animatronic Bugsy Siegel welcomes the sheep to the
MegaResort room, which gets a big reaction. Cameras start clicking

again. It's a miniature replica of the Strip right before the end of the millennium, waist high and encased in Plexiglas you can walk around. All the old monuments are there: the Eiffel Tower, the canals, the Pyramid, and the Empire State Building. The resort names roll off my tongue like gold coins: *Luxor. Bellagio. Monte Carlo.*

"And please check out our Wall of Fame, featuring some of Las Vegas's best and brightest entertainers." I've never heard of most of them. They all smile with their mouths open too wide, like they're waiting for someone to pitch something in—grapes, or quarters. Liberace's there, at the end. I know him, of course. He's not only a part of Las Vegas history, he's part of mine.

This is my favorite room, because it's the Las Vegas of my parents. I can replay their doomed history here in three dimensions. It's like a giant, unfolding pop-up book, spread out to tell my father's story of the time my mother was lost, and found, and lost again. In miniature, I can watch her enter the back door of the Venetian with the harlequin man; I can see my father chase the blue Volvo down Buccaneer Boulevard, feathers flying out of the window; I can pick the both of them up like tiny dolls and place them together, gently, in the little plastic gondola for their final meeting. . . .

The could-be-Vietnamese woman with the sunglasses is breaking the rules. She's bent over, looking straight down at the Venetian hotel. Her hands are pressed hard against the glass, her face so close she could kiss it. The DO NOT TOUCH DISPLAY sign is under her right elbow. My mouth opens but the words jam up in my throat. I know it's not my mother, I'm sure of it, but the woman is so intent on seeing what she's seeing—what *is* she seeing? My ghosts? Hers? She's so still; to disturb her would be wrong, it would be like waking a sleepwalker. *She could be. She could be.*

"Could we move on?" a voice bleats in my ear. I Love Texas, mint green, is looking at me with a worried expression. I feel my face blotching red: I've been wandering; the sheep are anxious. Time to wrap up.

By now, even the Koreans have realized how ripped off they've been. Luckily, the tour ends with a movie, so I don't have to face their disgusted looks. In the tiny auditorium, they arrange themselves on rows of hard benches. I flick the switch. The movie's basically one big infomercial, courtesy of the Las Vegas Tourism Board. "Vegas Now!" swoops in with a helicopter view of the Strip, then a series of quick cuts. All the new attractions of the last five years are included: the Fallen Twin Towers Memorial Statue and Light Show (mournful bagpipe interlude); the giant Laughing Buddha of the Shanghai Hotel (Chinese zithers plinka-plinka-plinka-ing from speakers in his elbows); and the magnificent Green Dome of the New Baghdad Palace (live Middle Eastern ululation, set to a salsa beat). Pick a world, any world.

Smirky Boy and Pouty Girl are going at it. They've been waiting the whole tour for just this moment. At my place by the door, I can see them sitting in the dark in the back row, body pressing hard against body. Their limp arms slowly animate themselves, slithering into each other's shirts. I can't look away. His tongue flickers in her mouth; he writhes against her leg and his shirt rides up, revealing new, white skin. I should throw them out, but I can't move. Smirky's eyes open. I see them glittering in the dark. He watches me watching him, and smiles, mouth open, and dives in again. I jerk my head away.

That's when I realize—the woman with the sunglasses is missing. I do a head count. She's definitely gone. I leave the auditorium and retrace my steps quickly, room flowing into room flowing into room, back in time to the beginning, but all the spaces are empty. Rafael stands alone, scouting for no one. And then I'm running, fast-forward now through the years, arriving into the darkness of the movie ending and me flicking the lights on just in time, pointing the way to the gift shop and trying to figure out exactly how I missed her leaving me—I missed her leaving me again.

It was outside a rest stop in Cozad, Nebraska, that Emily's destination became clear to her. Until then, she hadn't really considered where she was heading; Emily was keeping thought to a minimum. I-80 was the perfect highway for just that—no deviation, no decisions along the route, and nothing to stir up memories, either: the endless array of farm and field, and farm and field, reminded her of nothing but farms and fields. She was able to just drive, noting the mile markers accumulating along the way, the steady press and release of the accelerator under her foot. The monotony was a blessing.

And not once did she feel the need to shake a finger out the window and yell, "Moo-cows! Look!"

Watching the odometer tick off the life of the Volvo gave Emily a grim kind of pleasure. She liked imagining how the speed, the dust, and the miles were all conspiring to wear down the car. Emily, she of the faithful three-thousand-mile oil and fluids checkup, the woman who kept an extra three-ounce bottle of metallic blue paint in the glove compartment for touch-ups, was, in effect, hastening the car's demise, and it gave her satisfaction. She could punish *it*, at least.

She needed to leave for everything to stop. She had thought going to Vee's in Wisconsin would help put life on hold, but that was impossible with Walt around. Life didn't stop for a four-year-old. Vee could take care of the cooking, the cleaning up, could even help with Owen, Emily's sedated husband, but she was no comfort at all to Walt, who wanted Emily, and only Emily, just at a time when the touch of anyone was enough to make her stomach clench.

She hadn't felt that way since just after Walt was born. During those terrible months, the merest hint of exuberance in her husband's smile was enough to send her reeling to the bathroom. She had such an acute sense of panic then, of being responsible for everything when all she wanted to do was sleep.

But this time it was worse. Much worse. After arriving in Wisconsin, Emily would stare at Owen's inert, drugged body lying in her childhood bed and imagine screaming at him, "Get up! Get up! Do something!" even though she knew that wasn't fair. Her husband was sinking fast into a depressive episode, which she understood was a) clinical, b) diagnosed, and c) perhaps unavoidable, but more than that, she knew there was nothing he could do that would make her forgive him. It was she who needed to get out.

The Lucky Stop was exactly what Emily was looking for: a local trucker's hangout, small, ramshackle, three loose boards shy of condemned; no place for children. Her previous stops for coffee and restrooms so far had been hit-and-miss: truck stops were generally safe; Mickey D's were out, of course (play structures and Happy Meals), and so were the more well-known fast food establishments. Too many station wagons in the parking lot and she veered away immediately, no matter how full her bladder was. No, the Lucky Stop was perfect: nobody in sight but a muddy pickup truck at the pumps and a woman in a dirty green apron chatting with the driver. The name on the front sign was so faded it might have been part of the wood grain.

No one was inside. The Lucky Stop contained not only a gas station and a convenience mart, but a lunch counter as well. It was a tiny one: three torn gray vinyl stools patched up with gray duct tape, a dusty countertop, one small grill, and a deep-fry basket. A grimy box fan blew hot air into the hot air, and a yellow fly strip hung above the cash register, lazily revolving. Four flies, two flies. Four flies, two flies.

She stood in the doorway, dust particles floating down a shaft of light like a screen between her and the counter. She was a movie archaeologist, stepping into an exotic, long-forgotten temple. Years of calorie counting, label watching, and nutritional vigilance fell away. She sat down.

The menu, posted behind the fly strip on a board with removable letters, was a model of economy:

HAMBRGER $2
ADD CHEESE .50
GRILL CHEESE $1.50
CHI KEN FRIED STEAK $4
FRIES $1
ONION RINGS $1
PENNZOIL SALE $3.50
LOTTERY TIKS HERE

A piece of cardboard was tacked up next to the menu board with the beverages listed: coffee (two sizes), Coke, and Diet Coke.

The door flapped open and the woman with the apron bustled in. "Sorry, sugar," she called out as she made her way behind the counter. Her hands were smudged from leaning against the truck's tires and she tried wiping them onto the still-green spots of her apron. "That man just goes on. What can I do you for?"

Emily studied the board intently. "Chicken fried steak," she enunciated carefully.

The woman reached down into the small refrigerator (without washing her hands, the old Emily noted) and pulled out a gray breaded oblong, tossed it into the wire basket, and set the basket into the oil, where it bubbled weakly. "You want fries with that?"

Yes, Emily would have fries. And coffee.

"No problem," the gas attendant/waitress/cook said, grabbing a handful of frozen fries from a crumpled bag in the freezer and throwing them after the steak. The oil barely registered the addition. "M'name's Lydia. Where you comin' from?"

Lydia looked to be about the same age as Emily, pushing toward mid-thirties, but with much more mileage clocked in. Her hair was the shade of sand, pulled back into a loose ponytail. There was a mole, liver-colored, by the side of her mouth.

"Chicago. I mean, Milwaukee," Emily said.

"Mm. Milwaukee. That's nice. Never been there." Lydia took a plastic jug from the refrigerator and poured some thick, coagulated white liquid into a plastic cup. To this she added a spoonful of Heinz chipotle sauce from a glass jar. "This is my secret," she told Emily, winking. "Gives the gravy some kick. You like it hot?"

Emily usually avoided anything spicier than Dijon mustard. "Hot. Yes," she said.

Lydia plopped an extra spoonful of sauce into the cup, then set the cup into the microwave and punched in a minute. She poured out a cup of coffee. "You Filipino?" she asked brightly.

Emily offered her a tight smile and a shake of her head.

"My brother's wife is Filipino," Lydia said, by way of explanation. "Where you headed to?"

Emily fixed her eyes on the coffee mug set in front of her, then raised her gaze up the arm that placed it there to Lydia's grease-stained shirt to Lydia's mole. "I have no idea."

"Mmm." Lydia turned away, hoisted the fry basket up, gave it a shake, and pulled out the cutlet with metal tongs. She slapped it down on a hamburger bun upon which a translucent sliver of tomato and a leaf of iceberg lettuce nestled, waiting. Two quick stirs of the heated gravy, then that was slathered over all. A rainfall of crisped fries, and the plate was complete. Lydia slid it over to Emily. "Enjoy."

Emily paused, head bowed over her food to avoid Lydia's gaze. The thought of eating this gargantuan, deep-fried, trans-fatty mess in front of its maker seemed suddenly too intimate, too obscene. Her stomach churned.

A car honked twice out by the pumps. Lydia wiped her hands on her jeans and excused herself, leaving Emily alone.

She started off slowly, nibbling on one fry—hot and crisp. Then another, dispatched in two bites. She took up the sandwich carefully with two hands. Gravy was spilling along its seams. She brought the unwieldy mass up, opened wide, and dove in. The softness of the bun sinking under her teeth gave way to the sudden crispiness of the breading, and as her teeth bit down, the squirt of hot oil and juice exploded in her mouth. The smokiness of the surprisingly tender meat, the sweetness of the bread, the silky saltiness of the gravy, and the fiery sauce igniting all: it was the worst and best thing she had eaten in five years. She devoured it in less than a minute.

"The condemned ate a hearty meal!" Emily turned to the door still pinching a cluster of gravy-swabbed fries; she hadn't even heard Lydia enter. "Must have been hungry."

Emily nodded and quickly shoved the fries into her mouth. She swallowed and reached for the napkin dispenser.

"Good. Good," Lydia said. "Glad you liked it." Her words were light, but her eyes fixed hard on Emily. "Saw what you did to your Volvo out there," she said in a friendly voice. "You got lots of space now, without them back seats."

Emily looked back at Lydia, her eyes expressing only the mildest interest. Lydia stayed by her side, rubbing the vinyl of one of the stools with her hand, back and forth. "You could sleep in there," she went on. "That's what I did, first time I got out here. Slept three months in my car, and it weren't near as nice as that one."

Emily focused on the crumpled napkins in her hand, carefully wiping each finger. "I don't sleep," she said quietly. Which was true; she couldn't remember the last time she slept for any significant amount of time.

Lydia continued as if she hadn't heard. "What's that in the back? An instrument?"

"An accordion."

"Funny thing to take, and no suitcase." Lydia kept twiddling with the stool in front of her, as if she were waiting to be invited to sit down. "I remember when I run out of my house, five years back, I grabbed my KitchenAid hand mixer. Forgot my address book, forgot my underwear, but took the mixer. Don't know what I thought I'd be mixing, but . . . your brain don't think of those things." Again, the hard look. "No, no it don't," she said aimlessly, and then, sharply, "You got kids?"

Emily felt her stomach constricting. She kept looking at the coffee mug.

"I got three," Lydia volunteered, as if Emily had answered her. "Two little girls and a boy. We all slept in a Chevy wagon. Three months. Me in the front seat, boy in the backseat, girls in the way back. They were young, it was all right. Long time ago. Sometimes you gotta do what you gotta do, right?"

Lydia slipped onto the stool. Her knee touched Emily's. "Look, honey," she said softly, "you don't look so good. You in some trouble?"

The knocking of knees sent Emily sliding out of her body and to the furthest corner of her mind, where she could watch her corporeal self proceed from a safer distance. Emily was pushing her plate away from her. Emily was taking up another napkin. Emily was wiping her mouth.

Lydia leaned her face closer. "You don't have to tell me." She fingered the little silver cross around her neck. "There's all sorts of places you could go. If you wanted to"—here her voice lowered—"get safe. If you wanted to."

Emily made no move, which Lydia took as a sign of complicity. She leaned closer, so close that Emily could smell her unwashed hair. "You know what helped me? What really helped?" Emily registered the touch of Lydia's fingers on her shoulder. From her distant corner she willed her body not to flinch. Lydia gave a glowing smile and lowered her head, conspiratorial, almost flirtatious. "Let me ask you this, honey. Have you been saved?"

Emily's eyes widened. She almost laughed. Here was one avenue she was quite certain she wouldn't be traveling down. She had dealt with this kind of thing many times before: Jehovah's Witnesses, Baptist evangelicals, Emily had turned them all successfully out from her gate in Chicago for years. She had defenses for this, well practiced and obdurate. It was almost a relief.

"Don't worry about me," she said coolly, pulling her purse close and getting out her wallet.

Lydia didn't move. "I just know, it sure helped me."

Emily flicked out a ten. "I'm fine." Her condescension was mighty.

As she sailed out of the Lucky Stop, restroom key in hand, Emily did feel fine, and mighty, leaving Lydia and her wide-open mouth to catch flies and other people's souls. Emily was not going to be saved, not at all.

She turned the corner and began running for the bathroom door but already knew it was too late. The twisted knot in her stomach finally released, and with it, her beloved sandwich. A moment later she was kneeling on the ground, arms wrapped around herself, heaving out the last remnants of chipotle gravy and bitter coffee.

And it was there, next to the bits of once-again steaming sandwich, that she found the feather. It was by her knees: a bright patch of color amidst the totality of bleached dirt and gravel. The feather should by all rights have blown away, but there it was, its vermillion brilliance held fast by the merest wisp of scrub. The feather was unsullied, and when Emily picked it up she could tell by its softness and texture that it was the real deal—an exquisite, fan-shaped marabou feather, big enough to cover her palm. She looked up immediately, as if expecting more to rain down from the sky, or to spot the large, exotic bird that could have shed such a treasure.

Instead, the sky yielded up a vision. Set dark against the fierce radiance of the sun: a man's face, wreathed in an effusion of burning feathers. The kindest of smiles beamed down upon her, perfectly even teeth glowing white from the shadows. Soft, black eyes twinkled like bright rhinestones. "Come," he said breathily. The sound was everywhere. He was Comfort. He was Forgiveness. He was Liberace.

Liberace, come not to save her, but to offer guidance. In a moment of dizzying clarity she realized where she was heading. Where she had been headed to all along. Her wheels were already pointing south.

- She would drive to Las Vegas.
- She would find Liberace's museum.
- She would take the pills.

Emily looked down at the feather she held in her hand, and then up again, but he had disappeared, leaving nothing else behind but the vast blue sky.

When I get back to the apartment, seven hours later, everything is exactly the way I left it. Not a good sign. Even the open package of Double Stuf Oreos I've laid out as bait on the kitchen table has been untouched. Usually, by this time, he's made an appearance.

The floor tilts, just a little.

"Hello," I call out.

No answer.

My shirt's soaked from the five-minute walk home from the bus; it's that hot out. I strip off my work clothes. There's a Holy Reckoning of laundry to do—my pants are getting crusty and the apartment is taking on the delicate aroma of dirty socks. I throw my clothes in the hall closet and grab a pair of gym shorts from the pile. Sniff. They're okay.

I hear him in the next room. He's turning himself over slowly under the sheets. I know the sounds: one small grunt, pause; a long exhale.

Dinnertime. I crank up the fan, cook without a shirt on. Grilled cheese. I have to use the bread ends, 'cause that's all we have. *Bread*, I scratch on a list pinned to the fridge, while I'm waiting to flip over the sandwich. *Do Laundry!* I draw a sock with stink marks floating up the page.

Pickles, chips, sandwich, on a tray. How professional is that? There should be one of those small institutional white bowls with Jell-O in it, little red blocks of Jell-O with a crusty rose of whipped cream stuck on top. Or fruit cocktail, I could get him that next time, the kind with the one half cherry slowly bleeding pink onto all the washed-out blocks of pear and peach and those three gray grapes, all tasting the syrupy same. But we don't have any of those small, institutional white bowls. Next time I take him to LV Med Center, maybe I'll swipe a few. Maybe it'll make him feel more at home, at home.

"Your turn, Georgia," I say, but there's no one going in but me.

The bedroom is dark and sour-smelling. Curtains open, curtains closed, he doesn't care. Lunch is still on the nightstand, untouched. Next to it are the plastic cups, yellow and blue, Morning and Night, for his medication.

The air conditioner hums steadily. He's on his side, eyes closed, but I know he's not sleeping.

"Ready for dinner?" I ask.

There are two long breaths before he answers. "Hey, champ," he croaks. His eyes don't open.

"Get up. You gotta eat something."

He shakes his head.

"Look, don't be stubborn. Eat."

But he won't be persuaded. Five minutes of pleading and bullying and he isn't even talking anymore. We've gone down this road before. Maybe I'll be getting those white bowls sooner than I thought.

I sit next to him on the edge of the bed, munching on half of the grilled cheese sandwich. There are more patches of gray in his hair. They spread out in blotches on his shaggy head, like mold.

"Hey," I say, "they almost finished renovating the Luxor. The pyramid's back up. It's bigger. And there's a big eye on the top. They're gonna call it the 'Deluxor.'"

No answer.

"Hey," I say, "you know that big sphinx in the front? They got a new one." I'm talking too loudly. "It tells riddles. And if you guess the right answer, it spits out a poker chip in between its paws."

No answer.

"You know that sphinx?" I say. "Is that the same sphinx as the *Oedipus* sphinx?" I know damned well the *Oedipus* sphinx is from Thebes, he's told me the story enough times, but at last his forehead furrows, and though he keeps his eyes shut at least his voice has some prickle to it.

"No. You know that," he grumbles. "Different sphinxes." He sighs. "Originated in . . . Egypt. Monuments. Named by the Greeks." When I was younger, this would have been the beginning of at least thirty minutes of Oedipus, birth to blindness, but now, his voice is already fading.

"Yeah, but do they both tell riddles?" I ask quickly.

He shrugs one shoulder. "History's . . . fluid," he says distantly.

"But—"

"Sorry, Walt. Sorry." He waves his hand like he's rushing off to a meeting.

"Yeah, okay." I stand up. "Look, I'm leaving the food here. Eat it before you take your pills."

I mean to leave, but the next moment my hand's on his shoulder and I'm whispering in his ear. "You know, at work today, there was this woman . . ." I'm twelve years old again. "I don't know, it could have been her."

His breathing stills, and I think, it's worked, he'll turn and say, "How exciting! What did she look like?" and the game would begin again, but instead he gives an indistinct moan and settles deeper into the pillow. Dismissal complete.

I grab the tray and swing it toward the door. Almost out, I turn around just in time to see a small smile creep onto his face. He thinks I've left the room. It's a sly smile, it's the tail of a secret swishing over his face. He doesn't want to come back, I think. Maybe I'm keeping him from a fantastic dream. Or oblivion, maybe that's what he's after, and he's shuffling toward it eagerly, like this big water mammal pushing through the mud, about to take a sudden slide into the river.

He wants to be light again. He wants to be free.

———

Snow. I think of snow. White, pure, obliterating snow. I heard there were once occasional flurries around here, years back, but global warming's taken care of all that. It's about time for the Strip to invent some. I imagine a casino shaped like an igloo, with gaming tables made of ice slabs and cocktail waitresses with fur-lined miniskirts and hooded sealskin parkas. Every hour on the hour, in the hotel atrium, there would be snow: big, white, glorious flakes descending from the ceiling in manufactured, five-minute blizzards that would taste only slightly of plastic. The hotel would be called Tundra, and I would work there, pouring frozen drinks at the bar, or training the penguins to sweep away the flakes with their furry feet. I'd be known as the Aleutian; I'd squint off into the distance, and no one would ask me what I was.

My Oreos are melting.

I'm wedged into a little green plastic lawn chair out on our balcony, waiting for coolness to set in. Balcony's too fancy a word for this tiny space I'm crammed into; it's more like a playpen made of iron railings and concrete. My back presses up against the wall, my legs are folded up onto the rusty bars—it's the only way this baby'll fit. I stare out at the magnificent view: the dusty parking lot littered with candy-colored X-rated flyers; the identical rusty playpens on the other side; and far, far off, on top of a building, the glimmer of red neon that's Lady Luck turning her back to us.

I wish I could remember snow. After all, I'm supposed to have lived in Chicago for the first five years of my life, you'd think that would have laid down some kind of imprint, but all that time's down the sinkhole. Life began at five.

This apartment building, La Marguerite, is the only place I can remember calling home. It used to be this hot flamingo pink, with all these bright plastic flowers sprouting in the courtyard. Over the years, sun and neglect have bleached it out to the color of a dirty Band-Aid. The flowers have all been plucked or pissed on. The building's faded like the rest of the neighborhood, and it sits, squat and tired, like all the other ugly *brujas* on the block, another lost cause.

My father and I have watched the flow of tenants here come and go: the tide of Mexicans, El Salvadorians, Nicaraguans, and various other -ians, swept from their countries by poverty or plague. They settle down here, and a few years later, it's either up or back; they sweep out to make way for a new wave of immigrants. Five building custodians have left during our time here; two have died, one by his own hand. Only we remain. Those mildewed stains on the back of our shower wall haven't lasted as long as we have. I'd like to call it stability, but really it's just inertia.

My father used to talk about us making our own exodus from the place, about getting an apartment with a bedroom for each of us, but we never could afford it, not with his job history. Even when he was working more or less steadily, that stretch of years at Premium Outlet as a security guard, we were always just getting by. That was when I was still in elementary school, and my father would get the women in the building to look after me while he worked, a succession of brown-skinned, kindly-faced *abuelas* who never seemed to mind, though they were settling down themselves after a long day of scrubbing toilets and making beds. He wasn't asking for too much, though: he left for the Outlet after I went to bed and would get home in time to fix me breakfast. He just needed someone to keep an eye on me in case the unexpected happened; if a fire broke out or if I spontaneously combusted in the middle of the night, I'd know which door to knock on to get help.

Every night except Sunday, after I brushed my teeth, my father would lead me across the open walkway to whichever apartment was acting as sentry. We'd tap on the door, and I'd present my pajama-clad self to Mrs. Hernandez/Alvarado/Trini/The-One-with-the-Mole. My father would mouth "thank you" and they would get their chance to take pity on the Motherless Boy. *"Pobrecito niño!"* they'd cry, stroking the side of my face with their leathery palms and cupping my chin. Then back we'd go to our apartment, where I'd pad off to bed (this was when the bedroom was still mine), vaguely embarrassed.

My father would switch on the lamp and sit at the edge of the bed. I'd say, "Tell me a story," and he'd say, "Well . . ." and then off we'd go, halfway around the world. My father and I would set sail with Jason and the Argonauts, follow Orpheus to the gates of Hades, enter the maze with Theseus. He knew all the myths, and never from a book. I asked him once why he had so many stories in his head, and he told me, "That used to be my job," and for the longest time I thought that meant he got paid for putting kids to sleep.

When it was all over, when the last monster had been slain or the final nymph had turned into some kind of tree or flower, my father would pat me on the shoulder and lean in for a kiss good night. He'd flick off the lamp, and then, every night, always, he'd stand by the doorway in the dark for the longest time; I'd almost forget he was there. I'd be well on my way toward sleep when his voice would float over to me in the darkness: "I'll be back. I won't forget."

And he'd always be there in the morning.

Now, of course, he never leaves.

Evening. I don't realize how dusky it's gotten until the outside lights pop on. The yellow bulb glaring over my shoulder darkens the entire parking lot, even though the sun is still lurking somewhere out there, beyond the buildings, where the mountains live.

My row of cookies is done. I set down the package and wipe my hands on my shorts. Within finger's reach is my black notebook, where I've pulled it out of my backpack. Clipped inside is a mechanical pencil and a pen, extra fine tip, black. I leaf through the pages, telling myself I'm looking for inspiration, but already I know what I'm going to draw. I click my pencil, once, twice.

A clean, white page. I work to get it just right. The black hair cascading down, wave after wave of swooping pencil, hiding the already hidden eyes. The alien darkness of sunglasses I scratch in as they jut out from the strokes. Three lines become the mouth, pressed together in concentration, and a pair of parentheses frame them, arching from the smaller curve of the nostril toward the soft *V* of the chin.

She's complete. Now she can leave me alone.

I can do it automatically, this recording of faces. It's a habit. It started years ago, when I was seven, walking with my father downtown on Fremont Street. There was the usual crush of people staggering around us. He held on tight to my hand. There are no cars allowed on that stretch of Fremont, but my father kept me on the inside of the sidewalk, all the same. Suddenly, weaving in and out of the street chatter and casino noise: a jaunty, vibrating melody. I pulled at his hand. "Is that an accordion?" I shouted. My father nodded. I yanked his hand harder, bringing him down to my level, where I could whisper in his ear. "Maybe it's her," I said, because by this time he'd told me the whole story.

My father went very still, listening. Then he nodded slowly. His bright eyes matched my own. "It could be," he said.

We raised our heads quickly, listening for the song's direction, then set off, following the music. Halfway down the block: "That could be her. . . . Is it?" He pointed out an Asian woman with long black hair tucked into a corner of a building, chatting on a cell phone. No matter that she wasn't even playing an accordion, I galloped forward, but he held me back with a hand on my shoulder. "No, not her. Too tall." We continued on our way, and eventually found the source of the music: a middle-aged balding dude in a tux, playing for change.

"Oh well," I said, looking away quickly.

"Next time," my father said, patting my head.

That became the game, locating women who could-have-been-but-weren't my mother. And after each sighting, flushed with adrenaline and disappointment, I'd race to my room and drag out my notebook (black or dark green, college-ruled at first, then blank) to set down the faces before they disappeared from my mind. Next to each sketch I'd mark down the reason my father gave for her not being my mother: too old; too ugly; too skinny; too short; too not-her.

The idea was, back then, that if I could eliminate all the characteristics that weren't her, I'd arrive, eventually, at a picture of who she was. There wasn't anything else to go by. No photos of my mother in the house; no Web site or a scrapbook or a locket with a fragment of her face glowing inside. She exists only in memory, and not mine.

These days, I carry around a sketchbook. I draw lots of things, but not potential mothers, not anymore. Still, there she is, Mystery Woman with the Sunglasses, floating disembodied on the white page. What to mark down next to her? Too-what? I could catalog her with a question mark, or leave the space blank, but I've got no label for her.

These days, there isn't anyone to tell me who she isn't.

Sketch #1: Just the facts.

OWEN

WISCONSIN

EARLIER

He was curled up on the oily floor of the garage, just below the open driver-side door of the Ford Explorer, when the shoes appeared: scuffed and brown, possessing the merest undulation of heel. The epitome of sensible. They were waiting, expectantly, in front of his face. By this time the room had stopped its merry dance. Owen no longer felt the push and pull of gravity, the urge to bash his head against the concrete in order to slow things down. He had just managed to open his eyes (slowly—the heaviness was still there) when he noticed the scuffed brown brogues—was that a shoe name? Or just an accent? An Irish shoe?—mere inches away from his nose.

It took Owen a moment to realize that they were, in fact, attached to legs. He had imagined them to be a pair of little tan puppies (the looping brown laces floppy ears) who had come to nuzzle him awake. *Hey, boys, what's wrong? You say Timmy's in the well? Well, Timmy's going to have to wait. I've got a date with this floor right now, you see, and after that, I've got to find my wife.*

The shoes. Yes. He opened his eyes again (more difficult, this time) and they were still there. So were the legs. Apparently, they wanted something from him. He would have liked to have glanced upward, to make the acquaintance of the shoes' owner, but found even that small sweep of the eye really quite beyond him. He'd have to hazard a guess.

Vee? he whispered to the thick ankles.

The voice came from impossibly high. Voice of God.

You're not the victim, you know, she said.

And abruptly, she was gone, shoes padding off obediently with her.

Ah, Vee. Angel of Mercy. Sweet, sweet Vee. An Irish face to go with those Irish brogues. It wasn't a hard guess, really. No points given for that one. This was, after all, her house, and, by extension, her garage. She was the matriarch. *Matriarch.* Yes, that word suited her. Not mother, not even to Emily, her own adopted daughter; never mother. *Matriarch.*

The floor felt cool against Owen's cheek, and he decided to remain there, as if there were a choice. *I may need to rethink this plan,* he thought, though there really was no plan to speak of. He had awoken that morning to the radio announcement, heard Vee bellowing in the kitchen, Damn it, she's gone. Owen sat up instantly, Lazarus raised from the dead. That shot of adrenaline had miraculously transported him out of bed, into clothes, through the kitchen door, and almost into the Explorer before shutting off abruptly and dropping him onto the concrete. It was the smell—the humid, stale air that the car exhaled immediately upon opening (*a corpse's breath on a hot day,* he thought, falling)—that had clobbered him behind the knees and felled him to the earth, as effectively pinned as pierced Diomedes outside the walls of Troy.

Wait. Weight.

It was hard to imagine that not too long ago the process of movement wasn't such an agonizing event. His limbs used to be steady, once upon a time, his mind unfogged—why, he was tenure-track, after all— was—but the darkness hadn't yet settled down on him, Erebos crushing him molecule by dense molecule. He hadn't noticed how bad he was getting over these last hazy weeks (months?); because things were expected of him, he was forced to function. Wear the suit, sign the papers, make the deposition. He had become one of those trees that topple but slowly because of the mass of vines supporting it. And there, in the car on the way to his mother-in-law's house, Chicago to Milwaukee, curled up in the passenger seat, he felt the vines release and the tree come crashing down. It was dead inside, but he had only just realized. Up the milligrams, was the verdict of his doctor. It'll pass. May cause dizziness. Ergo, the floor.

The brogues. He missed those brogues. Unlike Vee, they were warm, companionable. He should have named them. And hadn't they borne the weight of those disapproving feet for so many years? It was something he understood. He wondered if Vee had always despised him, or only since recent events. Certainly, she had never been particularly warm to him, but warmth, he gathered, was not something she was known for. *That's just the way she is,* Emmie had said, one particularly horrendous Christmas visit, rubbing that aching spot between his shoulders. *Believe me, I would know.* They were sitting in her former bedroom, impossibly small, on the same bed he had been confined to these past two weeks. But nothing prepared him for this—this active, accelerating iciness emanating from Vee. Had that always been present, waiting for the right moment to manifest itself, or was it a new antipathy? *Antipathy.* It sounded like a small, barren island. *I am banished to the shores of Antipathy.* His just punishment. Better here than on that other rocky shoal—*Pity.* He didn't blame Vee. He didn't blame anyone. But himself, of course. For him, the lowest reaches of Tartarus. *Mea culpa, mea culpa, mea maxima culpa—*

And abruptly, she was back. (*Hello, little brogues!*) Those stern legs were bending; he could see knee, thigh, waist—Come on, come on, she said—and Vee's hands were clenching the bulk of him; he towered over her but she was determined and her grip was steel. Vee managed to lift him to his feet and together they tangoed into the living room, where she shoved aside the coffee table with one deft push of her foot and released him onto the couch.

He was panting and wet with perspiration. *Sorry, Vee, the couch might get a little soaked, why not slide that doily over here and save a cushion*—but suddenly she was grabbing his hand with both of hers, smoothing out his fist—*Why, you do care after all, Vee, or should I call you Mom?*—and only when she had pushed herself upright, jingling metal silenced by her closing fingers, did he realize that all along she was going for the car keys clenched tight in his right hand.

She paused, looking down at him. Her creased face displayed nothing but Purpose. Vee's arms were crossed in front of her, and she patted them twice, decisively, as if to rouse herself. He had seen Emmie make that same gesture, many times. A decision had been made.

I'll be back, she said. Another pause, and then: You rest.

She went away. A moment later he heard the car start up and then that too was gone.

He gasped loudly in the silence. She had set something off. It was the modulation in her voice, yes, that was it, the way her pitch lowered and softened with the two words, You rest, which reached inside and undid him. The flow of feeling—*feeling!*—coursed fast through his body—*no, no no no*—as the words echoed, not the meaning of the words but the tone, dark and forgiving, and his trembling began, and with it the sobs—large, painful, and without limit, Emmie, he cried aloud, over and over again, Emmie. Emmie. Emmie. And he needed her, and he wanted her to need him again, to fit in that hollow of his arms, but she was gone, just as he was coming back. *Yes, I am back,* he thought, his mind clearing, and this was followed instantly by *When did I last take my medication?* and then, in a moment of revelation (the cursed moment of revelation) he saw clearly the nightstand with no pill bottles on it and knew where Emily was heading, and soon he was lurching that way, too, by way of the kitchen where he had to, somehow, find a phone book and a way to the airport.

Hello, much better. Thank you. Owen was never so happy to see clouds before. Here he was, traveling at an oblique angle to the horizon, heading upward, *en route* as it were, when just hours before he had been inert matter puddled on a garage floor. Stowing his items in the overhead compartment, fastening his seat belt, returning his seat and tray table to their locked and upright position: he was master of all federal aviation requirements. Remarkable.

Owen shifted his gaze to the left. Not everyone, apparently, was as overjoyed by his presence at the coveted window seat as he. His traveling companion, for one: she of the cropped pink halter top with baby blue sequins spelling out ICE PRINCESS across her birdlike chest. Owen had plugged in the airline's headphones to maintain some privacy, but the gesture turned out to be largely redundant; the sour emanations of two weeks' convalescence mixed with the earthier aroma of his cooling sweat had apparently secured as wide a berth as possible from his hapless midriff-ed companion. She was at this moment twisted in what looked to be an incredibly contorted position away from him, jammed to the far side of her seat, her *Mademoiselle* magazine perched precariously on the distal armrest. This poor Ice Princess (a reference to lineage, temperament, or occupation?) was in obvious distress, and short of hurling himself out of his tiny window Owen could do little to alleviate her suffering. *Ah, but fear not, sweet nymph! Rescue is at hand!* For at this moment, just as the seat belt icon dimmed, Owen saw the ever-attentive male flight attendant leap to her side with catlike reflexes. Sensitive to her plight, the attendant whispered a few discreet words to her and pointed to an empty seat two rows ahead (Owen, with smooth jazz pouring into his ear, could not hear). Our princess fumbled frantically against her bonds, broke free, and catapulted herself into the unoccupied 16C. She smiled gratefully at her hero (her first smile of the flight), who in turn sauntered triumphantly down the aisle, his greater glory assured. Everyone was happy, the skies were never friendlier, and Owen was airborne and alone.

Which was all to the good. It was amazing how quickly and smoothly things had pulled together. There was seemingly no end to the amount of flights going from General Mitchell International (MKE) to McCarran (LAS); he had only to pick a time. Mrs. Steiff from next door, with a mere modicum of animosity, agreed to look after feverish Walt until Vee returned home. The taxi arrived when it said it would, and though getting into the cab gave Owen a few moments of vertiginous anxiety, he kept his eyes closed and it was over soon enough. Airport security was quick and painless. The gods were smiling, for a change.

Owen peered over the seats ahead of him. His recently evacuated neighbor was now happily ensconced in her spacious new accommodations, head bopping to some fantastically sunny music her Walkman provided, her hand flipping through the magazine pages with abandon.

Now then, am I really that hideous? Owen sank back against the headrest. He wondered what changes might have come over him in these last few weeks. Had, perhaps, the Accident transformed him, shifted his features in some imperceptible but unsettling way? Did he now bear a mark that drove people from their seats to get away from him? Children would now run screaming from his lumbering path. His arms would reach out to them stiffly, his teeth bared: *Run from me, I am depressed. Beware my depression.*

I suffer from depression, he murmured to himself, trying it on for size. This was the first time Owen had ever said those words aloud. He had been avoiding it, perhaps because to admit It meant to own It, having It branded on you forever. He is a professor. He is married. He suffers from depression. It became part of you permanently, like a son or daughter. More permanently, actually. *Ah, no, no, best not to go down that road. Too dark, wouldn't you say? Let's stay up here in the heavens, shall we?*

Peggy Lee concurred, crooning "Fly Me to the Moon" from his headphones.

Owen shook his head as if to rouse himself and jutted his chin forward, teeth gently clenched. It wasn't true. He wouldn't be like this forever. This was just an episode, that's what they called it: a depressive episode. Completely understandable. From the Greek, *epeisodion*, that piece of action between choric songs in a Greek tragedy. There it was. He was having a bit of a depressive episode, waiting for the next song to arise. Where was that song?

Let me know what spring is like on Jupiter and Mars . . .

He was going to save his wife. Glorious action had begun. All would be well, finally, and that last, awful episode would be in the past.

He thought of kissing Walt good-bye this morning. The boy didn't even stir from sleep—how long had he been sick? Owen couldn't even recall hearing his son's voice in Vee's house, these two weeks he had been sequestered away. *Bad father.* No, no. He had to go. Walt would be fine. Vee would look after him. With any luck, Walt wouldn't even realize his father had left, and Owen would be back, Emmie at his side. If all went according to plan. That, of course, was the fuzzy part; he had no idea what was going to happen once he touched down in Vegas. Now, Emmie, Emmie would have had maps and books, itineraries and schedules on hand. Before arriving at her destination she would be able to tell you what the best way out of the airport was, which route went where fastest during what time of day, and what the average cab fare to that destination would be. Owen was just happy to have found the correct gate in time. But all was not lost. He knew Emmie, and if he could just figure out what she would do, maybe he could follow. He would get there in time. It would all work out, somehow.

That is, if Emily was indeed heading for Vegas.

She is heading for Vegas. Owen adjusted his headphones, settled back into his seat, and closed his eyes.

Omnes viae Vegas ducunt. All roads lead to Vegas.

One Monday morning, my dad, at the age of seven, was in the backseat of the family Pacer, horsing around, while his mom drove him to school. He had woken up late and missed the bus. His mom, who was herself late for work, was going to be later still by driving three miles out of her way. Her hair was damp and in curlers, wrapped up in a scarf. A Salem menthol cigarette was dangling from her lips (for some reason, this fact was important to my dad). As I said, my dad was horsing around, singing the theme song to the *Batman* TV show at the top of his lungs. "Batman! Da-da-da-da-da-da-da-da-da-da Batman! Da-da-da-da-da-da-da-da-da-da—" he yelled endlessly, flopping up and down on the seat like a marionette. His mother, who had stopped at a red light, turned around and, clenching the Salem between her teeth, hissed at him: "You are going to be the death of me!" She was wearing her big, dark, tortoise-shell sunglasses. My father couldn't see her eyes, but he could see his own reflection, twice, and, a moment later when she looked up, the reflection of the truck that was about to plow into them. Twice. The truck knocked the Pacer forward with a jolt, into the path of a station wagon moving too fast. It slammed into the Pacer, spinning it around forty-five degrees and into a traffic light pole. My father's mother was propelled across the front seat into the passenger-side window. She died instantly.

My father didn't have much luck with cars.

That he survived that accident was something of a miracle; after all, as he himself stressed with a disbelieving shake of his head, back then NO ONE wore seat belts. But in the telling, my father never saw it as a miracle. He believes that day was the start of some kind of lifelong curse, incited by his mother's prophetic last words, which involved him and cars; one that would replay itself time and time again, with precise and deadly accuracy, over the years.

Curses might sound a little too B-movie horror, but, given his history, it's hard to argue with him. There is another explanation, though, I once pointed out. Maybe the curse began not with him but with his own father, Owen Sr., who was not killed in a vehicle but did die in one: an ambulance, to be exact. Owen Sr. tried to off himself (gun in the mouth, missed and shot out his throat) and had the good/bad luck to do it during rush hour: traffic was slow and he bled out on the way to the hospital. Who knows what dark karma was cast into the air before he gurgled his last? Two weeks later, baby Owen was born, three weeks premature. It doesn't seem like the smartest idea to name a kid after his suicidal father, but maybe that's just me.

My dad liked this theory, but it never seemed to stick. "It doesn't matter how it started," my father said. "What matters is that it ends with you."

All this goes by way of explaining why we don't own a car; why we know the public transportation system better than anyone in Clark County; why I've always tended to walk on the inside of sidewalks; and why, on this Monday afternoon in May, five weeks before my eighteenth birthday, I'm finally getting my ass into an automobile for a driving lesson.

I've had to lie like a meth addict to prepare for this. I applied for my learner's permit, shelled out the thirty-five bucks, forged my dad's signature on the permission slip, and presented my papers to the DMV, along with a notarized medical exemption for my dad, courtesy of the Nevada

Health and Disabilities Department. I'd taken, and passed, the driver's ed class at school, along with all the pimply freshmen who barely reached my shoulder standing up. All of this was done with my father thinking I was at a series of staff meetings. If he ever found out I was even thinking about getting behind the wheel of a car after he'd successfully kept me out of them for almost all my life, well, it's his worst nightmare. It'd kill him, literally. Then he'd be dead, I'd be responsible, and the curse would pass on to me. I know how this curse thing works.

I sailed through the whole process without thinking too much about it. All I know is, it seems crazy not to have a license. Who doesn't have a driver's license? Whack-jobs, the legally blind, and me. Enough is enough; it's time. So I'll just ignore the SUV dangling on a thread over my head and get on with it. To be honest, driving seems more like a theoretical concept to me than a practical one; learning about traffic signs, stopping distances, and defensive maneuvers is like studying a language spoken in a country I'm not sure I'll ever visit.

It's been almost half a year since I left Silverado High, and I have to say, looking up at its terra-cotta-colored bricks and windowless tower, I still hate it. The building has the personality of a parking garage merged with a penitentiary. I did three and a half years of hard labor here, time off for good behavior. The two-bus-ride commute every morning, the hallways with their particular smell of old sweat and marijuana, the daily doses of indifference and casual cruelty—there's nothing about school that I miss. If they weren't offering free Behind the Wheel classes I could have very easily never seen this place again, could have let the whole experience congeal into one big putrid mass and slip down the sinkhole.

No one was sorry to see me leave early. My only friend here, Shifra Downey, she of the heavy eyeliner and vicious mouth, had disappeared at the beginning of the year. Her family moved to parts unknown; I'm guessing witness protection. That left me, one of those kids administrators are always profiling: antisocial misfit, intelligent but underachieving, a quiet loner, disdainful of team sports, always scribbling in a black notebook. I've got no Nazi manifesto Web page, but other than that, I was a classic case of someone who was going to walk in one day and shoot out the school cafeteria. Lucky for them, there's no way I could have afforded the black trench coat.

Today, I wear all black to the school anyway, just for the effect. I've got on an oversize hooded sweatshirt and a backpack that just might be concealing a semiautomatic rifle with two clips. I've got my best disgruntled face on. I'm back: this time, it's revenge.

But no one notices. No one scrambles for the intercom, locks the school doors, or calls security when I walk past the chain-link fence into the courtyard. Nothing's changed: the same kids are bouncing out of the doors, the same kids are lounging on the concrete benches, sneaking tokes and swapping spit and constantly chattering, like the monkeys on the treetop canopy of The Mirage. Even my old tormentors can't seem to be bothered. Two jocks who have been bouncing orange balls off my head since fifth grade come clumping down the stairs toward me. I brace for the inevitable insult (it's reflexive), but they sail right past me without so much as a smirk or a sneer.

I'm already a ghost to them.

Around the back, at the rapidly emptying school parking lot, waits Mr. Handy. He's by the car with a clipboard and a sky-blue folder tucked under his arm and a scowl on his face. "Mr. Stahl. You're late," he barks. "You want credit for the hour, you get here on the hour." Mr. Handy thrusts the folder in my direction. "Driving log. Know what it's for?" I'm taking a wild guess that it's for logging my driving. He barrels on. "Keep it. Use it. Don't lose it."

Mr. Handy teaches physics in the basement lab of the science wing, and only emerges from underground, like a bad-tempered groundhog blinking in the sunshine, to conduct Behind the Wheel training classes. He's been doing this for as long as there have been cars, I think. I took physics with him sophomore year but I have no recollection of it. Vectors, triangles, sines and cosines, they all jumbled together into a kind of basso rumbling intoned by Mr. Handy way up there in the front of the class.

"Today, the basics. Get in." Mr. Handy opens the driver's-side door.

My father liked to recount the story of Phaeton, the boy who found out his father was the sun god Hyperion (or Helios, or Phoebus Apollo, depending on the version). To prove his parentage (no DNA tests back then) Hyperion says he'll do anything the boy asks. Obviously the guy has never had dealings with a teenage boy, because of course the kid asks for a set of wheels: his father's Sun Chariot, to be exact. This chariot has way too much horsepower, literally, for someone without even a driver's permit, but the god has to say yes; he's sworn an oath. Phaeton gets behind the wheel, cracks the whip, and everything quickly goes to hell. The chariot veers out of control, singeing the heavens, scorching the earth, turning Ethiopians black from the heat. The gods lament, Zeus zaps Phaeton with a thunderbolt, and down the boy tumbles from the sky, dead.

I'm guessing there was some kind of message there.

"Today, Mr. Stahl," Mr. Handy says.

I get in. The seat sags in the middle, the upholstery worn where thousands of students' butts have been sliding in and over. The interior is bare-bones and stripped away, like it's really the fossil of a car, in taupe. The top of my head almost grazes the roof of the car, my knees are jack-knifed under the steering column. I take a deep breath. The space feels very small.

Slam. Mr. Handy disappears, and an instant later jerks open the passenger side. He crowds in. *Slam.* I still haven't touched the steering wheel.

"Basics. Adjust your seat."

All of Mr. Handy's face droops: his nose, his earlobes, the folds on the sides of his mouth. His sagging eyelids have tiny growths on them that seem to pull the lids down even farther.

The next thing I know he's grabbing my right knee and pushing it down. "Get your foot on the brake! Your foot on the brake!" My foot goes on the brake. "You're too far in. Adjust!!" He's now reaching forward between my legs and pulling up on a bar that slides my seat all the way back. "Push in! Push in!" Soon Mr. Handy's practically crawling all over me, manipulating bars and levers until he's got me in a position he's happy with. "Remember that," he growls, settling back onto his seat. He checks something off on his clipboard.

"Mirror. Mirror. Mirror." Mr. Handy stabs his pencil in three directions. "Use them. They can save your life." He proceeds to tap his pencil at everything. "Temperature. Oil pressure. Fuel," he rattles off. "Headlights. High beams. Turn lights. Warning lights. Got it?"

My father had a sister, Kathleen, who was fourteen years older than he was. She kind of took him in when their mother died, and when she got married a couple of years later, he came along, too, her only dowry. She was killed eight years later in a hit-and-run. No warning lights for her. Just a curse. And then there was Georgia—

Car keys are dangling in front of my face. "Let's get her started," Mr. Handy says.

He's handing over the reins. I'm Phaeton, feeling the leather straps pull against my hands. *Steer the middle course, my son, neither too high nor too low.* What kind of advice is that?

Mr. Handy settles back into the seat, clipboard at the ready. "Key in the ignition."

There's writing around the ignition: Lock. Acc. On. Start. Acc is right. *Acc! Acc!*

"Go ahead."

I hesitate, because it feels like a really, really bad move. Putting the key in its slot, turning my wrist, it's starting something I can't take back. For what good reason? It seems, suddenly, like an incredibly stupid idea.

There are tufts of gray hair growing out of Mr. Handy's ears. They're shooting out, like sparks. He moves closer. His breath is stale and smells like pepperoni. "Key. In the. Ignition."

Time slows. Mr. Handy's skin is pouring down his face, puddling around his neck. He's melting, that's what it is. Sparks are coming out of his ears, and he's melting. Mr. Handy's on fire, there's no air left to breathe, and we haven't even taken off. There's a woman walking on the sidewalk somewhere, about to step into the street. She doesn't even think about it. Zeus is drawing back his thunderbolt—

"Put the key in the ignition, Stahl!"

And he's grabbing my hand, trying to force it down toward the steering wheel column, but I'm way ahead of him. I've already thrown the keys to the ground and I shout, "I can understand English!" right into his melted face. He jerks back, eyes open wide, mouth gaping like a grounded carp, but before he can speak again I've opened the door and by the time he reaches for my arm I'm already out of the car and making my way onto the sidewalk. He's yelling for me, "Stahl! Stahl!" but I'm up and over the stairs, through the chain-link fence, and away, hoping I'll be in time to catch the 202 at 3:39.

The bus runs slow. It ambles from stop to stop, like a cow. An aged, injured cow. All of them are like this, even the express ones. You get used to it: the constant jerk, rumble, and halt as the bus sways down Charleston Boulevard. You don't even give it a second thought when smoke pours out of the engine, again, and you have to wait on the side of the road for twenty minutes until another 202 creaks by. Nobody jiggles their legs impatiently or sighs heavily or looks down at their watches. The reason for this is simple: nobody who rides the 202 has anywhere they want to get to fast.

It's different up and down the Strip, of course: there the buses are electric (courtesy of the casinos) and have bright spangly videos of showgirls and acrobats playing from high-definition monitors. Those buses are mostly for tourists who can't quite figure out how the monorail system works, but they also transport the Strip's workers to the Downtown Station in Old Vegas, where they can connect to these wheezing, diesel dinosaurs that'll take them home. It's kinda like a reverse Oz here: the moment you leave the Technicolor land of the Strip, you step into a world the color of sand. My world. Reverse Oz-mosis.

The bus lurches forward, prodding me toward the backpack at my feet. I take out my sketchbook and pen. Soon Mr. Handy's face is staring up at me, pocked in black ink, with drooping skin and fireworks shooting out of his ears. He's growling the words "Stahl! Stahl!"

That's my name, don't wear it out. I draw the rest of him melting into a puddle on the car seat. There. That'll show him.

I turn the page and stare at a great big sheet of nothing.

Who needs to drive, anyway? I live in Las Vegas. Where else do you need to go? Look, look what's here. I scribble out Vegas Vicky, smiling her crooked, gap-toothed smile, and her big blond curls bounce down to her big bouncing breasts; she's so full of Luck she's about to burst out of that white fringed midriff top. She's kicking her white cowgirl boots high, sending the colossal air balloon of the Paris Hotel soaring—

—over the Coney Island roller coaster of New York, New York, rushing around a giant goose in a cowboy hat, big as Godzilla. He sits on a pile of golden turds and waves a wing at—

—Vegas Vic, with his tight pants and cigarette-ravaged face, who gives a wink and a leer at Vicky. He's standing in the shadow of the Stratosphere, that giant prick looming over everything. Big dicks and big boobs. Las Vegas is the finest place on Earth.

The bus rocks back and forth, rumbling comfort. *You don't need a driver's license,* it's saying. *Stay with me. This is my slow croon, my mechanical moo, my lullaby. Who else will rock you?* The pen makes a little black trail snaking down to the bottom of the page. My head nods to the stopping and starting of motion. *The wheels on the bus go round and round.*

At age five, life began.

I'm lulling myself to sleep with my own bedtime story. Not the one my father used to tell, his Vegas Adventure, but the one of my first memory. The first memory I can remember. I see the details so clearly, it's as if a light had switched on—flash—and a photo had been taken— me and my father at the ruins of the Venetian:

Walking in the dusty air, my hand clenched tight by the bigger one. His palm is sweaty.

"It's wet! It's wet!" I say. I pull away; he wipes his hand on the side of his pants, then swallows up mine again.

Sun in my eyes.

A chain-link fence.

Inside, concrete and broken glass mounded high, metal snakes twisting out of the wreckage. White rubble;

a stone lizard's tail poking out.

Fragments of bridges jutting at odd angles, leading nowhere and everywhere, chunks of blue sky littering the ground, fallen from another landscape where it's cloudy and cool.

I want a piece of that celestial debris.

Suddenly I'm rising higher, higher, my father's hand tight across my chest, pressed into his body. His mouth by my ear, his other hand leading my eyes to a half-buried boat submerged in the stones. Its slim prow points to the heavens.

"There," he whispers, "there's where I last saw her."

And his story spins from there.

OWEN
VEGAS
EARLIER

Are you ready for Fun?

The relatively hushed calm of the airplane, with its constant but indecipherable babble of conversations and steady cabin drone, did little to prepare Owen for the festive bedlam that was McCarran Airport. Welcome to Las Vegas! it proclaimed, with its chromed and mirrored surfaces and the constant *ting!-ting!-ting!* of the slot machines, which seemed as incongruous in a terminal as a waffle iron in a public restroom.

Obviously, this airport did not want him to move dutifully and efficiently from checkpoint A to checkpoint B like a good citizen; it wanted him to linger and enjoy. Gift shops stretched out on either side of him, a leisurely sampler of everything the resorts had to offer. Brightly lit Wheels of Fortune spun and buzzed enticingly. *A modern-day street bazaar,* Owen thought, maneuvering past carry-on bags and the elderly, and it was true, there were palm trees and dried-fruit stands and yes, look, there were even a cluster of Arab sheiks examining some duty-free perfume. *All that's missing is a small chattering monkey in a little red vest. Now, that would come in handy.* Owen imagined it perched, chattering, on his shoulder. *Find Emmie, little Jo-Jo, go! Go!* And Jo-Jo would go-go, the little gold bells on his vest jingling, picking his way expertly through the crowds before landing on the one woven basket that contained his master's mistress: bound, gagged, but otherwise unharmed. *Good boy, Jo-Jo!* he'd shout, proffering a fig as a reward—

Shrieking. Twin stratospheric cries, making Owen jump. Behind him, two women in short skirts and frothy hair advanced slowly toward each other, their arms stretched wide. They looked ready for hand-to-hand combat. How long had he been standing there? Owen found himself parked in front of a glass window displaying the various wares of the Venetian hotel, including several blown-glass gondolas, small enough to fit in the palm of your hand, streaked with yellow and green. *Wouldn't Emmie like those,* Owen thought. I should pick one up for her.

Emmie. That was it. Focus. He had arrived. It was time to begin the search, sally forth, and so on. He had no monkey, sadly, but he'd have to make do. Owen followed the signs to Ground Transportation. He took long strides, hoping to inspire a feeling of confidence.

Why was he here again, exactly?

Emmie had always wanted to go to Vegas. This much he knew. It was on one of those internal lists she was constantly spinning up and adding to. This one was titled Places I Have to Visit Before I Die. Athens was on that list, and Bali, and Venice. Vietnam, oddly enough, was not. And Vegas, Vegas was on the top of the list. She was mildly obsessed with Vegas. Owen knew it had something to do with Liberace (look, there he was now on an airport kiosk, smiling from a poster advertising his eponymous museum), and with the accordion she used to play. Nonetheless, when he noticed his pills were missing (do not take more than prescribed dosage/illness or death may occur) it immediately jumped into his mind that she must be headed for Vegas. After all, if she drove away with his pills with the intention of swallowing them in more than the prescribed dosage (why would she take them otherwise, he reasoned) wouldn't she drive to one of those Places She Had to Visit Before She Died? Vegas was the only destination in the continental United States, she didn't have a current passport, and, even suicidal, Emily wouldn't want to miss a chance to strike something off her list.

Owen followed the signs overhead like one of the dutiful Magi, veering neither north nor south but staying constant in his travels west, west to Baggage Claim, west to Ground Transportation Exit 3 or 4, west to the promised Hut where presumably a taxi awaited, swaddled in blankets. *I come bearing tips.*

Choosing Exit 4, he was met with two equally strong and opposing forces: the crush of passengers propelling him through the door, and the wall of heat outside, which nearly pushed him back into the cool sanctuary of the baggage claim area. It was one assault of the senses after another, first of sight, then sound, and now feeling: how could humans exist in such extremes? Apparently, very well, thank you, judging from the accelerating chatter of his fellow travelers, the anticipatory set of their shoulders as they pushed forward into the Saharan heat, the shocked but gleeful *Whoa!*s exploding from their mouths like so many kernels of popcorn bursting around him. Owen took in a breath of dry, hot air and held it all the way to the taxi stand.

And there it was, a cab waiting patiently just for him. Exhaling, Owen grabbed for the chunky metal door handle. But it would not move. A jerk downward, a jerk outward; it would yield in no direction—

(*It yields in no direction. His hand pulls the slim molded plastic handle—Why won't it open? There's no time, no, he can't—think—the door won't open and—Why won't it open!—and his arm tightens, fuses with the plastic, jerking it, her eyes are closed—Open! Open! Let. Me. In! and a moment later he is sprawled on the asphalt, the door handle suddenly light and senseless in his hand, nonsensical really, this little disconnected piece of molded plastic, and all he can do is stare stupidly at it while inside it is so hot—*)

Chunk! The taxi door unlocked. The driver didn't even turn his head. Standing beside the cab, Owen turned the handle easily, and swung wide the door. He poked his head in, suddenly clammy—*Nothing scary here!*—then forced himself into the cool cab, onto the patched red leather of the backseat—so wide. So horribly empty. Owen pushed his head against the back of the seat and closed his eyes.

The gondolas, he said. Take me to where the gondolas are.

Craaank went the meter. The taxi slipped silently into the flow of traffic.

He had warned her. He had been quite specific about it. Yes, Owen remembered the exact location, all those years ago: it was at the Italian restaurant Anna Maria's. She always insisted on calling it Anna Maria Alberghetti; he never understood the reference. A small place, six tables total, and a counter to pick up and eat slices of pizza. They were at the spot by the front window with fake daisies overhead. They had ordered what they always ordered: Linguine Bolognese for him, Pollo alla Anna for her, not spicy, please. The tables were small and his knees would occasionally, thrillingly, knock into hers. It was, as they say, their place, and that was where he remembered telling her he was cursed.

He had to tell her. Owen felt the frequency of their dinners together was perhaps indicative of something more: five months' worth of dinners and movies; the two concerts in Grant Park; even that attempt to meet up at the overcrowded Taste of Chicago, which had failed due to a bad sense of direction (his); the long winter they had endured together and the gradual emergence from heavy parkas with bulky sweaters, scarves, and hoods to woolen coats and caps and eventually today—surprise!—to a light sweater and jacket (spring in April, always a miracle); all of these events together now added up to something more, or seemed to, in his eyes. The accretion of time spent together felt heavy, ripe, and ready to be redeemed for something of greater value. Which was why he was nervously tearing his slice of garlic bread into smaller and smaller chunks until he held what amounted to a crouton between his thumb and finger. He looked over his parsley-flecked fingers at her and smiled quickly.

They had met in November at his friend Larry's annual Orphans' Thanksgiving. Owen had a near-perfect attendance record to this event, dating back to its inception during Owen's first year of grad school, some eight (ten?) years previous. The usual double handful was there that year, plus a couple of attachments and minus a few who had decided to brave the trip home (an option not available to Owen) or who had managed to find better parties elsewhere. Of these attendees there was a nucleus of four that Owen saw regularly: undergrad friends who had not fled Chicago post-BA. This included his host, Larry, who was at the moment preoccupied with both the final throes of dinner preparation and his current squeeze, Richard ("squeeze" was no figure of speech; Larry could not pass by the languid Richard without impulsively kneading a shoulder or ass or arm, as if to convince himself that Richard was indeed corporeal; Larry had gone a long while without a lover, though not, as Larry was fond of pointing out, as long as Owen). Larry had only time for a quick peck on Owen's cheek (no hug, hands too covered with bits of pastry dough) before darting back to the kitchen, Owen's wine bottle tucked in the crook of his arm.

The house was warm and reassuring with its smell of turkey. As Owen was taking off his coat the doorbell screeched again. Larry's voice boomed from across three rooms, Could you get that? and Owen punched at the door buzzer. *Bang* went the outer door of the vestibule, *bang* went the inner door, and before Owen could wipe the condensation off his glasses the apartment door swung open and two women swept in.

They entered laughing and brandishing more wine bottles. One of them he knew to be Jillian, another Thanksgiving regular (her laugh was recognizable even from the landing below). The other woman, much smaller than Jillian and bundled up, was, as far as Owen could tell, unknown to him, but by the time he had readjusted his glasses she was revealing herself: slowly unwinding the long scarf from around her neck. The deliberateness with which she unwrapped herself, her arm slowly revolving around her head one, two, three, four times around (there seemed to be no end to the scarf) brought to mind those whirling dervishes from Istanbul, but inverted: her legs were still, but her head and arm were in constant, hypnotic orbit.

Finally the scarf was uncoiled, and with that, the dance ended: gloves, scarf, and hat were stuffed into her coat; the coat came off with one prac-ticed flourish; and like a magician's trick out emerged a small, slender Asian woman, eyes bright and coal-dark, her long hair whipping free. She smiled at Owen, and for the second time that evening his glasses fogged over.

Jillian stepped forward, both their coats piled in her arm. Hey, Owen, she said. Gimme your coat. This is Emily.

And as Jillian disappeared into the coat-dumping room (had he even murmured thank you—said anything?), Emily took a step forward and said, Another orphan? and Owen, peering from the top of his glasses, nodded too eagerly, as if that fact were the most wonderful thing in the entire world.

The subject of orphans came up again later on at dinner. Owen was too preoccupied to engage in much of the conversation swirling around the table (with his usually Teflon-coated grasp of names, he was silently repeating the name Emily, Emily to himself, trying to make it stick) when he heard her voice sharpen at the other end of the table. I don't understand, she said, who is this Thanksgiving for?

We're not *technically* orphans, said Larry, seated next to her at the head of the table. He reached for Richard's free hand, giving it a little massage. We're more *holiday* orphans.

It's wishful thinking on our parts, Jillian said.

Emily nodded slowly, then looked around the table. Are there any *technical* orphans here? she asked. Jillian laughed and said, Uh-oh, here comes the lawyer.

There were several shakes of the head, and Thomas piped in that he was halfway there, but it wasn't until Larry gave him a pointed look that Owen remembered to raise his hand.

Ah, said Emily, so I'm not the only one.

She went on to merrily describe her upbringing to the table, not only that she came from an actual orphanage (I'm afraid you have me there, murmured Owen to no one in particular) but that, *technically*, she had never had a mother. Apparently, the woman who raised Emily (was

V an initial or a name? Owen couldn't make it out) had some aversion to being called Mother. Ergo, motherless.

Jillian jabbed a turkey-laden fork in her direction. Now you're just trying to make us jealous.

Owen, having had his brief moment in the full glow of her attention, slipped back in the shadows of the other diners. Half in and half out of the flow of her narrative (raised in Milwaukee, John Marshall Law School, job at Arthur Andersen), he marveled at how easily Emily conversed with strangers. (*Emily. Emily.*) The way she tossed her hair over her shoulder, graceful as a water nymph, a naiad slipping silently from a rushing stream onto the quiet shores. Combing out her dark hair, *Long-Haired Emily of the Bright Eyes—*

To no woman born, intoned Richard portentously. Grad student, Shakespearean studies, Owen guessed.

Pie, proclaimed Larry, and rose from the table.

Later, seated in the blue armchair with the sides ripped away by Larry's cat Thiebaud, Owen stared at the fire and found himself settling into the dusky melancholy he always experienced during required holiday celebrations. The others were huddled out on the porch smoking or collecting dishes from the dining room in anticipation of dessert. Owen didn't even know Emily was by his chair until she spoke.

I'm not very good at the clearing-up part of dinner, she said apologetically, as if he were Larry's host-by-proxy.

Oh, Owen said, momentarily confused, until a large clattering of dishes in the kitchen gave him context. He smiled at Emily. It's better to stay out of there, he said. Larry rules his realm with an iron fist. I was banished from the kitchen years ago. Something about the wrong dishrag.

Emily nodded. It was obviously time for some kind of leading question or statement from Owen, but he was out. The conversation wasn't sparking. It was being smothered. Lack of oxygen. The fire was sucking it all away. Why did he have nothing in his queue to talk about? Why was his mind so dull? He sensed her starting to shift away, and despaired.

Fortunately, she was only bending toward him in order to save the situation, for which Owen was profoundly grateful. She whispered, in a mock-conspiratorial tone, I was a little disappointed to find out it wasn't a technical Orphans' Thanksgiving.

Yes, yes, Owen said, buying himself some time. Then, inspiration at last: Give them a few years, he said, I'm sure there'll be more who qualify. Thomas's father has been diagnosed with some horrible disease, so you might keep an eye on him.

She said, That's terrible! but she was laughing just the same. Owen felt relief, and a certain tingling travel up his spine. The next pause was comfortable; she sat down on the arm of the chair, and there was a sense, Owen felt it strongly, of a shared experience, however tenuous. Two technical orphans, staring at a fire. Dynasties had been built on less.

You've heard my orphan story, Emily said finally, and Owen was sure he could discern under the light tone a darker shading. What about yours? she asked.

But Owen couldn't, not then, and shook his head with a mock-rueful demeanor. There's so little of interest about me, he said, I need to keep what mystery I have to myself. Which was not altogether an honest answer but was acceptable given the circumstances: he didn't want to scare her away.

That's okay, Emily said to him, her hand on his shoulder. You keep your secrets.

And so he did, for five months, as chance group encounters progressed to casual meetings progressed to arranged appointments and now, to bona fide, scheduled dates. And here it was, on the cusp of something, a something that mattered, that he felt it was only fair, it was *incumbent* upon him to warn her, however stupid, or worse, alarming, he might sound. So there, with his parsley-flecked fingers and the shreds of garlic toast littering his bread plate, waiting for the entrée to come, he told her.

You know, he said as casually as he could, lifting a glass of house wine to his lips, I should tell you: I think I've got a curse on me.

And so he told her his entire sad story, of his mother and his sister and the rest, and though he didn't mean for it to happen (he swore he didn't), of course the warning didn't have the intended effect but quite the opposite: she grabbed his hand tight and didn't let go, and of course she didn't believe in the curse but was horrified nonetheless, not of him but of his circumstances, and this, of course, made her slip a notch deeper in love with him, and that, as they say in common parlance, sealed the deal.

I bet she believes in it now.

Owen looked out the taxi window just as a sphinx (the Egyptian varietal, not the Greek) reared its head over the horizon. He was suddenly aware of being besieged on all sides by pedestrians, cars, and buses, packed on the road, on the sides of the road, entering the road, reducing the taxi's speed to a crawl. *I might as well be riding on a camel,* Owen thought, as Giza's famous beast towered overhead. They were all on a pilgrimage, making their personal hajj to black pyramids and castles, giant golden lions, monstrous candy faces, and Lady Liberty herself, green with vertigo as she struggled to stay upright amid the twisted tracks of roller coasters and the giant Ferris wheel. The Vegas Strip was not like a street, with hotels. It was entire nations pushing up against one another, crammed. Civilizations jostling for space. These cities have gone to war, but instead of armies the buildings themselves have rushed forward into battle. Owen had never felt so lost.

EMILY & VEE
WISCONSIN
MUCH EARLIER

Long before she had ever heard him play a note of music, long before she had seen his face splashed on a tabloid magazine cover or watched him cavort with Muppets on television, Emily felt a special bond with Liberace that bordered on kinship. Her relationship with the flamboyant pianist began in black and white, under circumstances that led her to believe the man was, in fact, her father.

Not her biological father, of course, just as Vee was not her biological mother. Vee didn't even call herself Mother, never felt comfortable with it. The title just wasn't accurate. Anyone could see they weren't biologically related; to pretend otherwise was untruthful and made their actual relationship seem like something to be ashamed of, which it was not. She didn't want to confuse the child; she wanted the facts laid out, clear and simple: she was Vee, a mother figure in Emily's life, but not, in the strictest sense, her mother.

Emily's biological mother was presumed dead. No other information was forthcoming. There was no use in asking Vee because she had already stated flatly that she knew nothing about the woman, and why do you keep asking? Emily couldn't consult her own memory, either; she was less than two when the large lady from Milwaukee, United States, scooped her up from the orphanage in Saigon.

In those early days, when language was still liquid to Emily (English not yet formed and her memory of Vietnamese receding daily, its few remaining syllables and intonations remembered more for comfort than meaning), she would sometimes cry out *Ma! Ma!* in the middle of the night, terrified, and Vee would stride in immediately, as if on cue, ready to pat Emily's back, shush away the fears, and murmur in her growl of a whisper, "I'm not Ma. I'm Vee. Call me Vee." This continued until the word Ma, in English or Vietnamese, no longer had any meaning to Emily at all.

As for Emily's biological father, it wasn't that he was missed, exactly. Raised by female caretakers and then Vee, Emily had little interaction with men who were not doctors, immigration officials, or principals. And if those stern, frowning officials were any indication of the gender, the less interaction she had with it, the better. Young Emily had no need for a male figure in her home, and neither, apparently, did Vee.

Still, by the time she finished kindergarten she began realizing that not every child's household was like hers. Many, most, had homes that were much more populated. There was a Mommy, a Daddy, frequently other children, and sometimes animals. Emily could easily point to Vee as the Mommy, in function if not name, but shouldn't there be the Daddy?

By eight, these impressions had solidified into Fact: one or more children equaled two parents. The Farmer took a Wife; the King lived with his Queen; even Bears had a Momma and Papa. Sometimes Daddies or Mommies died (or, in one case, were banished to the shadowy netherworlds of Divorce), but they still existed at some point. Who was the phantom mate of Vee? While Emily couldn't imagine a farmer ever grabbing Vee and pulling her into his circle (not without being given a good what-for) she could envision Vee taking a Farmer. She would take him by the shoulders and give him a good yank in; Vee was very good at yanking. But what had happened to this yanked-in man?

Asking Vee directly resulted in a swift, equally direct rebuttal, followed by a stern admonishment to get her fanny into school clothes, and quickly, too. Emily, not so easily dissuaded, had to resort to more circuitous methods of discovery to get her question answered.

One Saturday well into October, when the Wisconsin air was just cold enough for Vee to consider pulling the big comforters out (the furnace wasn't even an option until the day after Thanksgiving, or the first snowfall, whichever came earlier), a call came from one of the neighbors. The widowed Mrs. Steiff had broken her leg cleaning out the gutters, and she asked Vee to perform a mission of mercy for her. She was in need of some necessities: Kitty Chow, Campbell's cream of tomato soup, and a carton of Parliament 100s.

Sighing heavily, Vee grabbed her plaid quilted jacket from the hook by the kitchen door. Switching on Saturday-morning cartoons, she pointed to the couch and told Emily to stay put. A jingle of the car keys, and Vee was gone.

Emily, who had overheard the entire phone conversation, realized a golden opportunity when it presented itself. The roads were twisty, the A&P was fifteen minutes away, and Mrs. Steiff was a talker. Emily had plenty of time. Time to explore.

She remained obedient, perched on the couch, exactly the length of one cartoon. During the commercial she quietly made her way down the hall, ready to dive immediately into her own bedroom should Vee return unexpectedly. And then, with the cheery patter of cartoon characters providing backup, Emily slowly pushed open the door to Vee's bedroom. The soft *whoosh* of the wood moving over the carpeting was more felt than heard. She stood for a moment, frozen, peering into the silent room with equal parts fear and excitement. Vee's room was off-limits; Emily understood this without ever having been told. It was not a room for visiting, it was not a room for playing in—it was a room for sleeping, and only for Vee.

Two steps, and she was in.

There wasn't much to explore. Vee kept her room as spare as a nun's. Nightstand, dresser, bed, chair. All of it made of rough pine, stained dark, and all of it almost exactly like the furniture in Emily's room.

Emily knelt by the bed, as if saying her bedtime prayers, except that instead of her hands clasped in front of her she had them jammed under the mattress up to her elbows. She was sawing her thin arms back and forth, trawling for anything hidden between box spring and mattress. Nothing. She ducked her head beneath the bed, found only a gloomy darkness residing there. The bed yielded no secrets.

Emily moved her little fingers quickly and efficiently along the bottom of each drawer and in between folded layers of clothes without disturbing a crease; she knew instinctively to observe how many fractions of an inch each dresser drawer was open to begin with and to close it by just that much. All her skill, however, yielded her nothing. No secret packet of love letters, no incriminating wedding photo. Not even the underwear was alluring.

Then she opened the closet door.

It was all the way in the back, below the flannels and denims and poly/cotton blends, behind the three pairs of sensible shoes that Vee owned: a bruised cardboard box big enough to fit Emily, were she able to contort herself in the way the little Siamese girls did on those circus shows. It was too dim to read all the faded letters on the side of the box, but she could make out the faint red outline of a smiling chicken holding up an egg with the fingertips of its wings. RANDALL FAMILY FARMS.

Emily marched Vee's shoes out and lined them up in their respective places away from the closet. Holding her breath, she dove back in, hunched over, sidling along the wall to the back of the closet. In the darkness she could see that the box was unsealed, its top flaps crisscrossed shut. The gap in the center invited disclosure; it wanted to be opened. Emily inched the box forward, then got behind it to shove with all of her weight. Hanging pants and jackets batted at her face, warning her, but they flapped unheeded. Not even the smell of Vee, so rich inside the closet, could deter her. The weight of the box was too promising. She unmoored it from the confines of the closet and propelled the box into the bedroom. It floated adrift on the powder-blue carpeting, a treasure chest recovered from the deep, ready to be plundered.

Opening the flaps, the first thing to catch her eye was a bundle in white tissue paper. Emily picked it up carefully; the bundle was light but insistent, each soft crinkle of the paper a whisper: *Open me, open me.* She meant to unwrap it carefully, but at the first provocation the paper gave way and green fabric slipped free, cascading onto Emily's lap like water.

It was a dress. Silky and soft, and Coke-bottle-green. It was so delicate it looked like it might float away, but instead slid from her hands onto the floor, where it shimmered. A faint pattern of magnolia flowers blossomed in an even paler shade of green over the blouse of the dress, with tiny jade buttons serving as stepping stones down to the skirt, which rustled with pleats. Emily had never seen anything more beautiful.

She might have stayed with the dress longer, fingering each button and stroking the shiny material, but a pair of eyes inside the cardboard box would not be ignored. They stared at her from within a gilt-edged frame, which jutted upward, half buried in folders and photo albums. The eyes followed her as she lifted the frame out. Emily gasped.

The man in the black-and-white photograph was no farmer. He was dressed in a black tuxedo, every bit the match of a Coke-bottle-green dress. His hair was full and wavy and dark as his eyes. He had a gaze that was intense but welcoming, tempered by the full, soft lips and round cheeks. His hands were poised over an ebony grand piano with a gleaming candelabra stationed on top. And scrawled to the side, in a bold, looping signature, the words "All My Love, Liberace."

All My Love. Emily clasped the frame to her chest. This was the man she had been looking for. She had found Mr. Vee.

OWEN

THE VENETIAN

EARLIER

It would seem improbable, standing in the grand opulence of the Venetian Resort Hotel Casino, with its marble columns and Italian frescoes on domed ceilings, shimmering golden chandeliers and Puccini arias wafting down from hidden speakers like sweet perfume, that Owen would be contemplating Polish sausages, but there he was, clinging onto the smooth white marble banister at the top of the second floor, thinking of nothing else.

It was a specific Polish sausage, one that came out of a steam table on a corner by the bridge at Jackson Boulevard and Michigan Avenue, one sweaty day in Chicago. The aroma wafted out from under the yellow-and-blue umbrella, enveloping Owen like a steamy, meaty mist as he scanned the crowds for Emmie on the advent of what was going to be their first official getting-together without the protective safety net of friends. Owen was waiting, had been waiting, for her on this particular corner, it was the agreed-upon corner, he was certain, but she was three-quarters of an hour late already and another fifty minutes would go by before he finally gave up and headed for home. The corner by the Indian statue, she told him later that day, when they met up at Anna Maria's. Don't you remember I said the Indian statue? He did not. She had left two messages on his machine. *I'm here, by the Indian statue. Where are you?*

I'm in Venice. It's magnificent. I'm about to throw up.

Finding her would be impossible. He couldn't even find the lobby anymore. As far as he knew, he was inside (which looked like outside) and upstairs, which was on the ground floor. He had wandered up and down two levels, over bridges, through passageways, onto carpeting leading to cobblestones leading to marble tiles back to the carpeting, gondolas appearing and disappearing from out of nowhere. The only place he could find with any regularity was the casino, which seemed to appear, blazing and buzzing (*ching! ching! ching! chunk-a-chunk! Wheel! Of! Fortune!*) around every corner. This wouldn't be like meeting someone in the lobby of the Best Western. This hotel was a municipality unto itself, and the second floor was another place altogether, one of canals and strolling minstrels and lampposts lit against the perpetual twilight painted on the ceiling. Walking toward St. Mark's Square (he hoped), he was acutely aware of passing through a city within a city within a city; it was like being in one of those little Russian dolls that disgorge the smaller dolls inside of it. And with any luck, in the center, tiny but intact, he'd discover Emmie.

Unless he was, once again, on the wrong corner.

Let's stop for a moment, shall we? Let the dizziness pass. He was sure he had it right. He had listened. She had always wanted to go to Vegas, and if she were in Vegas, she would be at the Venetian, because Venice was also on the list. They had actually planned a trip to Venice for their belated honeymoon (well, Emmie had planned it, she had the stacks of books and brochures, had circled hotels and *ristorantes,* pinned down the right airline and the best fare) before an unexpected bump under the proverbial cabbage leaf knocked that idea out of the canal. The pregnancy, several years early according to Emily's timetable, put life into a crisis zone. She would leave her job (her choice) for at least a few years, and that would mean implementing the most draconian of measures: there could be no honeymoon, no trip of any kind; a bigger apartment and a safe car were the priorities. Still, the travel guides and brochures stayed on the bookshelf and made the cut of several rummage sales. And, AND, less than a year ago, he remembered her pointing to a story she was reading in the *Tribune* travel section; she had made him remember it by opening the spread in front of his face while he was grading papers and eating breakfast. There it was, a full-color, half-page photo of sparkling aquamarine water and ebony gondolas, and she said, We should go there, and he said, Venice? and she said, No, no, it's in Vegas, it just opened, and when he said nothing she said, We could kill two birds with one stone, and he said, Okay, when? and she said nothing, only sighing and snapping the newspaper away, no doubt for future clipping and filing in some color-coded folder.

Get to St. Mark's. That's where she'd be. Owen hurried on, trying to follow the canal but thwarted by meandering streets, which inevitably veered off into another alley of high-priced souvenir shops and blown-glass galleries. He had the feeling that if he stayed in one spot too long everything would change. All the landmarks were shifting; even the painted sky above seemed to continually darken, warning of impending night—what time was it anyway? Always darkening, never dark; there was no rest to be had in this underground (second-floor) kingdom. He was Orpheus, wandering through the Stygian realm, searching for his lost love, Eurydice, among the damned souls. Here was the River Styx, bright aquamarine, passing under marble bridges. There, floating past Owen, went Charon the ferryman, in a red bandanna and straw hat, crooning "O Solo Mio" to two enraptured passengers with coins on their eyes. The only thing missing was Orpheus's song. Owen couldn't sing a note to save his life, let alone his wife's.

He crossed another bridge onto a large cobblestone square. It was the exact match of the newspaper photo Owen had seen spread out over his cereal bowl, only more densely populated. Restaurants ran along the perimeter; faux second-story buildings glowed with evening light. A gelateria occupied the center, swarming with customers pointing to various brightly colored bricks of ice cream. Wheeled wooden stands were set up, laden not with tomatoes and sweet basil but with gondola snow globes, Venetian masks, and dice. Was that the faint scent of lilies in the air?

Finally, after two hours, he had made it. St. Mark's Square, bereft of actual Italians. And Emily.

There wasn't any sign of her. It was then Owen realized she might not have arrived yet. He tried to calculate how long it would take to drive from Milwaukee to Las Vegas, and hadn't the faintest idea. Would it be tomorrow? The next day? Wasn't it a drive of several days? Why hadn't he thought of that before? And what was he going to do, sit by the canals for three days waiting for her to show?

A sudden susurrus of wings, a collective gasp from those along the canal, and out of nowhere, a flock of pigeons exploded into the sky. *Of course,* thought Owen, *St. Mark's Square. They thought of everything.* The pigeons fanned out across the square, soaring upward. People applauded. *There isn't much sky for you to fly into,* thought Owen, but the birds had anticipated that. At the last minute they swerved away from the ceiling in perfect sync, gliding gracefully to the ground.

Except one. A lone pigeon continued its trajectory upward (Rebellious? Suicidal?) until it became acquainted with the finite and rigid qualities of this particular sky. With much violent flapping of wings it smashed into a wispy cloud. Immediately the bird fell downward, its body compressed into a streamlined missile, picking up speed, heading straight for Owen, who could only gape, frozen, as it dive-bombed in his direction.

The pigeon landed square on his chest. He was expecting the softness of gray wings, or the sharp point of a beak to bore into him. Instead, the hard nub of the bird's head slammed into his left clavicle, not hard enough to hurt, but enough to throw him off balance and knock him down. He landed hard on his tailbone, and a second collective gasp sounded from the crowd. The bird lay beside him, dazed, but miraculously not dead.

He'd been attacked by a pigeon in Venice. It was time to get a room.

As if on cue, three men in dark blue uniforms and epaulets appeared by his side, helping him up, murmuring soft but urgent apologies in his ear, whisking the bird from sight. And just like that, his wish was granted. Fifteen minutes and a signed release of responsibility form later, he held in his hand a plastic hotel key card, complimentary, emblazoned with the glowing lights of the Doge's Palace.

This is perfect, he thought, sitting on the luxurious king-size bed with winged lions glowering regally from underneath the nightstand lampshades. He would find her tomorrow, he would stake out the canals all day until she arrived. And when he found her, there'd be a room for her to stay in, to recuperate. It would be their long-delayed honeymoon.

He needed to make a call. His hand hovered over the hotel room phone. Emmie would never approve. She'd say, Phone charges? That's where they get you. And she'd whip out her long-distance calling card, like it was her talisman against evil. We'll call from the lobby. Owen didn't even know where his card was. There was nothing to be done. He pressed the hotel prefix, then, with reckless abandon, dialed the Wisconsin number. *I guess they got me.*

Vee picked up on the first ring. Where the hell are you? she demanded when he announced himself. I'm looking for Emily, he said. He half expected her to interrupt him and say, Emily's here, you idiot! When she did not, he was, foolishly, relieved. He said, I'm in Vegas.

Where? she asked.

Vegas, he said, I'm in Las Vegas.

What on earth would Emily be doing in Vegas?

I, I have a feeling, he said, instantly sensing Vee's eyes rolling to the back of her head. He continued, saying hurriedly, Emily said she wanted to go to Las Vegas. Now? Vee asked, getting to the heart of the matter, and Owen said, No, no, but Vee was already tired of talking to him. How long will you be? she asked, and Owen said, Until I find her. And what am I supposed to do with your son? she asked, and Owen stammered, I, I was hoping you could look after him. I won't be long, and Vee gave a laugh, short and bitter. How do you know?

He needed to get off the phone. How is Walt? he asked. How's his fever? She said, It's there, and when he asked to talk to him she said, He's sleeping, and from her tone, he could tell that she wasn't about to go waking him up.

Well, if you could tell him, tell him I'm, we're coming home soon.

I will tell him no such thing.

Please, Vee—

How can you find her? You can't even get out of bed.

Owen felt his jaw clench tightly. Well, I'm here now, aren't I? he said hotly. She's my wife.

Vee exhaled loudly. You don't know her, she said, and hung up.

He put down the phone carefully. It had not even been two minutes, he was sure of that. The charge wouldn't be too much. Owen felt strangely victorious. He had made it all this way. He had navigated himself all this way, down to Las Vegas, and had secured a free room in the finest hotel, to boot. He would find her.

She would want to be rescued. She'd arrive at the canals and he'd be there, waiting for her, he'd extend an arm and beckon her into a gondola. Soundlessly, they'd float, in each other's arms, and all would be well. Like Orpheus, he'd lead his Eurydice out of this underworld and back to *terra superus,* to Chicago.

And he wouldn't look back, no, not once.

Bridges, gondolas, lampposts. Stores. Bad opera singing. Stores. A painted sky.

It's pretty much as I remember it.

My foot's about to step onto cobblestone and the Great Indoor Shopping Experience known as the Grand Canal Shoppes. There are two life-size statues flanking the archway to St. Mark's Square, on blocks of marble atop seven-foot pillars. A Young Apollo and Diana, in classic positions: slim Diana bending down to retrieve what looks like an arrow, foot pointed and arm outstretched; hunky Apollo seated on the block, one leg out and one leg bent, lyre at his side, face raised toward the eternal blue sky projected above. I don't remember them being there before, but it's not like statues are a big deal on the Strip. You can't go two feet without running into an imitation *Thinker* or *David*. Apart from a few gawping tourists, most people pass through the archway without even glancing up. There's no time to stop and admire Beauty when Armani beckons.

No accordion players, though. We used to come here a lot, looking for them, the first years after the Venetian was built back up and rechristened Venice Venice. My father would take me by the hand and we'd go up and down the newly erected bridges, chasing after dark-haired accordion players. Then one day he said he didn't want to go anymore. It wasn't the same, he said, the Venice of Venice Venice wasn't the same as the Venice of the Venetian. It was too vast now, he said, the canals were too wide and there were too many bridges. She would be impossible to find.

I was also getting to the age where I realized that the chances of her making a return engagement were pretty thin, and I think he knew that. It wasn't long after that that he started staying in bed more and more, started the staring, and since I was too young to go myself, well, that ended that.

Strolling musicians at two P.M. The kiosk doesn't mention which instruments. Is there anyone in a Pierrot costume, wielding an accordion, black hair? I consider asking someone about it, maybe Security Joe over there, the big black man with the navy blue jacket and the wire looping over his ear, but he's already giving me a red-rimmed stink eye. He knows a vagrant when he sees one. I head over to the gelato stand across the square, the only place where I can afford to buy something. Single scoop.

So much for the Great American Consumer Experience. I pass back through the archway, tending to the chocolate drips, when all of a sudden a high-pitched squeal pierces my ears. It's one of those teenage-girl squeals I've encountered many times at Silverado High, a squeal that can only mean cruelty and public ridicule are about to follow. I brace myself for the onslaught, but it's not a teenager in front of me, it's a middle-aged woman with a freckled bosom and a pink Spandex top. Her mouth is open in a perfect *O* of surprise. I swipe at my face with my hand, figuring I must have had a major Nutella mishap, but then I realize that she's not even staring at me. Her finger is pointing above my head.

I look up, and there, on the block of marble, is Young Apollo's chiseled leg. His thigh. His bare hip. His haunch. The haunch of Apollo. There isn't any other way to describe it, it's a haunch, like nothing I've ever seen. Three and half years of mandatory high school PE had never before revealed a haunch like this one. My gelato-lined mouth falls open into an *O. O. O*. There is no *not* looking at this leg. It's powerful and sleek, massive without being crude. Every muscle is accounted for, every tendon and line can be traced from origin to end. It's so real looking I turn away, blushing. There's heat coming off the white stone.

And then it occurs to me: Wasn't his lyre on the ground, resting by his hip, when I passed through? Now it's in his hand. And wasn't that other hand, the one lifted to make a pass through the strings, resting on his knee before?

I think, I must not have been paying attention, but I swing my gaze over to Diana, and she's different, too. She's now crouched, hand resting on her fallen arrow, her back straight, head raised, like she's ready to leap up and resume the chase. I'm sure: They've changed positions. They've moved.

I notice that each pillar has a little carved-out nook halfway up, with a porcelain urn inside. There are dollar bills in the urns. Then it hits me. Hits me hard. They're real.

I shiver. If I had any hair on my body it would have stood up on end. These statues are too still, too perfectly proportioned, to be real; and yet, they are. I can see, way up there, life in Apollo's deep-set, unblinking eyes, even if they're not looking my way. It seems impossible, the way his wrist bends back with the fingers spread out, never trembling. There's not a nostril flare, no slow, telltale expansion of the chest. It's wild. He really is a god up there, trapped in plaster.

"Oh my Gawd," Spandex Bosom exhales.

It's hard to be impressed living in a place like Las Vegas, where they cart in the latest Wonder of the World for mass consumption every other Friday. And there are certainly superhuman feats performed twice daily in almost every hotel on the Strip. But these gods, they're different. They aren't like those other living statue posers that crowd the walkways, those with bodies hidden under white draperies and gloves and their herky-jerky movements like bad robot impersonators. This Apollo is something else. Art made Flesh. Or Flesh, transformed into Art.

"Damn," mutters a man beside me, "damn damn damn." He's wearing glasses and breathes through his mouth. Little beads of perspiration dot his hairline. "I've been watching her for an hour straight and I haven't seen her move a muscle." His eyes never stray from their heaven-ward trajectory. "She's doing it somehow but I can't catch her. I can't catch her. Ah shit! Shit! Her hand! When did she move her hand?"

Diana is now clutching the fallen arrow, which, last I saw, was lying on the ground. She has it lifted just past her anklebone. Whipping my head around, I discover Apollo's right hand now drawn past the lyre, as if he had just released a sweet chord into the air.

The man pulls off his glasses and squeezes his eyes tight. He runs his hand over his hair twice and then over his face. "I was watching!" he cries. "How is she doing that?" He sounds both amazed and angry, like he's been duped. He takes one last look up, then wrenches his body away. "I've been here too long," he murmurs, shaking his head. "I need to go gamble." And he flees.

I walk reverently up to each porcelain urn, dig in my pocket, and di-vest myself of my remaining cash. Happily. I've been converted. This isn't my father's Venice, after all.

OWEN

THE VENETIAN

EARLIER

Three A.M. With the curtains drawn, the room was comfortably tomblike (womblike?), but Owen could not sleep, not even in these soft, warm sheets, under the ornamental canopy positioned over his head. We could kill two birds with one stone, Emily had said. The Venetian, surely, was one of the birds, and Venice the other. Look, there was an actual bird, the pigeon almost killed by a trompe l'oeil. They had probably taken it away to finish the job, wring its neck in a discreet alcove. Pigeons are Forbidden to Attack the Guests. It was in their contract, right after Pigeons Will Not Defecate in the Square. Could a pigeon be potty trained? Walter. He sometimes regressed in his potty training, during illnesses. Ear infections he got, mostly. Is that what he had this time? Owen hadn't even known Walter was sick; Owen had been sick himself. Weakness. Damn Vee. Would she leave any kind of message from him, would she tell Walter that his parents had not left him, that it was only a temporary, a brief *epeisodion*? Not likely. He should have insisted that she wake Walter up, so he could have spoken to him, reassured him. . . . Vee wouldn't have budged. But he should have tried. . . .

Owen threw off the sheets to get a glass of water from the bathroom sink.

He had seen that picture of Liberace, on the kiosk in the airport. VISIT THE FABULOUS LIBERACE MUSEUM! Was that an omen? Or was it the pigeon (that's right, that's where he was going with the pigeon idea), was the pigeon the sign that he was in the right place, the place of the killed bird? He was no oracle. Was it telling him that the bird was already killed at the Venetian, that he needed to go elsewhere; maybe the Liberace Museum was the other bird, and she was on her way to killing that bird. *Oh, Emmie, Emmie, where art thou? We could kill two birds with one stone. . . .* Which birds did she mean?

It would be a long night, even in Egyptian cotton sheets.

Owen turned onto his side and flicked on the radio alarm clock by the winged lion on the nightstand. Electronic keyboards and a clarinet solo crackled softly from the speaker. Emily would have hated this New Age music, but it was the perfect soporific. Owen settled into the pillows and closed his eyes. Underneath the radio music—from another suite? or perhaps coming from the recesses of his pillow?—he heard the familiar tinkling of piano keys. Another song, snaking its way into consciousness. He opened his eyes, recognized it immediately. Another moment, and yes, there was Ray Charles's tobacco-and-honey voice growling softly into his ears alone:

Georgia, Georgia, the whole day through . . .

Owen found himself crying again, but this time it wasn't painful. Not at all. He didn't even notice the tears until the rivulets trickled into his ears, effortless. Like a soft summer rain. He felt relief. Here was his sign, unmistakable. Owen looked up into the blackness and smiled.

He whispered,

Little Miss Peach, you found me.

EMILY

HELL

EARLIER

Emily crossed the twenty-four-hour driving mark in complete darkness. There was no landscape, no horizon in sight; the headlights picked out black highway leading into a black sky. Even the stars were absent, covered by a thick, heavy cloud mass that stretched into the infinite, muffling light.

She met with very few fellow drivers, even while skirting late-afternoon rush hour outside of Denver. There had been the occasional solitary car accompanying her for various stretches of highway, but eventually she outpaced them all, watching them grow smaller and smaller in her rearview mirror and finally disappear, never to be met up with again. And for hours now—no one. Just her, the rattling Volvo, and night in Utah-soon-to-be-Arizona, which was altogether too vast, too replete with silences waiting to be filled.

She entertained the notion that rather than driving to her extinction, she was driving in it. Perhaps she had died without noticing. She had fallen asleep at the wheel, slammed into some majestic rock outcropping, and was at this moment driving a phantom car across the country toward whatever afterlife she deserved.

The thought was momentarily cheering, but Emily knew it was simply fantastical speculation. She dragged her upper teeth across her cracked bottom lip, repeatedly, until it drew blood. Yes, she was still alive. She could taste it. This flight into the paranormal, it was due to a surfeit of caffeine; it was the lack of sleep; it was the darkness. And, she admitted to herself, regripping the steering wheel, once you think you've seen a vision of Liberace, well, you've opened a door to almost anything.

For a while, Liberace had been an excellent car companion. She imagined his face turned to her, all openmouthed wonder and soft brown eyes perpetually widening, anticipating something delightful. Together, they played duets: "The Beer Barrel Polka," "El Cumbanchero," and "Kitten on the Keys" were her jaunty sound track across Colorado. Emily saw every glissando, arpeggio, and flourish as if his rhinestone Baldwin grand were there up on the dashboard. But when night began seeping into the landscape, the Utah terrain grew less and less hospitable to such frivolity. The music stifled. Liberace and his smile flickered, then disappeared.

It was just as well. Liberace was not a part of her adult life. Her childhood affection for the man was not easily reconciled with who he really was; by the time she was out of high school he had devolved into some kind of hoary, rhinestone-encrusted punch line; it was easier to just look away. She had stowed him away as completely as she had her accordion.

Still . . . She fingered the soft red feather tucked into the visor above her head. His company was infinitely preferable to the now-empty space next to her. There was also a whole lot of empty space behind her. When she looked into the rearview mirror the night sky seemed to have oozed into her car and spread out, black and cavernous, and in that blackness her eyes kept trying to form shapes, to reassemble the backseat, to discern the forms slumped and sleeping there. . . .

Lists. She needed lists. Thoughts arranged in bullet points: organized and controlled.

Things I Should Have Done
- Made coffee
- Gotten the dry cleaning the day before
- Taken the Echinacea and vitamin C, four times daily, at the first sign of cold or flu
- Called Owen at work
- Called the day care
- Divorced
- Always kept the gas tank at three-quarters or above
- Never said yes
- Called the day care
- Called the day care

It wasn't working. This list kept growing tendrils.

The yellow warning signs began appearing at intervals. Her headlights would pick them out, and they'd shout out at her upon discovery. STAY ALERT! they insisted. STAY AWAKE! STAY ALIVE! Emily found the signs darkly amusing; in her case, they were missing the point completely. But then the little white crosses began sprouting up at the side of the road, and these she could not dismiss as easily. They were inescapable. Mile after mile, another would spring up just as she was sure she had passed the last one. The crudely made crucifixes would glow suddenly in her headlights, only to fade out, ghostly, as she passed. The piles of stones, the little bunches of dried-out flowers at their base, the ragged photographs pinned up and curling in on themselves: they were all too personal, and much too close. She gunned the motor, hoping to distance herself from them, but always more appeared. It was as if a cemetery had sprung up around her.

How fitting, Emily thought, pressing hard on the accelerator, but she'd had enough. She would ignore them. She'd stare directly in front of the car, she would hum "Roll Out the Barrel," she would get herself out of this stretch of mortality.

And that's when the engine died.

She felt the pedal go slack under her foot, heard the sputter, and suddenly she was coasting. There wasn't anything to do—she wasn't driving anymore, she was play-driving. The car had finally given out. Emily could feel the adrenaline race through her body and her heart start to pump fast, but her mind remained curiously calm, even detached. Here she was, at the end of things. Events had been taken out of her control. She could only bear witness, fascinated.

After the initial drop in velocity the car took a long time to slow. It was so quiet she could hear the crunch and pop of every stone under the tires. The Volvo cruised along at an amiable pace for almost a quarter of a mile before coming to a stop, as if on purpose, before yet another small wooden cross.

The faltering headlights illuminated this marker as if it were showcasing a fine work of art. The cross was smaller than most, and weathered; the white paint had peeled away in strips and the whole thing was leaning precariously to one side. At its base were two large red devotional candles, partially filled with sand, and a bouquet of bleached-out plastic flowers lashed to the vertical board with wire. A few of the pale leaves had melted together. Farther up, tied by thin cord, a ragged communion dress clung to the horizontal board. Tatters of ruffles and lace flapped free, the pink of the ribbons and trim only a faint shadow.

"Oh come ON!" Emily shouted in disbelief. She threw her hands up in outrage. "Jesus CHRIST!" she shouted to the heavens, as if expecting Him to appear and explain Himself. He did not. She was alone.

The headlights began to dim. It was when the dashboard disappeared that she felt real panic set in. *It can't end here, not here,* she repeated to herself, yanking at the steering wheel, *not in this car, not in front of that scarecrow child. Not here.* Was there something there in the darkness, something small crouched behind the cross, rustling the fabric of the dress? She gasped for breath, teeth bared, hands clawing at the ignition. She was sure she saw movement out there. Something was walking toward the car, dirty-soled, naked, and tearful. Arms out.

Her foot jabbed down on the brake. She turned the key. Once. Twice. Three times. Emily's accelerating sobs mimicked the whine of the engine, unwilling to turn over. At her final try she let loose a full-throated scream that signaled the end of hope and reason, and that, seemingly, gave the engine the jolt it needed. The ignition caught on and the car roared back to life.

Emily pulled off at the Valley of Fire exit in Nevada. She was panting, as if she'd covered all seventeen hundred miles from Wisconsin on foot. The light from a truck stop shone out like a beacon. As she pulled into the lot, Emily wasn't thinking of food, or gas, or restrooms. She just needed to get out of the car. She propelled herself from the Volvo, a little unsteadily, and made her way to the OPEN 24 HOURS sign. The door swooshed open. A gentle puff of cool air hit her face. For a moment she just stood there. The glare and hum of the fluorescent lights, the merchandise, the utter normalcy of it all completely shocked her.

She must have looked alarming because the boy behind the counter got off his stool and took a step back. "You . . . all right?" he asked.

Emily grimaced to get the saliva working again. "I'm fine," she rasped, and entered.

She turned her attention to the nearest display (SNAX 2 GO!) as much to avoid the clerk's gaze as to steady herself. Her breathing had slowed, but she could still feel the tiny, insistent hammering of her heart against her chest. It was just exhaustion, she told herself, it was the sheer physical toll of staying awake for the entire drive. That was something near impossible to do, and her body knew it. When she told the checkout clerk where she'd driven from and how long (he would not stop staring), he told her the same thing.

"No way," he said. "You'd kill yourself doing that drive in one shot."

She grimaced. "No such luck," she whispered hoarsely, grabbing a packet of Slim Jims and heading down the cold aisle. She opened a cooler door. She spun a snack rack. She wandered through the store. Never had selecting a beverage seemed so alien, and so comforting. She just wanted to lie down in the middle of the aisle, there between the potato chips and the antacids, and cradle her plastic bottle of lemon-lime Gatorade.

Back at the front of the store, Emily was about to check out when the speakers overhead began piping in a pan-flute version of "Georgia on My Mind." It took her a full twenty seconds to consciously register what the song was, but during that time she froze, dropping the Gatorade and Slim Jims to the floor. When the chorus repeated itself her shaking began again. She ran out of the store, barely waiting for the door to clear.

Emily hurried back to the Volvo and popped the rear door, whispering, "I'm coming, I'm coming" over and over again, frantically, just as she had uttered those same words, lifetimes ago, rushing down a darkened hall late at night toward the sound of a wailing child. She crawled into the car and laid herself down, curled around her accordion, her head against the cool metal runners where the backseat would have been. She was certain she was about to die. She had done it, she thought, she had literally run herself into the ground. Emily waited, eyes wide open, for everything to stop.

But it didn't. After what seemed like an hour, oblivion had not arrived. Emily was still shivering on the floor of her car, the red glow of the store's flashing neon reflected in the windows above her. She was still there. Emily's breathing slowed, her body stilled. The boundaries of mind dissolved; it was as if she were standing in front of an open door, one not for passing through, but for receiving.

With a muffled moan, Emily uncurled herself and, still on her side, stretched out her arms. With a gasp of pure pain, she let Georgia in.

Enough.

There's no putting it off any longer—time to speak of the unspeakable. It really can't be avoided. Emily could never escape it. Owen will never rise above it. Even our young Walter, who at this point knows practically nothing of the particular circumstances of the event, can still feel its ripplings beneath his feet more than a decade later.

Omnes viae Georgia ducunt.

Let's talk about Georgia.

Better yet, let me draw you a picture. . . .

MOM! COUGH! COUGH!

MAYBE WITH GEORGIA FINALLY WELL ENOUGH TO GO TO DAY CARE EMMIE COULD WHEEL THE TV INTO WALT'S ROOM AND GRAB HERSELF A COUPLE HOURS OF SLEEP.

I THROWED UP AGAIN.

TWO HOURS, THAT'S ALL SHE WAS ASKING FOR.

7:35 AM

OWEN HAD A LOT ON HIS MIND.

YAWN

TERM PAPERS FOR 2 CLASSES TO GRADE, STUDENT EVALUATIONS, A GRADUATE SYMPOSIUM ON "EROS AND THE CITY-STATE" THAT HE'D STUPIDLY AGREED TO SPONSOR.

OH SHIT!

PLUS A MEETING WITH HIS DEPARTMENT CHAIR AT 9:30. HE WAS GOING TO BE LATE.

HONNNNNK

THERE IS A MOMENT OF STILLNESS, OF FROZEN TIME, BETWEEN THE MOMENT OF REALIZATION—

—AND THE BODY'S ABILITY TO ACT.

IT'S THE LAST GASP OF DENIAL.

IT'S TOO LATE. MUCH TOO LATE.

PART 2

WALTER
VENICE VENICE
LATER

Mondays are spent in service to the gods.

I arrive as soon as the concourse opens, and they're already in place; they could have been there overnight, for all I know. I give my customary wave to Security Joe, who nods back, and set up my viewing station on the marble banquette facing the archway to St. Mark's. I've got my lunch in a Food-4-Cheap plastic bag, my pad and pens and my bottle of water. I'm good to go.

I silently mouth, "Good morning" and take my seat. Not that these statues notice; they're aloof, as they should be. The masses don't deserve to touch the hem of their robes. Well, really, they can't; they're too high up. Also, there are no robes. In fact, the gods don't wear much at all.

Diana's got a short tunic plastered on, revealing marble thighs, and a quiver of ivory arrows on her back. Young Apollo's wearing even less, just a stiffened alabaster fig leaf that always manages to hide his privates and a length of white fabric that never flutters clipped around his neck, spanning his broad shoulders and draping down. He's got a crown of white laurel leaves nestled on his unyielding curls and a stone lyre permanently affixed to his hand.

They're monochromatic, but gorgeous.

Today Apollo is feeling bold. When I arrive, he's standing upright, one hand placed jauntily on his hip, the other holding his lyre up to the sky like an offering. His right foot is stepping in front of his left, knee bent slightly. Another difficult pose to hold, but I know he can pull it off. His head lifts proudly.

Diana, his sister, is more reserved, seated folded in on herself, head down. Her neck is long, like a swan. One hand is held to her chest, the other gestures out, warding off advances. She wants to be left alone, I can tell. She might remain like that the whole day. She's done it before.

The two look like they actually might be related. They both have the same strong brow, the deep-set eyes and the full lips. Apollo, though, likes to show off; he's brazen, befitting a sun god. Diana's more moon-melancholy, graceful but hidden, or as hidden as you can be on a giant column with a klieg light shining down.

I'm not in any hurry to start sketching. Monday mornings are usually slower, and today's no exception. Spectators are less frequent, and when they do come around, they only last about twenty minutes, tops. People are fascinated, but don't have the patience. When they realize the statues aren't going to start break-dancing they drift away. The gods would probably get more attention displayed in Banana Republic's fall fashion line: Apollo in a chocolate cashmere ribbed V-neck with brushed corduroy boot-cut jeans; Diana wearing a lightweight wool two-button blazer and matching gray pleated skirt. Celestial chic.

The painted sky darkens to a perfect sunset, thanks to the wonders of modern technology. Apollo's bathed in the golden light of late afternoon, tinged with dusky red. Forty-five minutes later, the sky begins to brighten, a dazzling morning glow. The painted day passes quickly again and again, and it's not even noon.

Apollo's feet are together now, the lyre pressed against his chest. Diana, like I thought, hasn't changed positions. Her out-flung arm is still out flinging, without a tremble. The first time I came to visit I told myself that I was only there to catch one of them moving. That was my goal, to prove that they were mortal, after all. It hasn't happened. As hard as I stare, I find myself lost in thought for a moment, and when I focus again, they've shifted. Or maybe they'd been shifting all along, only so slowly that I don't comprehend it as movement. It's beside the point now, anyway. I don't want to catch them in action anymore. I just want to be with them.

I wonder if they even know I'm down here.

The place starts to fill up. The room echoes with chattering tourist-talk and the rustling of designer shopping bags. Groups of people stream in, fill the room, and stream out again, consumer corpuscles pulsing through the chambers of Venice Venice's heart. And I'm the little clot that remains.

"Look at me! Look at ME!" demands a teenage girl in braces and braids. She's waving her scrawny arms at Apollo, whose face is, as usual, turned away. The rest of her friends, a gaggle of giggling ponytails, press together in a clump. Their leader gets emphatic. "Yoo-hoo! I'm talking to you! I've got a dollar! Look over here! Now!" Apollo doesn't dignify her with an answer. The Clump takes up the chorus. "Yoo-hoo! Yoo-hoo! Yoo-hoo!" they shout in yoo-nison. She gives one last "Hey!" then crumples the dollar bill defiantly in her fist and stuffs it into her purse. Yeah. That'll show him. She's got those dark hard eyes that are too close together and a beak of a nose that'll probably get fixed by junior prom.

I don't duck my head fast enough—she sees me watching. "What are you looking at?" she screams. I will myself into invisibility, but it's too late: Marble Eyes has got me in her sights. The group clumps around her in solidarity, all looking faintly horrified by the sight of me. Six lip-glossed mouths curl up.

Seconds drag on. Finally, Marble Eyes cranes her neck forward. "Fuh-reak," she sneers. Her mouth stays open in a grimace even after the word has splattered on me, pushing her beady eyes even closer together. Her sisters-in-destruction whisper together in agreement. Their laughter grows rapidly in volume until, propelled by one communal screech of pleasure, the half-size harpies push away from one another and scatter, only to merge moments later on their way out of the square.

I look up at Apollo but he's as serene as always. Mortals don't matter, apparently. It's time for lunch. I peel back the plastic on my "Snack-to-Go" tray: blocks of yellow cheese, brighter than nature intended, cubes of a ham-like substance, and salty round crackers.

I think, briefly, of lifting my tray to the gods. An offering. Apollo want a cracker? When do they eat? Don't they get hungry? For a moment they revert to human beings in my eyes, and I remember how much effort, how much sheer willpower they must be exerting just to remain still. And that blows my mind, which elevates them to godlike stature once again.

Apollo. I know this god; I've spent hours studying his body. He's not much older than me, I'm guessing, but the way his body's constructed, he might as well be a different species. He's got contours and angles that I couldn't begin to find on myself. The sharp jut of his cheekbone, the deep cleft of his hairless chest, the line that begins at his hip and swoops down to touch upon his fig leaf and curve back up the other hip, that shadow that runs along the side of his thigh from his knee to the perfect roundness of his ass . . . The white makeup he has on, or paint, whatever it is, never beads up or flakes off or smears. It covers him completely and reveals everything.

It's odd that I should be able to stare at him in this way; and that, in a way, I'm expected to stare at him. After all, what is a god without his worshippers? It would seem incredibly sad to me that no one would be sitting here on this banquette, staring up, bearing witness. These gods get contributions, sure, but no applause, no greater glory. Just me, fishing out a carelessly thrown gelato cup and some wadded-up paper napkins from Apollo's collection jar. Surely, they deserve better.

The sky brightens.

The sky darkens.

Two guys stumble in during an afternoon lull. Shiny ties loosened at the neck, dark blue shirts untucked, hair wildly spiked. They appear to be renegades from some frat vacation/real estate convention/bachelor party. These gents must have recently come from the Paris Hotel, because they're toting giant plastic cups topped by Eiffel Towers, straws poking through the summit. One of the guys, the blond one, drags his dark-haired counterpart over to Diana's pillar and whispers sloppily in his ear, something hilarious to be sure because his friend can barely stand, he's guffawing so hard.

"Yeah! Yeah! Yeah!" he says, each emphatic repetition the vocal equivalent of a fist pump in the air. And then he does raise his arm, only it's to point at Diana, who's still repelling all advances, but she can't beat away his voice, which booms up to the ceiling and echoes around the concourse. "You're right, man! That's one STONE-COLD BITCH!"

A mother watching nearby tugs her daughter sharply into a store, two ladies with shopping bags make for the nearest exit. Security's already on its way, I think; no one messes with the Great Shopping Experience. The two guys are oblivious to repercussions, though—they hoot with laughter and, yes, they high-five each other. Losers, I think, but I've hunched myself lower, head bowed down to my sketch pad.

"Come on, baby, don't let him talk to you like that!" the Blond One yells up, a Southern drawl in his voice. He's been emboldened by his friend's bravado. "Give us some sugar! Come on down, honey!"

They're swaggering below her pillar, hungry dogs sniffing at a tree. I half expect Diana to spring up suddenly, bow in hand, to dispatch two swift arrows into two impure hearts, but the Huntress has no response. Where's Security Joe? My eyes lift to scan the entrances, but no one's coming.

The two are getting revved up. The Blond One pulls out his wallet, waves it in the air. "Five dollars! I'll give you five dollars, you give me a little kiss, okay?"

The Dark One has found other quarry. "DUDE! What happened to your CLOTHES?" he bellows at Apollo. "COVER! YOUR! SHIT! UP!" He yells each word like he's calling out plays on a football scrimmage. "HEY! That's a pretty FUCKING SMALL LEAF, MAN!"

I'm standing before I know I'm standing. The blood's pounding in my ears. I lean forward on the balls of my feet, fingers clenched tight.

The Blond One has pried the Eiffel Tower off his cup and is weighing it in his hand. "Hey!" he yells up to Diana, breathing heavily. His bleary eyes have narrowed. "Don't turn away from me, you fucking BITCH!"

He swings back into a classic pitcher's pose, but his arm never gets to release France's most famous monument, because at that moment I have crashed into it. The Eiffel Tower's plastic point impales me just below the collarbone, painfully, and then bounces to the ground. I'm not sure how I got there, but somehow I am tangled in the arms of the Blond One, who yelps, "What the FUCK?" but doesn't fall down, not even with my weight and momentum pressed against him, and I see that even though I am probably a head taller than the guy he easily weighs two of me. I prepare myself for the inevitable pummeling that is sure to follow and by Jove there it is, not from the Blond One but from the Dark One, who has thrust his fist into my lower back so hard I feel his class ring digging into my kidney, and has also somehow managed to punch me on the side of the head at the same time. I haven't even figured out which way to crumple when two rough hands clamp down on my shoulders and pull me backward. My body tenses, waiting for the next installment of pain to begin, but to my surprise the cavalry's come after all. I'm looking into the red, watery eyes of Security Joe, who tucks his burly arm under my chin, choking me in the mildest way possible. His two compatriots escort Blond and Dark to the ground.

And the last image I see, just before I'm dragged away, just before I pass out in Joe's suffocating embrace, is of Apollo standing above, head tilted down. His lips are pressed together into a smile, a real one, with chiseled dimples, and for the first time, I am looking into the unblinking eyes of the Divine.

They're blue.

And they're staring at me.

My father isn't supposed to be awake. That's what I was counting on. I drift in quietly, just to get the lunch tray; I stay far from the bed, but damn if he doesn't look up and notice right away.

"What the hell happened to you?" His voice is cracked and has that raspy gurgling sound like our bathroom sink trying to cough up hot water.

"Nothing." I'm surprised he even noticed, but when I sneak a look in the mirror it's not too hard to understand: there's a purple-black relief map of Australia puffing up on the right side of my face, with a fissure running along the northwest end that's crowding my eye and threatening to erupt at any moment.

"You hungry?" I call out as I leave the room. Even I know that's a lame getaway line, but it's the only one I've got.

He's by the stove in forty-five seconds; fast for a man who's barely used his legs in more than a week, who takes an afternoon just to get to the bathroom. "What is this? What happened?" He touches the perimeter of my bruise and his eyes narrow farther into his puffy face.

I shrug him away. "It's like, nothing, nothing, I just tripped and fell."

"On what? Where?" He's getting that panicked stare, a faraway, far-inside kind of look. The last thing I need.

"It was stupid, I was coming off the bus, it was really crowded and I tripped on the last step and slammed into a pole—it was one of those bus stop signs, but there was a rivet sticking out or something and I kinda whacked my face onto that, there was blood everywhere." My lies always go on too long.

"Oh, Walt, you've got to be more careful." He's standing in front of the refrigerator, swinging the freezer door back and forth uncertainly; he's forgotten why he's opened it. I grab a bag of frozen peas and wave them in front of his face. He nods vaguely and then, after a moment's hesitation, shuts the door.

I head for the living room, peas to cheek. I want to be alone and there's nowhere to go in the apartment; it's way too cramped, there are too few steps between the kitchenette and the couch, and I'd head out to the balcony but he's already by my side, staring at me like I'm the Elephant Man.

"You . . . you could have lost an eye!"

I did lose an eye. Two of them. Two blue and luminous eyes shining down on me, intense and warming, the eyes of the sun. I want to fix them in my memory, to set them down on paper, because I'll never see those eyes again. The Powers That Be at Venice Venice's security office have laid down their judgment, and I have been set free, as were my fellow Disturbers of the Peace. No charges, no fines, but kindly refrain from ever entering our hotel or casino again. I am banished from the premises, now and always, amen. The most Security Joe can do is offer me a sympathetic eyebrow-raise and a small shrug—What can you do? Rules are rules—before giving me the boot at the back of the hotel by the loading docks. I've been exiled from Olympus, and I'll never see my gods again. Never again.

"What's wrong?" my father asks.

"Nothing. It's . . . the ointment, stinging my eye."

My father lifts the bag of peas off my face to look underneath. "Walt, you've got to be careful," he repeats, settling by me on the couch. I'm not used to this. Two weeks he's been comatose, and now the one time I want to be alone he's playing the Worried Father, sending me off to school with a bag lunch and a pat on the head. As if he were even aware of where I've been or what I've been doing, or how the groceries get put on the shelves or the sheets get washed or the disability checks get cashed, how the rent gets paid. As if the emergency numbers by the phone were for me.

I twist away from him and head back to the kitchenette, mumbling something about getting dinner started. This time he doesn't follow. "You've got to be more careful," he murmurs, and this time I wonder if he's talking to me.

Beans. There's always a can of beans. Self-pity and beans, that's what's cooking tonight. I make a big show of being busy, slamming cabinet doors, banging the fry pan down onto the stove, but when I turn around my audience is gone.

He's left. The empty living room has—*whooosh*—expanded three times in size.

Damn.

Well, he can't get any worse than he is now, I think, which is a lie. He can get a lot worse. But it's not my responsibility. Isn't that what that counselor lady told me, the social worker at LV Med, in one of the two appointments I actually went to? "You're not in control of your father's state of mind," she said, tapping her long fingernail on my father's file to make the point. "You're not responsible, and you're not to blame." I thought she was crazy at the time. Who else was going to be responsible? But maybe she had a point. Let him sleep the rest of his life, if that's where he's heading. It's not my problem.

"Your turn, Georgia," I say. I had a little sister once, victim of the Curse. An accident, never explained, never to be talked about. Sometimes I wonder what it would be like if she were around today, helping me take care of him. Would we be rolling our eyes at each other about now? Would I be washing up dishes while she'd have to be the one going in, giving me the finger but smiling all the same? Of course, if she hadn't been in that accident, well, well, there'd be no missing mother. No Las Vegas. No story. We wouldn't even be here.

I turn off the burners and head in.

He's already back under the sheet, one arm thrown over his eyes. I stay by the doorway.

"I'm fine," I say. "Really."

No answer.

"I'm sorry. You okay?"

Without uncovering his eyes, he pats the bed with his other hand.

I walk slowly over. As soon as my father feels my weight on the mattress he gropes for my hand and squeezes it.

"Don't scare me like that," he whispers.

"Sorry," I say.

"You've got to be careful."

"I know."

He gives my hand one more squeeze, then releases it.

"I gotta make dinner," I say. There's no answer. I think he must have gone away, but when I reach the door he speaks again.

"I love you so much, Walt," he says. "You're the best thing I've ever done."

I wait for a minute, but there's nothing more. I switch off the light and quietly close the door. Back to the beans.

I'm the best thing he's ever done. Yeah, that's probably true. At least, I'm the only thing he's managed to keep.

EMILY & ROSSETTI
WISCONSIN
MUCH EARLIER

On the same day she unearthed Liberace's framed photo from the cardboard box at the back of the closet, eight-year-old Emily, in her search of Vee's personal belongings, discovered another artifact hidden there, this one in a dark brown case deeply submerged in the box, beneath stacks of paperwork. The case's surface was pebbled and striated; crocodilian. The material invited tactile investigation, as did the two brass latches, which were not locked. Emily flipped them up quickly and flung open the lid.

It was an accordion. Emily had seen such an instrument before—there was a black-and-white photo up on the wall of Vee's father playing one—but this accordion, nestled in the blue velvet lining of the case, in such vivid color, was scintillating. The keyboard was mother-of-pearl; the minor keys and the body of the accordion were of a shiny, pearlescent red resin, the deep, alluring red of apples offered to fairy-tale princesses, and of bowling balls. To the left of the bellows, the word "Rossetti" was painted on in white, flowing script not unlike the looping signature adorning Mr. Liberace's photo.

Emily pulled at the dark leather straps. The accordion was heavier than she had anticipated and fell back into the case, her almost following. Emily took a wider stance, grabbed onto the straps again, and hoisted upward and back, pulling it toward her body. Once the accordion cleared the cardboard box she knelt down, resting it on her lap.

She slipped her arms in the shoulder straps; they hung loosely down her back. The body of the accordion covered her entire torso; she could rest her head on it. It felt solid, like armor. Emily hugged the accordion close. It was begging to be released.

She slid her left hand under the leather bass strap. With her head still placed sideways on top, she looked across at the metal clip holding the bellows together and traced its outline with her right hand. With one flick she unsnapped it. The top of the bellows stirred, pushing against her. Quickly, the bottom clip was felt and found and unsnapped as well, and with that the bellows loosened and the accordion became pliant, a breathing creature. She slowly let it expand with her left hand, feeling it engorge with air, her chest expanding along with it.

There was power gathering between her hands—sound and energy waiting to be released, and all she had to do was squeeze. She knew she would have to put all of her strength into her left arm to push back the bellows. Her left shoulder tensed, ready for the plunge—and that's when she saw the shadow of Vee in the bedroom doorway.

Emily froze, felt her fingers grow numb. Vee's eyes were narrowed, her brow clamped down over her eyebrows and her lower jaw jutted out. She, too, was frozen, but Emily knew it wouldn't be for long. She recognized that look; two strides and Vee would be upon her.

But, miraculously, the heavy hand of Vee did not come down, administering justice. Instead, the woman turned abruptly and left the room. Emily was alone in the bedroom amid all of Vee's plundered belongings and an accordion filled with air. Eyes liquid, chest heaving silently, Emily tried sneaking the bellows back into place little by little. It let out a disconsolate moan. Emily almost swooned. Suddenly, from the living room, she heard Vee's voice, low and measured: "Bring that in here."

The accordion moaned again. Emily managed to tether it shut and pushed it off her lap. She stood up and felt a trickle of cold sweat travel from her knees to her calves. The photo of Liberace stared up at her, his smile still beaming. *Help me, Mr. Vee,* she thought desperately, but she knew there'd be no salvation there. Emily picked the accordion up by its shoulder straps and slowly trudged to the door, the instrument weighing down her every step. She thought briefly of Sunday School Jesus, marching toward Calvary, wooden beams heavy on his shoulders. Could that Cross be any heavier than this accordion? Emily doubted it.

She finally made it to the living room. Vee was standing by the glass sliding doors. The curtains were closed. Her arms were folded. Emily stood before her, head bowed, her pearlescent red badge of shame resting at her feet.

"Look at me."

Emily raised her eyes toward Vee's face, from which nothing could be read.

"That was mine. My father gave it to me." Vee spoke without any emotion at all. "He played very well."

Emily nodded.

"He wanted me to learn." Vee's lips pressed together, puckered, and came to a rest. "I was never much interested. It's a good accordion, though."

She looked down at Emily. "You interested in playing?"

Emily nodded, eyes wide.

Vee frowned, exhaled, and patted her arms twice, quickly.

"All right, then."

The accordion needed work, though not as much as one might expect, given that it had sat in a box in Vee's closet for close to two decades. The reeds had to be retuned, the wax holding them in replaced. The bellows were in excellent condition. For Emily, Vee had the shoulder straps tightened and a back strap added. Even so, it was a ladies' full-size and Emily was small for her age. Her fingers had to strain to reach the farthest buttons. It would have been preferable to start out with a child-size accordion, but Vee would never have agreed to the extra expense, not when there was a perfectly good accordion that Emily just needed to grow into.

Finding an instructor was not difficult, not in Milwaukee, polka capital of the Midwest. Vee selected an old friend of her father's, a semi-retired professional polka player, to be Emily's mentor. Joe Wojcik, "the Accordion King," was stout, emphysemic, and barely limber enough to waddle across the room, but strap an accordion on the man and he would become as energetic and elastic as a fully inflated playground ball. He taught lessons in the mildewing basement of his ranch house in West Milwaukee. In the cool, damp space with a stained orange shag carpet, he'd set up a folding chair on one side of the room and place his seat on the opposite side, amid his collection of taxidermied birds and small mammals, which served as a mute but attentive audience.

Joe didn't know quite what to make of Emily, his first Asian student ("A little *chinska*, playing the accordion?" he would mutter in varying shades of disbelief several times a lesson) but in nine months' time she was his star pupil.

Emily practiced constantly, with great determination. Reading music made intuitive sense to her; after a month she could hear in her head the song emanating from the rapid rise and fall of notes on a page, and could translate that knowledge into choreography for her fingers dancing gracefully along the keyboard. What she had to work on was the timing: the pressing of keys, the pushing of buttons, and the flipping of switches, all coordinated with the breath of the bellows.

Physically, this was daunting for petite Emily. Managing the bellows alone took all her strength. Her size, though, became something of an advantage over time: Emily had to put so much of herself into making the bellows breathe that it became an extension of her own breath. This gave her playing muscularity, and passion. It also gave her the shoulders of a junior linebacker.

Once the mechanics of playing the accordion were mastered, the music seemed to stream effortlessly out of Emily through her instrument. After memorizing a piece she would enter into an almost trance-like state, her fingers flying along the keys of their own accord, the bellows pushing in and out like the tide.

"Did you hear that, my *wiewiorka*?" Mr. Wojcik would confide to a dusty squirrel perched alarmingly askew by his side, after Emily had finished a particularly daunting passage. "Perfect! That is how you play the 'Hoop-Dee-Doo'!" Emily faced the unblinking eyes of pigeons, jays, crows, and squirrels, as well as the blank, sightless stare of one unfortunate, patchy mole she was particularly fond of. That creature, no bigger than her hand, was one of Wojcik's first attempts at taxidermy, and proved to be too small and delicate for his sausage-like fingers. As a result, the inexpert stitching, the odd bulges in its back, and the loss of its two front paws made it look more like a rolled-up sock than a creature. Emily liked performing for the mole above all the other woodland fauna; it loved her no matter how she played.

Wojcik introduced Emily to the mysteries of the European ballad, the passion of the tango, and the complexities of the world's jolliest music, the polka. "There Is a Tavern in the Town," "Little Brown Jug," the polkas of Karolinka, Julida, and Jenny Lind, her fingers conquered them all. Her hunger for music seemed to have no satiation; each time she successfully completed a piece she would look up at Mr. Wojcik and his fat green binder, hungry for more.

The only thing Mr. Wojcik couldn't teach his student to do was smile. Emily took her playing dead seriously. The look on her face was one of pure concentration. Whatever song she played, "La Vie En Rose," "Sentimental Journey," or "Choo Choo Polka," she attacked with the same intense focus. "Listen to this music, my *ptaszku*, my little bird," he would implore after wincing at her severe expression, "it is dancing! You are making the bubbles in your heart! Light! Happy! Smile, *ptaszku*, smile! This is the 'Champagne Polka'!"

Emily tried to oblige, but the effect was even worse: her brow continued to pull down while her mouth muscles strained upward, creating an expression that looked like she was ready to chew off her own leg. Worse yet, it interfered with her timing. Wojcik soon realized it was best to leave well enough alone. What her face lacked in buoyancy her nimble fingers more than made up for.

Just after her tenth birthday Emily played her first public performance. Seated on the back of a flatbed truck serving as a float, Emily, wearing a white milkmaid's dress, her hair in two black braids, solemnly knocked out a flawless, continuous loop of "Beer Barrel Polka" for the town's Oktoberfest parade. Five pimply boys in leiderhosen sat behind her, trying in vain to keep up. At first she was something of a curiosity to the crowd, with lots of pointing and smiles hidden behind hands, but soon they were all clapping along. Emily noticed none of it, until the end of the parade, when she played her final flourish. She gave a relieved, gap-toothed grin, and the crowd burst into applause. Cheering loudest was Mr. Wojcik, who bounced forward to help her down from the truck. Farther back was Vee, who smiled and gave Emily a gentle swat on the head. The three of them headed for the bratwurst tent, and later went out for ice cream.

After that success, Mr. Wojcik encouraged Emily to hone her skills in public, finding her opportunities over the next few years at various nursing homes, hospitals, and VA events. These older audiences were particularly appreciative. Even those not afflicted with eye disorders got weepy at her World War II–era repertoire. Their arthritic hands clapped gingerly but enthusiastically, and they liked to reach out from their wheelchairs or aluminum walkers and make contact with Emily, patting her head or stroking her arm as if she were a touchstone to bygone, better times.

As the performances grew more numerous and farther away, Mr. Wojcik volunteered to drive Emily in his banged-up boat of an Oldsmobile. It reeked of smoke, and Mr. Wojcik was an erratic driver at best, but he was far more enthusiastic than Vee about Emily's playing. He would shout his evaluation of the day's event over his shoulder at Emily, strapped in the backseat next to her accordion. He'd veer widely across the highway as he recalled a particularly fine moment in Emily's playing, losing the steering wheel for seconds at a time.

After they arrived home, more or less in one piece, Mr. Wojcik often stayed for coffee while Emily got ready for bed. She'd enter the kitchen in her nightgown to say good night, and they'd be at the table, Mr. Wojcik with his Sanka and Vee with a mug of darker brew warming her hands. He would have just finished recounting the night's triumph, and Vee would look over at Emily and nod her approval. "Off to bed," she'd say.

At the Junior High Talent night, Emily played "Stairway to Heaven" on the accordion, all eight minutes and two seconds of it, flawlessly. She won first prize and the ridicule of her entire school, except for her three friends from biology and a cadre of second clarinetists, who thought she was a god. Mr. Wojcik stood up and cheered loudly from the back row, and Emily blushed, not entirely from embarrassment.

The following year, Wojcik entered Emily into the American Accordion Players Association's (AAPA) Wisconsin Youth Competition. Though participation had been steadily eroding over the years, competition was still fierce in a state known for its champions. Emily was competing against fifty other accordion players, all under the age of eighteen, 80 percent of them male. The judges initially dismissed this serious-looking *chinska* as an oddity, much like Joe Wojcik had, but they could not deny her virtuosity. Her musical selection was a polka version of "Hey, Look Me Over" followed by a stirring version of "Come Back to Sorrento" that was melancholy beyond her years. Two of the most hardened judges teared up. They awarded her first prize.

Vee was in the audience for that victory. "That was my father's favorite song," she told Emily, and for a long moment Emily didn't know whether it was a compliment or an accusation. It was a compliment.

Emily's photo was printed on page eleven of the *Milwaukee Herald*. Mr. Wojcik snapped up ten copies of the paper from the newsstand; Vee picked up her newspaper from the front porch.

Mr. Wojcik was overjoyed. Before the regional competition, which was to be held three months later in Chicago, he insisted on additional lessons for Emily—on his own dime, of course. He set up a little stage in his basement, just for her, stopped wearing his stained white shirts, and combed his hair. He even dusted the animals. "Listen to me, *ptaszku,* this will be no problem for you. To win Wisconsin, very hard. The rest, pah!"

Emily did listen. They disagreed only once. Three weeks before the competition, she wanted to change her musical program. Instead of "Hey, Look Me Over" Emily wanted to play the notoriously complex "Clarinet Polka." Mr. Wojcik could not think of anyone in the junior competition that had ever opened with "Clarinet Polka."

"*Wiewiorka*, why would she do this?" Wojcik demanded of the perpetually shy squirrel hiding its head beneath its paws. "That polka, it is no good for the nerves! No one expects a fourteen-year-old to perform 'Clarinet Polka'!" He addressed a group of crows clustered by the water heater. "Why not the 'Pennsylvania'? The 'Friendly Tavern'? Why not 'It's a Small World'! They love to hear the young ones play this!" Finally, he thrust his shaggy brows in her direction. "The 'Chihuahua,' for God's sake, play the 'Chihuahua'!"

But Emily was adamant. She knew that if she could put over the "Clarinet Polka" it would give her the edge. She also knew that she could play it, and play it well. Finally, she knew that Mr. Wojcik knew this, too, and would relent. He did.

A week before the event, Vee bought Emily a formal black velvet dress, as per the regulations. Emily had hoped Vee would pull out the green dress from the cardboard box in her closet and have it shortened, but Vee never offered, and Emily didn't dare ask. In the fitting room, Vee was surprised by how much Emily had grown. "You've got legs!" she said, almost reproachfully. Emily blushed and smiled.

The competition started at nine in the morning. Emily needed to wake up at five thirty to get dressed and ready for Mr. Wojcik, who was going to be driving her to the Hyatt Regency in Chicago. Vee, in her flannel robe, combed Emily's wet hair, something she had not done for almost seven years. She gathered Emily's long black hair with one hand and pulled it away from her face, which served to accentuate Emily's newly prominent cheekbones. Vee slipped a rubber band tight around the ponytail. "Look pretty," she said to Emily, and took out of the utility drawer a new emerald-green ribbon. Vee slowly wound the ribbon around the ponytail and tied it off in a bow. She smoothed Emily's hair, sighed, and gave Emily's head a little squeeze with her fingers. "There. Pretty." They both stared in the mirror, for proof.

In the early-morning quiet they heard the screen door creak and Mr. Wojcik knocking lightly. He stood on the porch in a new white shirt, already darkened with sweat, and a light blue striped bow tie. Vee handed him a mug of coffee and Emily's gown, shrouded in plastic. "Be careful with the dress." She gave Emily a paper bag with sandwiches, apples, and a small carton of milk. "Have fun. Don't talk to anyone," she told Emily, and disappeared into the house.

Through most of the ride through Wisconsin, Emily found it difficult to breathe. The air in the car was thick with stale smoke, and the windows were all rolled up to protect her dress and hair. Her ponytail pulled tight against her head, like someone had a hold of it and was yanking her back. She couldn't concentrate, not with the smoke and the yanking and Mr. Wojcik in the front seat tapping out polkas on the steering wheel with his fingers. *Bum bum-bum bum-bum.* He had applied aftershave, and it wafted over to the backseat like a noxious cloud of alcohol, menthol, and sweat. She tried going over her program, getting back into the music through her twitching fingers, but they kept losing the way. Emily started to panic.

She took out the accordion from the case beside her and pulled it onto her lap. The accordion no longer engulfed her, but she could still put her head down on it. It felt warm on her cheek. She took a deep breath and blew out slowly.

Her dress was hanging in the plastic on the hook above the car door, blocking her view out the window. Emily reached out and slipped her hand under the plastic, fingered the soft black velvet. It felt like the misshapen mole in Mr. Wojcik's basement. She wished she could have taken the mole along with her, for company; it could have perched on her shoulder, a knotty little extension of her dress, while she played.

Emily thought of the photo, buried in the box in Vee's closet, of Mr. Liberace in his dark tuxedo. His bow tie was white, glowing like his shirt and his teeth. He wouldn't smell of aftershave, or smoke, she imagined. He would smell clean, like soap. Mr. Liberace played the piano, which was not so very far away from the accordion. They could play duets. He would nod his head and they would simultaneously place their hands on their respective keyboards, and the music would flow out. Emily smiled.

"*Ptaszku*, look, we are here."

The car turned down Michigan Avenue, toward the bridges over the Chicago River. The Magnificent Mile spread out before her, vibrant and bustling with people. The Tribune Tower loomed to her left, the Wrigley Building's clock tower dazzled in the morning sun. Flags along the bridge waved her closer. Emily was in love.

She changed in the lobby bathroom of the Hyatt. When she stepped out, Mr. Wojcik, waiting with her accordion, appeared stricken, like he'd been betrayed. "Who is this, this beautiful young lady?" he said in disbelief to a floral arrangement on a table beside him. He squinted at her and shook his head. "Oh, my *chinska*, my *chinska*," he whispered. She took the accordion out of his trembling fingers and entered the Grand Ballroom.

Emily stepped onto the stage at 9:45 A.M. Fifteen minutes later, she was done. At 2:02 P.M., she and her Rossetti marched up the steps again, this time as the Great Lakes Division Youth Accordionist of the Year. She received a small trophy, a certificate, three hundred dollars, and an invitation to the Frankie Yankovic National Competition at the annual AAPA convention that fall. Wojcik grabbed her tightly and hugged her for so long she thought she might suffocate in his humid embrace.

She rode in the front seat on the way home. Mr. Wojcik had insisted: "You are big girl now! The front is for champions!" Emily felt like a champion. Her trophy was beside her; the accordion rode solo behind.

On the long stretch of stop-and-go traffic leading out of Chicago on I-94, Emily began to yawn. "Sleep, *ptaszku*, you deserve it," Mr. Wojcik said. Instead, she closed her eyes and thought about Chicago. She knew already she wanted to live there, it was just a matter of when and how. She could see clearly in her head, just like musical notes on a page, the steps she would need to take to get there:

1. Win national competition
2. Get scholarship to music school
3. Become famous
4. Meet Mr. Liberace
5. Move to Chicago
6. Get a cat. Maybe a mole.
7. Perform for

When Emily woke up, eyes still half closed, Mr. Wojcik's hand was on her leg, midway up her thigh. It rested on top of the velvet, just where the dress ended and her skin began, very casually, as if he'd been patting her leg and forgotten to remove his hand. Emily couldn't see his face, but the rest of his body was still and the car was running smoothly down the highway. The only movement came from the soft, soft pressing of his fingertips into the velvet: middle finger, ring finger, pinkie, index finger; middle finger, pointer finger, middle finger. It was a polka he was caressing into her leg. The fabric gathered under his fingertips; each note pushed her dress a little farther up. The thumb and pointer landed on skin, passed the hem of the dress to the middle finger, which slid it along to the ring finger. Another verse, and his pinkie was burrowing under the velvet. It crept forward like a fat worm. Ring finger, middle finger, thumb. Pinkie. Pinkie. Pinkie. Pinkie.

Emily jammed her eyes shut and shifted her body abruptly to the right, as if she were settling into a deeper sleep. The hand leapt from her leg at the first movement and didn't land again. Soon Mr. Wojcik began humming, and she could hear his fingers tapping on the steering wheel—the "Clarinet Polka." Emily stayed pressed against the passenger-side door for most of the rest of the trip, only opening her eyes when she heard the familiar *crunch crunch* of the car pulling into the gravel driveway of her home. "Good nap?" he asked her lightly as she shoved open the car door and jumped out.

Vee was cooking pot roast, Emily's favorite dish. Emily could smell it as she ran past the kitchen into her bedroom. Whether Vee had prepared it as a celebration or a consolation, Emily didn't know. Emily kept her thoughts on Vee and dinner as she stuffed the black dress deep, deep in the back of her closet and clawed the green ribbon out of her hair.

When she entered the kitchen Vee was by the stove, forking the meat and shuttling it to a cutting board. Mr. Wojcik was by her side, mid-expostulation, waving a bottle of Pabst Blue Ribbon for emphasis. "Ah! Our champion!" He turned to Emily, and he smiled wider than she had ever seen him smile; a gaping smile, a smile that could swallow her whole.

Vee wiped her hands on a dishcloth and took measure of Emily, head to toe, crinkling her forehead at Emily's oversize T-shirt and baggy sweatpants. "Well, you don't look like a champion," she noted dryly, but there was a lightness to it. She beckoned Emily closer and gave her a hug. "Congratulations. Did you hang your dress up?" Emily nodded into Vee's collarbone. Vee gave her a quick pat on the back, but Emily didn't let go. "Biscuits," Vee said, releasing Emily and grabbing an oven mitt. "Set the table."

Emily kept her eyes focused on the floor and went around the counter to the silverware drawer. Mr. Wojcik continued his narrative. "Let me tell you, Vera, you should have seen her, up on the stage—" But Emily was no longer listening. She gathered up three forks in her left hand and three knives in the other and carried them slowly to the kitchen table.

"—when she goes to the national competition—"

The three forks, each nestled smoothly into the other. A little fork family. Emily pressed her thumb slowly onto the tines of the forks and watched the skin turn white, then red upon release. White, red. White, red. The fleshy part of her thumb was dotted with tiny indentations. She pressed down again, hard, but it would only go down so far. It was impossible to force your thumb down hard enough to break the skin. A knife, though, would be different. A knife could slide through the skin easily. That's what it was made for.

"Absolutely not!" said Vee.

Emily froze. Vee had raised her voice. There was a silence, and then Emily could hear Mr. Wojcik trying to muster up words, the sounds sticking in his throat before exploding out. "But, but, but she could win a *scholarship!*"

There was no answer, but Emily could feel the shrug Vee must have given.

"Frankie Yankovic himself will be there!"

Emily could hear Vee pouring a pot of egg noodles into a colander in the sink. "I don't care if Jesus, Mary, and Joseph will be there. She's not going to Las Vegas."

Emily held herself still. It was as if her slightest breath would sway the decision being made.

Vee continued. "It's no place for a little girl and you know it. No way I'm letting her set foot there."

Mr. Wojcik spoke. "It is for the national title. She must go. Not to worry. I will make sure she is safe."

"NO!" The word shot out of Emily's mouth faster and harder than she had expected. Silverware rained onto the table.

Emily lifted her eyes slowly. They were both staring at her. Mr. Wojcik's face reflected, in rapid succession, surprise, concern, and finally, with a sudden loosening of muscles, understanding. The color drained from his red face and he turned his head away, but by that time Emily had eyes only for Vee.

Vee was looking intently at Emily; there was something in the girl's gaze she couldn't identify but knew she should. It troubled her. "Manners," she said to Emily, knowing that she was missing something vital.

Emily was breathing fast. "I want to go with you."

"Well, I'm not going," Vee answered, "and neither are you. End of discussion."

Usually that would have ended it, but Emily kept staring. Vee stared back, and Emily saw in Vee's eyes something she had never seen there before. Uncertainty. Emily jutted her jaw forward but said nothing.

Vee took a deep breath in. "Vegas is no place for decent folk. There's gambling, drinking, *murders*—" Her pursed lips would permit no further vices to escape. She continued in a more conciliatory tone. "Not going is not the end of the world. You can still play, you can still take lessons—"

Emily stamped her foot down. "I don't want to take lessons!"

Vee actually flinched. She had never seen Emily stomp her foot, and didn't like it. "What's wrong with you?" she demanded, eyes narrowing. "'I want,' 'I don't want.' You too high and mighty for lessons?"

Wojcik intervened, keeping his head down and mumbling to the oven mitt in Vee's left hand. "Please, Vera, she don't need no lessons from me. She is magnificent. Let her go to Vegas with someone else, maybe. Anything, as long as she keeps playing. She must play." This last he directed straight to Emily, and there was pleading in his voice, but Emily kept her eyes on Vee.

Vee was having none of it. "Nonsense. She's just getting the big head."

"I am not!" yelled Emily.

Vee lowered her head and glared at Emily, like a bull about to charge. Insubordination was something she understood. "Listen to me, you stop this nonsense right now or you can forget about playing the accordion at all. Now set. The table."

Emily knew the signs: the hardening of the eyes, the stillness, the furrows in Vee's brow. She knew if she were to look down she would see Vee's hand balled into a fist, slowly clenching and unclenching.

Emily stamped her foot.

"No," she said.

Vee's hand swept up and cracked Emily on the side of the head, but it was Mr. Wojcik who cried out. Emily stumbled sideways, hitting her right ribs on the side of the kitchen table. Vera turned her back to Emily and walked slowly to the stove.

"Set the table," she said.

But the blow that sent Emily back three paces also sent her out of the kitchen and into her bedroom, where she shut herself in for the rest of the night. She missed the compulsory meal of pot roast eaten by Vee and Joe Wojcik in stony, miserable silence. Emily didn't come out until much later, after Wojcik had slunk home to his frozen *ptaszkus* and *wiewiorkas*, after Vee had gone to bed without so much as a pause by Emily's bedroom.

Emily tiptoed out of her room, grabbed the Rossetti that was still by the front door, and shoved it onto the shelf of the hall closet. She knew that it would stay there until she apologized—Vee never backed down. She'd be safe: from lessons, from Wojcik, from the "Clarinet Polka."

She wouldn't take the accordion out again for another twenty-four years, and Vee wouldn't say a word about it that entire time. On the night of the victory dinner turned no dinner at all, Emily lay in her bed, covers pulled up and gripped tight, her eyes absorbing the darkness of the room until she was floating in it. She no longer felt her heart beating hard against her ribs, or her fists pressing down; her body seemed to have dissolved into the particles of night she was staring into. She was free. She didn't need anything; she didn't need anything at all.

EMILY

VEGAS

EARLIER

She woke up falling. Her head was inclined downward into a dip along the car floor's contours, where the backseat would have been. Emily jerked awake and pushed hard against the ground, tensed, like a cat flung from the bed. It was still dark. Above her, through the windows of the Volvo, she could see the night thinning out into murky gray.

She hadn't slept, not really, only skated along over the top of sleep, dipping in now and then but never plunging deep. Emily laid her head back down. It was very cold, there in the pit of the car. If this were Chicago, if this were the middle of a Chicago winter, they'd find her frozen there, curled into herself, blue-skinned and stiff. But here, she knew that if she were to remain in the Volvo for only a few hours, the car would turn into something else altogether. The sun would climb higher into the sky, heating up the glass, the dashboard, the steering wheel, and the seats, which would in turn radiate heat into the trapped air (this, an example of a localized greenhouse effect) and in a matter of minutes the refrigerated car would become a slowly heating oven, the air molecules speeding faster and faster, and within an hour there would be enough energy (total kinetic energy of an object's molecules = heat) to slow-cook a standing rib roast. Given a body weight of about twenty pounds and an outdoor temperature of ninety-five degrees Fahrenheit, a child (with its higher ratio of body surface area to mass) could undergo hyperthermia in surprisingly little time.

Emily knew all of this.

She knew all of this because she had done the research.

She had done the research because she needed a timeline.

She needed a timeline to know how many minutes she would have had to save her daughter.

It was lonely, lying in the car. There was a Robert Frost poem, something about the world ending in fire or ice. She couldn't remember how it went. This is how the world ends, she thought, shivering. It ends in the backseat of a 1998 slate-blue Volvo. Emily tucked her arms tighter into her body. *Let me give you some of my cold, Little Peach, and you give me some of your heat. Mommy's here.* But that was a lie. Mommy wasn't. Not then.

Georgia's head was perfectly round when she was born. Her downy, red-pink head was small and perfectly round. Emily had called her Little Peach right away. Owen insisted on the more formal "Little Miss Peach," but to Emily, she was only ever just Little Peach.

The sun was definitely on the way up. Emily could see the silhouette of a wayward Cheerio right in front of her face. It was either a Cheerio or a lost button. She reached out and popped it into her mouth. Cheerio.

Time to go. The last stretch.

Emily crawled out the back door and stood up on the gravel outside. Her shoulder complained but that was as it should be. She trudged toward the truck stop for the restroom key. Heavy steps. Heaviness and haze.

Who was she?

She was the pain in her shoulder.

She was the dull ache in her stomach.

She was a mother of two.

Scratch that.

~~She was a mother of two.~~
She was someone who had to pee.

In the grimy bathroom mirror she caught sight of a hideous bag lady by the sink, a crazy Asian woman you'd find skulking around Chicago's Chinatown, spitting on the sidewalk as she ransacked the trash cans. The desert sand had etched lines into her face; her matted hair had brambled outward into some kind of tumbleweed configuration. Bright red eyes, the skin around them bruised and swollen. It actually worked out well. She now looked like someone who should be found dead in a public bathroom. She might not even be recognized, provided she threw away her identification beforehand. Emily patted her bag, feeling the three prescription bottles pressed against the leather. She didn't know the exact dosage of an overdose, but figured that if she took all the pills at once it would surely do the trick.

Returning the key, Emily noticed in the free rack in front of the counter a magazine with Vegas showgirls splashed on the cover. There were three of them, all arched, sequined eyebrows and red-rouged lips snarling at the camera. And in the corner, a dog-eared image: a man in a giant cape playing the piano against a turquoise background. It wasn't Liberace, but he had the same candelabra, the same rhinestones, and the same openmouthed smile. "Liberace Competition Winner Tony Sherbé Plays This Weekend ONLY!"

Emily picked up the magazine. An imitation Liberace on the cover of a Las Vegas weekly didn't have the same revelatory impact as an enormous head smiling down from the heavens, but at least it gave her directions. She tucked it under her arm and paid for a large cup of coffee and five dollars' worth of gas. It would get her to Vegas, with enough left over for admission to the museum, a postcard for Walt, and a stamp, plus a soda to wash down the pills.

Emily flipped through the magazine as she waited for her tank to fill up. Mr. Sherbé was playing selections "in the style of the great Liberace" at the museum, one and three P.M. The location of the museum: East

Tropicana off Spencer, JUST MINUTES FROM THE STRIP! She could be there within the hour, and it would all be over.

Finish the task. Finish the task.

It was fitting that Liberace be the last person she saw. As a child, he was the nearest thing to a relative she had. Well, there was Vee, of course. But she had had enough of Vee. During the last two weeks, during this entire ordeal, Vee remained exactly who she had always been, and this enraged Emily more than was reasonable. What was it that Vee had said when Emily and her family first arrived on her doorstep two weeks ago? Shaking her head, staring at the ground by her feet? "It's a shame. Such a shame." It seemed to Emily that it was Vee herself who was shamed, by Emily, who had allowed this tragedy to happen. Except for one dismissive glance she barely looked at Owen; all of her pursed lips and furrowed brows were reserved for Emily alone. To others her demeanor might seem like sorrow, but Emily could tease out the accusations from the silence. Every movement contained a message, even the efficient, capable manner in which she hoisted the suitcases out of the trunk and hauled them into the house single-handed was a rebuke to her adopted daughter: I saved *my* two-year-old girl. Mine lived.

Her eyes were burning again. The gas nozzle handle clanked loudly. Emily noticed the Volvo's front bumper was curling off the frame and there was a large dent by the passenger-side door. She had no idea how they got that way, but she was glad nonetheless. Emily gave the bumper one vicious kick and it fell off entirely. It lay twisting in the dirt as she sped west.

She'd be there soon. Through the morning haze she could already spot the spire of the Stratosphere tower rising from the dust. "Hold on, Little Peach, I'm coming," she said quietly. It was a statement of fact.

The miles to Las Vegas were in the single digits now.

Sketch #2: I called this one Deus ex Liberace. It's so much easier to blame the gods.

OWEN

INSIDE VENICE

EARLIER

Good morning, cooed the voice on the phone.

Owen knew it was Emily. It had the same cool timbre, the slightly mocking upward inflection he had often heard whispering in his ear as he slumbered late on Sundays, back before the kids, right before she got up to grab the newspaper and switch on the coffee. His heart galloped forward, gaining momentum (*You've found me!*) but before he could stammer out her name the voice continued, upbeat and strangely artificial: This is your wake-up call!

It certainly is, Owen thought, as he thanked the operator, or machine, who had already clicked off. He had forgotten all about placing the wake-up call, and in fact hadn't even needed it, since he had spent most of the night turning his head toward the nightstand clock, afraid he was going to miss the start of day.

Despite that, Owen felt remarkably focused. He had already showered before the phone rang, had been able to dress and organize his thoughts at more or less a normal pace, was feeling—how should he put it?—mentally agile this morning, whereas for the past few weeks he had lumbered about in a semi-sentient state, Neanderthal. It had to be his medication, or rather, his lack thereof. Perhaps he had been better all along, and now that the clouds of pharmacology had lifted he found himself healed underneath. Or, maybe, this unexpected adventure had given his brain just the jolt it needed to right itself. What did they say about the restorative powers of travel? New sights, new vistas, new air to breathe. The poisonous vapors dispelled and so on. Either way, Emily had been instrumental in kicking him back into gear. He had to remember to thank her for it when he found her. *Thanks for taking my pills. Thanks for leaving me.* They might be able to even laugh about it, later. How things came together. How they came together. Later.

Emily and the pills.

Owen hurried down the hotel corridor. He was able to locate the elevator, pass through the casino, ascend an escalator, and find St. Mark's Square on the second floor, all without so much as a map. Maybe it was the lack of crowds, but Owen found the Grand Canal and its environs much more manageable this morning. Not that the time of day mattered much; here, under the dome of illusory skies, it was always day. That felt oddly comforting to Owen; the same ominous clouds he had watched the night before were benevolent now, shading him from the harsher rays, lazily wheeling above but never actually moving. The sky might darken, but only to a degree. This city was protected, encased. No plague would ever dare enter. No rats would swarm its docks. It was safe.

He had given himself plenty of time. He read the signs carefully and repeatedly, because he knew Emily would have. The gondola rides did not begin until ten A.M., but the ticket office opened fifteen minutes earlier. He was there a full hour before then, to get a fix on his surroundings before the boats started making their rounds. Nothing would be left to chance.

The shops were mostly closed this early (with the exception of the small food kiosks, from which he had gratefully purchased his croissant and coffee), and that was immensely helpful. Owen started at the farthest end of the canal and walked the loop from one end to the other three times so there would be none of the aimless wandering of last night. From leather shoes to evening gowns to art gallery with framed sunsets, from magic shop to Murano glass, Owen touched on each landmark (*this must be how blind people feel walking about their homes*), and managed all three times to find his way to the same bridge leading to the welcoming sight of the gelato stand in the middle of the Square. He had become a denizen of these cobblestone streets and arches. When nine forty-five arrived and the gondoliers, singing lustily in Italian, marched through the labyrinthine mall up to the boarding dock, he felt like they were singing for him.

People were beginning to accumulate up and down the canals. There was only one place to board the gondolas, and Owen could watch the cordoned line from his marble banquette. By ten the queue was full. Emily was not in it.

Owen took a sip of coffee, tore off a piece of croissant, and stuffed it in his mouth. An odd breakfast choice, here at the Venetian. Weren't croissants French? Of course they were, the pronunciation, *cwa-ssawn*, was unmistakably Gallic, with that nasal intonation that the Italians always laughed at, and yet here he was, tearing into one such *cwa-ssawn*, crumbs floating down as he sat on a marble bench in St. Mark's Square, watching the people queue up for their rides. *Where was Emily?* I'm here, by the Indian statue, where are you? *I'm here with Johnny.* Johnny, yes, that was it; it was Johnny's Devil Dog cart, name emblazoned on the yellow-and-blue umbrella. Owen remembered feeling it improbable that Johnny was going to be selling any kind of dog on this particular corner, not during Taste of Chicago, where just a scant half block away there were tables and tents filled to groaning with the best delicacies the Windy City had to offer, yet there was Owen, unable to abandon his post (she might arrive at any moment), fishing in his pocket for change, because he had been hungry ever since boarding the El at noon, and it was almost two, he let Johnny ladle on the spicy mustard and sautéed onions and then crammed the whole thing in his mouth (what if she were to suddenly appear, ready to begin their culinary promenade, and him with crumbs in his beard and nitrates on his breath?) while continuing to scan the streams of people going to and from the festival's entrance, not a one of them Emily. It all could have been averted with a cell phone. Not that either of them had one. Oh, they had seemed such a luxury, a frivolity, especially with such a regimented schedule as theirs. He remembered a colleague recounting his trip to the West Coast and laughing at all the people walking about with large rectangles of plastic plastered to their ears, but they were making inroads into the Midwest. Emmie wasn't convinced. It would be a waste of money, she announced in that clear, concise way of hers. You'd never remember to turn it on. Still, for emergencies. That's how the ambulance came. Someone had a cell phone. What would we have done without one? Someone would have gone inside a building, to a pay phone, probably, fished about for change—though weren't 911 calls free? Regardless, that would have taken longer. Not that it would have mattered, but still. It was his student, that girl, Maggie, who had the phone. That was her name. Maggie. She made the call. Very smart girl, good in an emergency. Now that he recalled it, it was she who took the keys from his hands—was that right?—yes, they were shaking too much—and opened the car door.

He hadn't told that part to Emmie. There was no reason not to tell her, but he hadn't, all the same. It was one of the things he had forgotten, omitted, during the interrogation sessions, in those days after the funeral and before the inquest. The endless hearings before the actual hearing, after Walter had gone to bed, with Emily acting as Prosecutor, Defense, Judge, and Jury, all for the supposedly benign purpose of her *understanding,* of her wanting *to make sense of things.* She would preface her nightly disembowelment with the softly spoken *I just want to understand,* a statement meant to explain why she would be clawing into his liver yet again with her unending list of inconsequential questions about that fateful day. She would be sitting upright next to him, fully clothed, so tensed she barely made an impression on the bed, while he just sank deeper and deeper into the mattress. How low was the gas gauge registering? How long was the line at the bank? What size coffee did you get? For God's sake. And while extracting her talons from his side, she would always bookend her *I just want to understand* with *I just want to make sense of things.* As if any of this could be understood. Could make sense. He should have been the one to open the car door. Shaking hands or no. Emmie, he was fairly certain, would see it that way. She would have opened it. She would have wrenched it from the frame. She would have gotten there in time.

An hour had somehow passed. Owen swiveled his head back and forth, from loading dock to St. Mark's Square to loading dock to St. Mark's Square. He would be vigilant and she would appear, Bright-Eyed Emily of the Long Hair. His diligence would be rewarded. *I'm on time this time,* he thought, slowly shaking his head no.

WALTER
FREMONT STREET
LATER

Back on the bus. All I need is a destination.

There's an official-looking envelope in the backpack at my feet. University of Las Vegas letterhead. We are pleased to inform you, la la la . . . I've been accepted. Being one of probably ten people who'll actually graduate from high school around here, my chances were pretty good. It's my first college acceptance, and since I haven't applied anywhere else, it means I've got a 100 percent success rate.

I guess I should celebrate.

Will I go? Probably not. Everyone around here knows the only continuing education worth having is to be found at the casinos. I could get some training and become a dealer. Then I'd be set for life. Or graduate from busboy to food-runner to waiter. There are a lot of opportunities just a bus ride away, which is an important thing for me since there's no way in hell I can get anywhere else without knowing how to drive.

The wheels on the bus go round and round.

We pull into the station, right outside the Plaza Hotel. The Fremont Strip is gearing up for its nightly excursion into FUN! and ENTER-TAINMENT! known as the Fremont Street Experience! That might sound fun and entertaining, but this is Old Las Vegas, so it mostly means more smoking and less ventilation. No roller coasters, no dancing fountains. Stickier floors. This old Downtown Strip is what the real Strip would look like after she's gone home at the end of a long night, wiped off her makeup, thrown down her wig, and slipped out of her support hose. And she's sitting around in her underwear, scratching herself in front of the TV. That's Fremont Street.

It's as good a place to get off the bus as any. Of course, this is also where I work, but there aren't many good options on the 202. At least you can walk around Fremont Street for free. It's Freee-mont.

The street's filling up. It's five o'clock, and the tourists who couldn't afford rooms on the Strip have begun packing into Fremont's hotels. It's a flood of people. Usually I can navigate the crowds. I can slip invisibly between the tourists and get to where I need to go. But trying to be one of them is harder. Four steps, and I'm tangled in the Mardi Gras nuns in halter tops passing out beads. Then I run smack into a crowd watching a graffiti artist speed spray paint landscapes and naked ladies on canvas. I spend ten minutes staring at the the Lucky Horseshit, which beckons with its promises of fried delicacies. Deep-fried Oreo? Deep-fried Twinkie? What about a molten Fudgsicle? Too many decisions.

Half a block later I get caught up in another crowd, this one watching the twice-nightly humiliation ritual known as Vegas Popstar! It's a karaoke competition sponsored by Bunions, where lucky tourists get a chance to sing to prerecorded tracks and get voted off one at a time by the audience until a winner is announced. Instead of a recording contract the lucky schmo receives fifty dollars' worth of chips and two free drinks.

Two contestants come and go before I even realize I'm watching. The next singer (using the term loosely) staggers up onto the stage, a bulky dude with a greasy ponytail. He tears into the song, screaming half the words and swallowing the other half along with the beer he's constantly swigging. His free arm pumps the air, and with each pump a little more of his hairy, perfectly round belly protrudes from under his

T-shirt: we're witnessing a man giving birth to an extra head. Then he gets sick (who didn't see that one coming?), which I take as my cue to pack it in. Once you've seen someone throw up into the mic singing "Celebration" you know it's time to go home. I'll grab the 202 eastbound, stop by the Food-4-Cheap, get some dinner, and then it's back to the apartment.

"There you are."

Behind me and to the right: a deep, silken voice that has managed to find the frequency between the screeching of the singer and the thumping of the bass, and slide smoothly, distinct and clear, into my ear alone.

I turn my head but there's no one I know behind me, just some young Euro-guy in a turquoise shirt and a woman with short hair holding onto his arm, but it seems the woman is looking at me, expecting something. I turn around a little more, pretending I'm looking way *over there,* and there is something familiar about the guy, but still no bells go off in my head. Maybe it's because of context, or the difference in perspective, or his size, or the fact that he's in color, or that he's wearing different clothes, or any clothes at all, but it's not until he cocks his head to one side and the tendons of his throat form a recognizable *V* pointing down into the shadows of his open-necked shirt that I begin to realize. My eyes widen, travel up to a familiar jaw, lips, and nose, and when I finally reach those unmistakable azure eyes he reveals himself to me in a dazzling smile. It's Apollo. He's come down to Earth.

It's a visitation.

Apollo is speaking again, but this time I can't hear a word he says. The noise, which had parted like the Red Sea to allow his voice through, has come crashing down in a roar of sound. Also, a massive wave of adrenaline, not unlike fear, tsunamis up and down my spine, cutting off all bodily functions. I'm inches away from having a convulsion. Also, I'm unable to stop staring at his teeth, one of his few body parts I've never seen. They're strong and white and a little sharp and when he opens his mouth they give his face a wolflike look. I stare at them helplessly, my own mouth halfway between a smile and a gape.

Diana (of course it's her, I should have recognized her graceful arms, her profile) pulls Apollo close and speaks into his ear. He smiles, laughing that wolf-laugh, and shakes his dark, curly hair, which shimmers almost to his shoulders. Where has all that hair been hiding? He's not nearly as tall as I had imagined (a little shorter than I am), but his body looks coiled and powerful, even under his civilian disguise: a turquoise silk shirt and tight blue jeans. She's petite, dressed in a simple rose-colored summer dress that hugs her body. They're both so full of color it hurts my eyes.

"It is you, yes?" Apollo leans closer and amps up his voice. He's got an accent, Middle Eastern or Slavic. Apollo mimes sketching in a notebook and staring upward. I nod, thinking, they did notice me. I made an impression.

Apollo claps his hands together and shakes them in front of his chest, then spreads them wide, like he's releasing a butterfly. "Fucking crazy, eh?" he asks Diana. She smiles up at me with her eyes crinkled closed. She's still got her hands on his shoulder but she's arching away, her arms long and fingers spread. She's a cat stretching on a scratching post. I notice that she's older close up than she looks eight feet in the air. Apollo, though, Apollo looks a lot younger; when he smiles he looks like he's barely out of high school. He could be my age.

"Where you have been?" Apollo demands, as if I've stood him up.

I finally find my voice. "I, I can't go back there, to the hotel. They won't let me, because of the . . . the—"

Apollo makes a *"Pfff!"* sound with his lips and throws his hands in the air. "This is bullshit, yes? This is—" And he can't find the words his hands are trying to grab.

Diana releases Apollo and places one languid hand lightly on my chest, as if she's awarding me a medal. I have the feeling that she would have preferred to touch my face but found it too far up. She looks at me with narrowed eyes. "What you did for me," she says severely, also with a strong accent. She pats her own chest with her other hand. "This,

I will never forget it. Those two men, those *choiros*"—this word she spits out—"I did not see, but my brother, he has told me all."

Brother. I was right. He's her brother. They're siblings. For some reason, this knowledge gives me great joy.

Apollo again grabs onto my shoulder, proudly, comrades in arms. "This is my sister, Acacia." He grabs his chest with the other hand. "And me . . . Chrystostom." Chrystostom. He makes the name purr. A lion's purr. No, a panther. The purr of a panther.

I notice them staring at me and take a quick breath in. "Walter. My name's Walter."

"Walter," Chrystostom says, and my name has never, ever, sounded so good.

I shake hands with both of them. "Acacia," I repeat, "and . . . and, Chriss-so—"

He laughs at the mangling. "Call me Chrysto. And also, you must please to allow us to buy for you a drink, for to thank you."

"Oh, but I, I don't really drink," I mumble, feeling myself redden.

Chrysto's face lights up. "Wonderful! Then you will buy us a drink!" They both laugh heartily, and I join in, because it must be a good joke, in their country. My newly named deity claps me on the back, and the three of us set off down Fremont. On the stage behind us someone is launching into "When You Wish Upon a Star" and damn if they're not getting all the notes right.

The bar they're thinking of, the tavern, they tell me, is only about a mile away, but I don't have time to worry about how I'm going to get in and get served because by now we're at the curb and I'm looking down at the proposed mode of transportation the two are offering: twin electric-powered red Vespas. Acacia is already strapping on her helmet and Chrysto is offering me his, saying, "Is not far. I am very good driver."

I've never learned how to ride a bike. Death on two wheels. A vehicle with no armor, exposed to the elements and every swerving automobile and truck. And a motorbike? To my father, I might as well wander up and down the highway on a July Fourth weekend night, dressed in black and blindfolded. He has never specifically warned me about these, because it would be inconceivable that I would even think of getting on one.

"Okay," I say.

I strap on the helmet and slide on the seat behind Chrysto and there is a moment of utter and sheer terror when he starts off and I can't find anywhere on the seat to grab onto, but Chrysto pats his side and yells back at me, "*Edo!* Not to worry!" and I grab onto his jeans where his belt would be, and I suddenly feel safe, I feel the warmth and solidity of his body and I know he's not going to let anything happen to me. And we set off for their favorite bar, stopping by the Money2Go! just in case, and even though we're not driving fast at all, to me it seems like flying.

The bar has no name that I can find, just some Greek letters scrawled vertically on the side of the doorway. I guess they're not too concerned about carding, or maybe the fact that I'm just about the tallest person in the bar makes me look older, but no one asks for my ID. It could also be because of whom I'm with. Everyone seems to know Chrysto. We haven't even taken two steps into the dark bar when some burly guy grabs his shoulders and bear hugs him. They exchange kisses on either cheek, two quick lunges of the head. Chrysto whispers something in his ear, and both of them roar with laughter. From there, he slides across the small space, high-fiving a middle-aged man sitting at a table and curling his arm around the woman next to him. He's got that easy, athletic grace to his limbs that I could never imitate, moving fluidly from one person to the next, like it's all part of a choreographed dance he's performing.

Acacia completely ignores her brother and floats into one of the booths toward the back, and I'm standing alone in my first bar ever. It's a high. It doesn't even matter that I don't know what anyone is saying around me, though judging from the mandolin music, the blue-and-white flag by the cash register, and the white plastic relief map of the Aegean Sea and its bordering countries running along the wall opposite, I'm guessing it's Greek.

The man behind the bar gives me a long hard stare. I'm gawking too much. I skitter off to join Acacia, who's lighting a thin brown cigarette with the red-globed candle at the table. She holds it up in her long fingers, exhales slowly. "You like this music?" she asks me.

"Sure," I answer.

"Is crap," she counters mournfully. "Someday they will play something from this century, eh?" She looks at me, as if I might be able to supply the answer. "Ah well," she sighs, disappointed, and takes another long drag. The bartender appears without being beckoned, sets a small liqueur glass with a clear liquid in front of her, as well as a glass of ice water and a small plate piled with green olives, feta cheese cubes, and radishes. He looks at me expectantly.

Acacia gives the slightest shake of the head. "He does not drink."

Clearly offended, the bartender scowls at me and withdraws. Acacia pours a small amount of water into her liqueur glass and it slowly turns a milky white. She lifts it to her lips. "*Yasas*," she whispers to me, then takes a sip. She's still again. The only thing moving is the curl of cigarette smoke wafting into the air.

Suddenly, she speaks again, as if we had been conversing all along. "But, the *kafe*, this they make here very good. *Sketos*." She hovers her hand with the cigarette over the plate of food, waves her ring finger (and only her ring finger) toward me. "Please." I grab for a radish and nibble on it nervously.

Chrysto finally arrives, plunks a bottle of Heineken down on the table, and slides in next to me. He's glowing with energy. He could be a college soccer star celebrating a winning game. Being so close to such masculine bravado makes me instinctively duck and lower my head, until I remember that he's not here to mock, thump, spit at, or hoot at me. I've been invited.

"Hey!" he says. "Is a good bar, yes?"

"Oh, yeah!" I say, neglecting to mention that I don't have a lot to compare it to. "What's it called?"

"Lethe," he replies, mysteriously. "A place where you can forget."

He glances at Acacia, but she's pouring more water into her drink and doesn't meet his look. Chrysto swings his shaggy head back to me and fixes me with his alarmingly wide blue eyes. "Come, you must drink something," he pleads. He speaks rapidly to Acacia in Greek. She responds with a lift of the right eyebrow. "Beer? Wine? Metaxa. This one—five star." He gives me an "okay" sign. I shake my head again. "Ah!" he says, understanding, and bends toward me. "You—AA." He puts his hand out between us—he won't say another word.

"I'll have a Heineken," I say.

Chrysto smiles, then his face lights up with a better idea. "No! Wait! Even better. Spiro!" he calls out toward the bar, waving two fingers. "Barbayannis!" He turns to me. "This ouzo—from Plomari." As if that's going to seal the deal.

I notice two men at the bar, old and grizzled, staring at Chrysto. Their eyes are narrowed, their lips are twisted shut. One opens his mouth and hisses something into the air; the other's mouth curdles even more. Chrysto isn't a favorite with everyone at this bar. Or maybe it's me they're objecting to.

Chrysto doesn't notice them at all. He pops an olive in his mouth, chews with great satisfaction.

"So, you're from Greece?" I ask, dazzling them with my powers of deduction.

Chrysto bounds up again and takes two steps to the frieze across from us. He smacks his hand over the part of Greece that looks like a hand, covering the peninsulas pointing downward with his own fingers. "Here. This is our home." He trots back and shows me the back of his hand, points to a spot just above his wrist. "Patras."

He smiles and returns to his seat. "And you? You are what?" It doesn't seem as offensive when someone from another country asks you about your own heritage. It's like fellow travelers meeting at a crossroads. "I'm American, but I'm half Vietnamese."

"Vietnam, yes." Chrysto nods. "And the other half? Maybe Greek?" He playfully grabs a handful of my thick, curly hair, and gives it a shake. "This hair very Greek!" He pulls at his own hair in comparison.

Even Acacia laughs. I shake my head away. "I don't know. Maybe.

My dad is . . . many things." I have no idea what my dad is. I can't stop grinning.

Chrysto nods. "Yes. Maybe Greek." Acacia sighs, but looks amused.

"How long have you been here?" I ask.

"In America?" Chrysto answers. "I have been here since one year."

"Do you like it here?"

Chrysto again looks at Acacia, and this time she tilts her chin up and meets his stare. He holds his gaze while answering my question. "Sometimes, very much."

Acacia makes a small sound in the back of her throat. "What times?"

The bartender bangs four glasses down in front of us. It's the same drink as Acacia's: a small glass of clear liquid and a side of ice water. Acacia's, though, looks like milk. Very soothing. I wonder if I should add the water, too, but Chrysto has already lifted his glass. "To our very brave new friend." Acacia lifts her glass. It's do or die. I lift my glass. It smells like licorice. I like licorice.

"*Yasas!*" proclaims Chrysto.

"*Yasas,*" Acacia murmurs.

"Yesyes," I whisper.

Chrysto's glass is heading for his lips. I hesitate, and out of the corner of my eye I see the bartender, still standing by our booth, watching. He's skeptical. He's onto me. He's about to ask me for ID. He's going to bounce me out of here. I figure, better to jump all the way in and get it over with. I figure, if I don't like the taste it'll be gone before I know it. I figure, it'll look impressive and manly, like in those movies where the hero snaps back shot after shot until his opponent has slumped under the table. But I only have to do one. I snap back my head and wrist simultaneously and let the drink pour in.

I figured so wrong. The pleasant sensation of licorice gives way to the not-so-pleasant sensation of licorice-flavored napalm searing a hole in my esophagus on its way to exploding in my stomach. My eyes water, and my body tries to cough the alcohol back up, but it's too late: I feel like I'm drowning in a lake of fire.

Chrysto is patting me on the back. "Slowly, my friend, slowly!" I notice he's only taken a small sip out of his glass. Even Acacia's eyes have widened a fraction. She pushes the food plate two inches toward me.

"I'm fine," I sputter, trying to control my grimacing. "I'm fine." I chug down the entire glass of water.

Acacia delicately brings her glass to her lips for another sip. "Americans," she says sweetly. "Always in a hurry."

Chrysto waves a hand at her. "Next time, Walter," he says conspiratorially, "I show you how. We drink together, very slowly. But now—"

"Not now!" I gasp.

"No no, now you must wait."

"Yes," Acacia chimes in, "wait."

A certain warm sensation has begun spreading out along my limbs. I have the sudden realization that my stomach is entirely empty except for the recent remains of half a radish. It's not a comforting thought. I stuff a handful of olives in my mouth, trying to stave off my alarm and the tingling sensation developing in the back of my skull.

". . . we missed you." Acacia has been talking.

"Yes," agrees Chrysto. "Every week you are there, and then, *puh!* Gone. Was very sad. You are . . . different than the others—"

"Very quiet—"

"—very quiet. You give to us respect. The others, always click click click click with cameras, always talk talk talk—"

"Pigs."

"Yes, pigs!"

I nod. "They are pigs," I say sadly. The tingling in the back of my head has grown into an iron mallet tapping on my brain.

Chrysto again mimes scribbling in a book. "You . . . write?"

"A little," I hedge. "I draw."

"Ah!" Chrysto smiles knowingly. "You like to draw us?"

I'm not even embarrassed by it. "Yes." I nod at Acacia, and then wish I hadn't; I feel the nod reverberating in my brain like a ball bouncing back and forth in an empty room. Things are getting a little bit swirly.

Chrysto wills me back to attention with his gaze. "Why?"

The words come out coated in ouzo, the answer pours out of me thickly, slow and sweet. "It's because . . . you're so beautiful. Both of you. But it's more than that. You're . . . pure. You're exactly who you are, and who you want to be. You live in your bodies, and you don't want to live anywhere else. You're the purest, truest thing in all of Las Vegas."

And that's when I pass out.

I open my eyes a moment later and find my head resting on the cool table, and it really seems the safest place for it to be, given the circumstances. The bar is rushing in and out and up and down, and when I see Chrysto it's like I'm looking out at the wrong end of the telescope: he looms big and small, big and small, and sometimes his head is big and his body is far away and sometimes he's all teeny teeny teeny. "I, I think I should go," I whisper to the water glass in front of me.

Teeny Chrysto zooms in large and his blue eyes are wet, like it's rained in the pool. "Everything, all right," he reassures me. His eyelashes are enormous.

At this point, as I am being scraped off the table, everything becomes very unclear. Time is sped up, and distorted, and the voices don't match with how the lips are moving. Lots of commotion, and me managing to stay upright, and someone fanning my face and at one point I feel a piece of feta cheese being slowly but insistently pushed into my mouth. I look at Chrysto and even in my misery I'm so happy, but mortified, too; these feelings are muffled and distant, way over there, on the far side of the moon, I remember seeing a check being presented and everyone getting very very quiet, time standing still, and me feeling like I was supposed to be speaking but I pull out my wallet instead and then everything speeds up again, the white check is covered with bills and whisked away, Chrysto's arm is on my waist, his steady grip propelling me out the door, the long terrifying motorcycle ride back, my stomach clenching at every bump in the road, my head resting on his back and his shirt is wet with sweat and I can smell the spiciness of his scent, like cloves. And even in my haze I don't want him to see the scary neighborhood I live in so instead I insist he drop me off at the Plaza Hotel at the end of Fremont

Street, where, finally alone, I stumble into a taxi and head off home, always and ever on the verge of puking my guts out but never quite going over the edge, and my father's awake, how can that be, and he's got a look on his face that I can't address, not right now, but a straight dive onto the couch, where I curl up, only my shoes kicked off, and let sleep come, come, but first, let me remember this pounding in my head, this heat on my breath, and forever, the faint but indelible impression on my cheeks where Chrystostom has planted two kisses that send me into the night, into sleep, into oblivion.

It was just before seven, and nothing was as she thought it would be. The gray, deserted strip mall she was stranded in looked like any other run-down strip mall in the country. The parking lot was empty, with the exception of a rusted orange Chevy Impala, haphazardly parked. Most of the surrounding stores were boarded up or in imminent danger of becoming so: the flagship Liberace Museum had apparently lost its fleet.

The museum itself tried to conjure up a bit of flair amid its surroundings. A neon piano rested on top of the tilted roof and a keyboard sculpture undulated around the building and spiraled into the air, with the words LIBERACE MUSEUM unfurled in mauve neon script, unlit. Even with these ostentations, though, the museum could at best muster a muted flamboyance against the gray, wan morning.

And it was closed.

Emily turned away because she couldn't bear to look at the words stenciled under a swirl of notes on the frosted glass door. CLOSED MONDAYS. It was inconceivable that she could have missed so important a detail. She had just assumed that everything in Vegas was open 24/7, even Liberace. Emily wandered past the museum and made it as far as the faded Hearts and Roses Wedding Chapel storefront. She stood under a peeling white trellis covered with plastic ivy and rubbed her forehead with her grimy hands. The neon rose and heart behind her were dimmed; the chapel also shut down on Mondays. She couldn't see Liberace, and she couldn't get married. There was nothing for her here.

Emily made her way back to the front door of the Liberace Museum. Along the wall, the score to the "Beer Barrel Polka" was painted, huge, onto the bricks. The song played repeatedly in the back of her head, muffled but constant, a dull headache that wouldn't go away.

She was at a loss. There was no contingency plan. Was it enough to have made it all the way to the museum, without actually having gone in? That seemed absurd. In her plan, she had seen herself entering the museum and finding a framed photo of Liberace, a serious shot, black-and-white, glamour lighting, dark probing eyes that would follow her wherever she stood, much like the painting of Jesus's head in agony that Vee had in the basement, only Liberace would be in a tuxedo.

She'd have a silent conference with him.

He'd absolve her.

She'd go into the bathroom, in the privacy of a stall.

She'd take the pills.

She'd fall asleep to the sound of tinkling piano music that would be piped in.

The end.

All of that was, of course, out of the question now. She couldn't even OD in the shelter of the doorway; she had no drink and didn't think she could swallow that many pills dry. The thought of getting in her car again, or even walking to Terrible's gas station across the street made her nauseous. What would be the point? There was no resolution—she hadn't finished the task. She'd failed again. Emily slumped in the doorway, head in her hands.

Bam! The door to the museum swung open, fast, cracking Emily's knees and knocking her head hard against the glass wall. She cried out in pain.

"Dear God! What are you doing there?"

She looked up. Looming large over her, blocking the sun, was an enormous, shaggy bird-lizard man. Layers of ostrich feathers, in various shades of violet, billowed out from a scaly hide of silver and lavender sequins. Flaring from the neck was a crest of stiff white cock feathers tipped with purple. The brown hair, swept up and back, the round face, the dark eyes—

Emily gasped in horror. She'd gone insane, after all.

"Honey, you don't look so good yourself."

It took her a good five blinks before she realized that of course it wasn't Liberace. For one thing, this man leaning over her was Asian. His face was broader than Liberace's, his nose smaller. He looked nothing like an Italian-Polish pianist from Milwaukee, except for the feathered and sequined cape, which, she guessed, had to be the Master Showman's—

"I wouldn't stand there, if I were you. The Bangs are coming out." The imitation Liberace swept away from the doorway into the parking lot. His posture was impeccable; he could have been walking down a fashion runway.

Emily got to her feet and out of the doorway just as a small Latino man, completely engulfed in what looked like a giant, ruffled American flag, teetered out. He was short enough for Emily to see the top of his bald brown head as he stared down, trying to gather up the fabric trailing on the ground and fling it over his shoulders.

"Shit," he said, "I should have worn my boots." He pinioned one side of the cape with his right elbow and was flapping his left arm, trying to free it from the sea of Stars and Stripes. "Lee, help me, Goddamn it!" he said, turning to Emily. When he realized his mistake he gave a little scream. "Who-the-fuck-are-you?"

Emily ducked her head down and tried to figure out how to get past them to her car, but before she could shrink back a third man strode out of the museum, a mustached giant, wearing no cape but carrying at least four over one arm, including one that appeared to be the pelt of a drowned black monkey. He didn't even look at Emily. "*Mariposas*! Stop dancing around and get in the car! *Ahora*!" He had a rough, pockmarked face. A scar puckered the skin above his right cheekbone. The giant strode over to the Chevy.

"Big Bang, relax!" the small one said, attempting to sweep his arms upward and keep the fabric in place. "This is my moment!"

"Your moment, Bang?" hissed Big Bang, stuffing the capes into the trunk. "This is your moment? Little B, this will be your moment with *la policia*!" He slammed the trunk door down. "It's fucking seven o'clock!" he shouted. "Who makes a break-in at seven o'clock?"

Little Bang tossed his head defiantly but walked to the car. "You know I'm no good in the mornings, *bruja*!"

Big Bang hurled a stream of Spanish invectives as Little Bang stuffed himself into the passenger side of the car. Emily thought of running into the open museum but Big Bang suddenly turned and in four paces was upon her. "What, you bring your sister, *chino*?" he snarled at Lee.

"Calm down, Big B," Lee said evenly. "She's not going to say anything." He turned to Emily. "Right?"

Little Bang called from the car: "Look at her, Bang. She's *loca*. Get in the car, let's go."

Big Bang spat on the ground. "You people are amateurs. Amateurs!" He pushed his way past Emily. "Start the car," he told Lee, and returned into the museum.

"Where are you going, Big B?" Little Bang yelled. He propelled himself out of the Chevy just as Lee was getting in. "Where is he going?"

Lee shrugged. Little Bang hesitated, then scurried to the doorway. "Get me a candelabra!" he yelled inside. He strutted back to where Emily stood, and suddenly laughed. "Hah! Fuck the museum. They can go to hell! And Tony, too!" He stroked the red, white, and blue ruffles. "What do you want?" he asked Emily. "We can get it for you. Once-in-a-lifetime opportunity."

Emily shook her head. "You'll never be able to sell those clothes," she whispered.

"Who wants to sell them?" Little Bang leaned closer to Emily and took a small stack of business cards out of the folds of his robe. "This is revenge." He flicked one card up so Emily could read it. Before she could even register where she had seen the name Tony Sherbé before, Little Bang flung the stack of cards into the air toward the doorway.

As they hit the ground, several loud events happened almost simultaneously. The Chevy's whining engine was trying, unsuccessfully, to engage. A large crash could be heard from inside the museum, followed by a heavy thud and the bellowing scream of Big Bang.

Silence.

An alarm began wailing from inside the museum, sharp and pulsing. Big Bang staggered out, hopping on one foot, carrying a silver candelabra. "*Ai!* Motherfucker! Motherfucker! Motherfucker!" he screamed.

"What the hell did you do?" Little Bang shouted, shoving Emily aside and running to Big Bang's side.

"I crushed my fucking foot! You said you turned off the alarm!"

"Not the one for the Swarovski! It has its own alarm! I told you not to touch the giant rhinestone, *pendejo*! Did you touch it?"

"It broke my foot! Do you know how much that thing weighs?"

"Of course I know how much it weighs! I hear that fucking question fifty times a day! It's 23 kilos, 115,000 carats, and I told you not to fucking touch it! You deserve to break your foot!"

Big Bang started weeping. "I did this for you, *mijo*! Here's your fucking candlestick!" He thrust the candelabra at Little Bang and sank to his knees, grimacing.

Little Bang grabbed Big Bang and pulled his head down in an embrace. "It's okay, it's okay, *mijo*."

This would have been the perfect time to escape, and Emily felt her heart beating hard against her chest, but she could only stare, transfixed.

"It's not okay! I don't want to go back to jail!" moaned Big Bang.

"You're not going back to jail," said Little Bang fiercely.

"It's not okay!" Lee yelled from the Chevy. "The car won't start!"

Little Bang pulled away from Big Bang. "What? It won't start?"

"It won't start!" said Lee.

"*Chingada!*" screamed Little Bang into the air.

Lee got out of the car. "Let's run."

"No! Not without all of these!" said Little Bang, running to the car and popping open the trunk. He began pulling the costumes out and piling them onto his shoulder.

Big Bang, however, was very still. He scanned the parking lot, eyes settling on the Volvo. He turned, looked toward the museum where Emily was standing. Limped up to her slowly. "Is that your car?"

Emily refused to answer, clutching her bag tighter to her body. Big Bang towered over her. He was at least as tall as Owen, and much thicker. Black serpent tattoos curled themselves around his biceps, which were as big as Emily's thigh. "Give me your keys," he demanded.

Emily shook her head, gritting down with her teeth. Little Bang was already piling clothes in the back of the Volvo. The museum alarm continued to blare. Lee started forward toward her, yelling, "Bang! Leave her alone!" but by that time Big Bang was already lunging for her bag.

Emily found she couldn't bear to let go of the car she had been trying so hard to destroy. With renewed energy, she tried punching Big Bang away, but it was like pushing against the side of a mountain. She stomped on his crushed foot. He roared to the skies, elephantine, and she was able release his grasp on her bag. A swift elbow to his solar plexus knocked the breath out of him. Big Bang crumpled.

Emily ran to her car, grabbed Little Bang by his collar, and easily yanked him away. She reached for the driver-side door but Little Bang was already back, his arm with the candelabra swinging in the air. "He's NOT going back to jail!" he said between his teeth. Emily ducked back, but too late; one of the silver arms caught her just above the left eye, gashing her forehead and sending her reeling back. She fell to the ground.

A moment later, when she could open her eyes, blood pouring down, Emily could see the Volvo making a wide circuit in the parking lot, feathers flying out of the window. Big Bang was driving, and Little Bang had his ruffled arm out the window, shaking the candelabra and shouting, "My name is Tony Sherbé!" at the top of his lungs. They made a tight curve and screeched out of the parking lot. Emily's bag was a few feet away from her, contents strewn on the ground.

She crawled to the bag, and, gasping, stuffed her belongings back in. The alarm continued to sound, this time echoed by police sirens in the distance. She looked up and saw her accordion four feet ahead of her. Behind it, feathers.

"I thought you might want it." The accordion was resting at Lee's feet, who was standing in front of her, impossibly tall and grand in his cape. He came toward her and she flinched, but he was holding out a handkerchief. Lee knelt down, wiped the blood out of her eyes, and pulled her face toward his. His feathers tickled her cheek. "Time to go, my dear."

"I can take care of myself," rasped Emily, but her voice sounded weak, even to her.

Lee shook his head gently. "I don't think so."

It was hard to resist a man in plumage. He pulled her to her feet with one hand and took the accordion with the other, and soon Emily was flying down a back alley with the feathered man into the wilds of Las Vegas.

When I wake up, I can barely lift my head. Apparently, it's been filled with concrete. Someone's covered me with a sheet and given me a pillow. I'm still in my clothes, which smell like I've been dragged across the floor of a bar. Which could have happened, for all I can remember.

I'm holding something in my hand.

I bring my hand up to my face and uncurl three fingers to reveal a crumpled business card. Even in the gloom with bleary eyes I can read whose it is:

Chrystostom, it says in the middle, with a phone number on the bottom left corner.

Chrystostom.

The night's events flash in my brain. Images both thrilling and cringe-worthy flicker in rapid succession, like one of those flip books of ladies dancing the hootchie-coo or a shark attacking a baby seal.

I've got his number.

"Back from the dead, Orpheus?"

Jesus Christ, my father is awake. I feel like I've been caught jacking off. I quickly palm Chrysto's card and shove it in my pocket. I don't remember the last time my father has woken up before me. It's unsettling. With a mighty effort, I manage to sit up.

"What did you do last night?" my father asks mildly. He's sitting at the kitchen table without the lights on. He's still in his robe, but he's awake, and aware. He's even made himself tea. I'm not the only one back from the dead.

"You're better," I say, on the way to the refrigerator to find something to wash my mouth out with.

He nods slowly, thoughtfully. "Maybe. Maybe . . . I am."

"That's good." I finish off the OJ, straight from the carton.

"Where'd you go yesterday?" my father asks again. He's back on track. Again, a little freaky. Where's that medicated fog when you need it?

"I told you," I mumble into the fridge. "Staff meeting."

"And then?"

"Um, we, there was a birthday and we, the staff, went out."

"Where?" he asks quietly.

I'm deliberately vague, keeping my options open. "A place. I don't remember."

"Did you drink?"

"Nah," I mumble quickly.

"Walter?" His voice is soft but expectant. The whole conversation's been leading to this. I know what this is. This is what it's like in a house where the father looks after the son, and the son does things that need looking after. I've seen this on TV. Here's my cue. I hang my head and nod sadly, a model of exposed shame.

"Walter." My father shovels as much grim disappointment into my name as it can hold. "You've got to be responsible." I'm surprised he remembers the lines. "It's okay to have a beer or something. Just let me know next time, okay, champ?"

I smile and nod, hoping we're going to cut to commercial, but then a horrified look comes over his face. "Walt," he says, panicked, "did someone drive?"

There's my dad. Happy to see his son swilling alcohol, but terrified that he'll step into an automobile. "No cars," I say. That, at least, is true.

I see the fog rolling in, finally. "Good. Good . . ." My father stares off somewhere to the left of his tea mug, picking at the skin around his fingernails. "You know about us and cars. . . ." He says it like they're some newfangled contraption. "We're not lucky with them. Ever since your grandfather—"

But I don't have time to hear about the family curse again—I've noticed the kitchen clock. "Shit!" I yelp. It's rounding toward eleven. "I gotta go." I'm due at work in fifteen minutes.

"Did you have fun?" my father thinks to ask, but I'm already in the bathroom. Two minutes later I'm dressed and heading back to the kitchen. "Walter!" my father calls out as I rush past. "When you get home, let's work on those college applications, okay?"

I quickly shake out his meds into the Morning and Night cups. "Don't worry about it," I tell him, running for the door and stepping into the hall.

He yells out, "Promise me you'll be safe!" but the door's already closed.

202. 202. I love you, 202. You're my getaway, my hideaway, my private space in a public place. I love you, 202.

I've got the window seat, no one next to me—optimal conditions. Four times in three stops I've tried putting away Chrystostom's card, tucking it into my notebook, slipping it into my pocket, only to find it—presto!—back in my hand again. There's nothing more to read on it, just a name and a number, but I can't help studying it, trying to decipher the deeper meaning. It's a golden-yellow card with dark purple lettering. Plain and exotic all at once. What does a living statue need a business card for? Maybe he does birthday parties. Charity events. Why has he given me a card? That's even more mysterious. The likes of me.

A name. A number. That's all. But an entire world spins out from this card, like a yellow brick road. One telephone call.

I am not the giddy type. Swooning does not come naturally to me, yet here I am, palpitating. I might as well be scribbling *Do you like me?* notes with little curlicue clouds on the borders and a heart dotting each *i*. *Do you like me? Yes No Maybe—check one.* I've never been like this. Even at Venice Venice, my obsession with the statues was always in the service of Art. Now, I look down at my sketchbook with its pages full of Chrystostom and it's different: this is no longer a god I'm looking at, or a study in shadows and geometric planes; it's a man, a nearly naked man, in parts and whole, who I've spent my time staring at, transcribing.

I want to see him again. I want to see him now. My mind is full of Chrysto, there's no room for anything else. There's a pain, right below my breastbone, that catches my breath, but feels like relief. I guess I know what this means. Surprising, but not surprising. This has been waiting for me my whole life.

A hardened husk is cracking open and something inside is wriggling loose. This me. Being released. The bus ride is short but my life has changed.

I touch his outline on the page, the pencil lines I've used to try to capture him in two dimensions. The line smudges, leaving a little of his mark on my finger. But he's not here in the drawings, he's escaped. He's become flesh; he's real, somewhere out there. I've got to punch the numbers in and he'll appear suddenly, in a wisp of smoke, genie of the card. I just have to call. My long-neglected cell phone is in my backpack pocket, waiting to be used. It would be easy enough.

Yes No Maybe.

Lee had just managed to close the security gate to his apartment complex when the police car raced by the building. His home was five blocks from the museum and they practically sprinted the entire distance. How he had managed to guide Emily, carry the accordion, and not trip over Liberace's enormous cape was beyond her, but he never faltered—he flowed.

"Don't bleed on the feathers" was his only instruction. Emily kept his handkerchief plastered to her forehead.

The outward appearance of Lee's building—the chipped concrete steps, the rusty railing, and the thin wooden front door with the peeling blue paint—didn't prepare her for the oasis of greenery inside. Plants grew everywhere in Lee's apartment. From pots, in concrete troughs, on shelves, twining around the arms and over the backs of chairs. Greenery cascaded from tables and formed dangling curtains from containers hung on the ceiling. Succulents spiked out of stone-filled jars; ivy insinuated itself down the walls. Somewhere, a fountain burbled.

"Welcome to my jungle," Lee announced, pushing aside two elephant palms and uncovering a couch.

Emily sat, breathing in the heady, humid odor of dirt and oxygen, her hand still pressed to the stiffening handkerchief, while Lee disappeared. She wasn't alone: there were faces staring at her from every wall of the room. Crude wooden African tribal masks with slashes of paint looked down their trapezoidal noses at her; brightly colored Mexican coyote and Thai lion heads snarled mutely. There were Mardi Gras masquerade masks, Beijing opera masks, and Caribbean horned devils glaring in red, yellow, and black.

A door banged open and Emily could hear a small animal clattering down the hall, its nails clicking furiously against the hardwood floor. It ran into the living room and jumped onto the end of the couch, a tiny Balinese demon mask come to life, all bulging eyeballs and open-mouth glower, yammering.

"Mercutio, down! Down!" Lee commanded. He was carrying a large glass bowl filled with water and a washcloth. Lee had taken off the cape and was wearing a simple black T-shirt and jeans. *He's a lot thinner plucked,* Emily thought. She couldn't figure out what age he was; the skin on his face was unlined but stretched tight over the bones, his full hair had receded far up his forehead. Lee could be thirty; he could be twice that.

"Don't worry about him, he doesn't bite."

The dog vibrated with anticipation at her feet, but she didn't move to pat the creature's waggling head, no matter how eagerly he stared up at her. Her accordion was on the floor, too, next to the dog, as if it were expecting to be pet as well.

Lee sat next to Emily. He pulled the washcloth out of the bowl and wrung it out. Gently, he pulled down Emily's hand to look at the gash created by the candelabra. "*Tsk*. Another victim of Liberace's excesses," he murmured, pressing the warm washcloth to her forehead while cupping the back of her head with his other hand. She winced, instinctively trying to wrench her head away, but his hands were firm.

"What are you doing?" she said hoarsely.

"Still, still," he whispered. He began blotting up the dried blood. The pain above her eye blazed hot, then slowly subsided. "Calendula water," he said, dipping the washcloth back into the bowl. He looked up again and stared at the wound. "You'll live."

Emily felt the laugh rise up her windpipe, dry and bitter, but forced it down. "What?" Lee asked, catching the momentary twitching at the corners of her mouth. "Disappointed?"

He wrung out the washcloth once more and this time wiped down the rest of her face, tucking his free hand under her chin to tilt her head up, like she was a little child back from the playground. Emily closed her eyes and let it happen. She felt the warmth of the cloth gently scraping against her face, her pores opening, giving away something of herself. She was feeling her skin again. She could almost fall asleep this way, chin resting on the palm of his hand, but he let go and she heard the washcloth dip back into the water.

Emily opened her eyes. The water in the bowl was gray. Lee placed his hands, still damp, on the top of her head, like a benediction. He smoothed down the tangle of her hair. "I knew it," he said. "There's a good haircut underneath all that."

Emily jerked back, batted his hands away. "Stop it, please," she said, reclaiming her hair with her own fingers.

Lee got up and poured the water from the bowl into a large potted ficus. "What's your name?"

"Emily."

"Emily, would you like something to drink?"

"No."

"Hmm." Lee picked up the glass bowl and disappeared down the hall. The dog stayed by her, panting, face inches from her knees, demanding attention. His saucer eyes stared up imploringly, his quivering tongue flicked in and out between the sharp teeth, pink and moist.

I could still do it, she thought suddenly. It wasn't the best in guest etiquette, but she could think of nothing better than to lay herself down amid all this greenery and never get up. Emily swiped her bag from the couch and stood up, Mercutio barking at her side.

Lee reappeared at that moment, carrying a tray set for tea. "For heaven's sake, Mercutio, let her be," he said mildly. The dog turned two circles and lay down. Lee placed the tray on the coffee table in front of her. The two cups were different from each other, and neither of them matched the teapot. "At least have some tea."

Emily shook her head. "I don't want any, thank you," she replied. "I really have to leave."

Lee raised an eyebrow. "You have some place you need to be?"

Emily didn't answer, but didn't sit down, either.

"Have some tea."

"I don't want—"

"Sit, please."

"Could I just use your bathroom?"

"Certainly. But leave your bag."

She opened her mouth in indignation, ready to protest, but looking at Lee, with his steady, placid gaze, she felt exposed. How could he know? Had he checked her bag?

"Why don't you sit." It wasn't a question. "You have time for a little tea." There was a touch of mild impatience to his voice. "It will fortify."

She sat.

"Honey, with no lemon," he said, smiling. That was exactly the way she drank it.

The parking lot. Of course. He must have seen the bottles of pills rolling out of her bag in the parking lot. She didn't remember any of them falling out, but they must have, just the same.

"You picked exactly the wrong time to visit the Liberace Museum," Lee observed, pouring the tea.

Emily said nothing. There was a long pause as Lee drizzled some honey into Emily's cup and slowly stirred. He held it out, looking at her expectantly. She took it.

"Thank you," she said.

Lee poured his own tea and gave a sad shake of his head. "Poor Little Bang," he said, as if they'd been talking about him all this time. "You must forgive him. He'd worked at that museum for more than ten years, was absolutely devoted. He knew more about it than any of those blue-hairs and no-hairs running the place. Of course, they never saw him in this way. Little B was strictly *custodial* to them, but he never minded, because even if he was just washing the floors, he was washing the floors near the things he loved. And they let him polish the pianos, which he considered a great honor."

Emily took a sip of tea and grimaced. It tasted of clove, and fennel, and something pulled recently from the earth.

"Buckthorn leaves," Lee said, answering a question she hadn't asked. "Keeps away the ghosts."

The tea was dark and bitter and astringent at the same time. When she finally swallowed, though, Emily felt tendrils of warmth spread throughout her chest. She breathed deeply.

Lee continued. "His love of Liberace wasn't ironic, you see. All the gaudiness, the superfluity Liberace lived by, none of it was kitsch to Little B. He believed in it. He thought Liberace was the most important entertainer of the twentieth century."

Lee lifted a teaspoon. "I wouldn't go quite so far myself," Lee said. "Liberace was an excellent showman, and I do like his choice of couture, but my musical preference runs toward the more traditional—"

Suddenly Lee was opening his mouth into a perfect oval and singing an Italian aria. His voice was a dark mahogany baritone: rich, resonant, and obviously trained.

Credo in un Dio crudel
che m'ha creato simile a sè
e che nell'ira io nomo.

The air was filled with his singing: every molecule surrounding her expanded, luxuriating in the sound. Emily's eyes widened, space clearing inside her head. A fog had been blasted away. She was awake, and alive. The skin on her arms tingled. *This is why the plants grow so green,* she thought. *To be bathed in such music.*

And then, just as suddenly, it was over. Lee was scooping Mercutio up to the couch and scratching him behind the ear. "I trained in Milan," he tossed off. "Now, about you . . ."

Emily shook her head, his singing still reverberating in her body. She asked, "Why should I feel bad about Little Bang?"

Lee smiled at Emily, almost coquettishly. "Ah. Yes. Let me tell you a story." He took a sip of tea and set his cup down. Mercutio yawned and settled into Lee's lap. "He's heard it before," Lee said, stroking the dog's fur.

"Imagine, Emily, a teenage son of immigrant hotel workers, ushering, for a lark, at Liberace's bicentennial show at the Hilton. He has no expectations, he only knows that this is one of the biggest tickets in town. He hands out programs, he closes the curtains. The house darkens. Suddenly, a man appears, glittering and fabulous. Fanfare. A red, white, and blue Rolls-Royce convertible drives onto the stage. Little Bang's life is changed forever.

"He watched the show, many, many times, to see the magic Liberace created every night. He taught himself to play the piano, to emulate that glittering man on the stage. Little Bang's family couldn't afford a piano, of course, but he practiced every day on the organ in his parents' church. Every day but Sunday. He had to bribe the priest with . . . oral satisfaction in exchange for time on the keyboard. Little Bang told me that fat old padre would push his head down and whisper, 'an organ for an organ,' right there in the sanctuary! Ah, *Jesú*! The kneeling that boy had to do to learn his craft!"

Lee laughed, but Emily felt only a sharp sliver of recognition for the boy who wanted to practice that badly.

Lee swirled his teaspoon in his cup and tapped it gently against the rim. "When Liberace died, Little Bang was devastated. I remember him coming to me, crying. 'Oh, Lee,' he said, 'if only Liberace could have picked me up in a parking lot!' Not that Liberace would have ever chosen Little Bang—my poor friend is too squat, his face too *brutto*, with his teeth all flying away from each other—Liberace would have recoiled in horror. But he played beautifully. He was a natural."

Lee fell silent, sipping his tea and lifting his gaze heavenward, as if he could hear the music. Emily picked up the thread. "And then he started working at the museum?"

"Yes, yes! Exactly." Lee set his cup down. "It gave him such solace, to be there among the things Liberace loved. They would show tapes of the Vegas shows, and Little Bang could really watch Liberace's technique on the keyboard. There were the pianos there, too, of course, but Little B could never bring himself to play a note on any of them, as much as he longed to. He didn't consider himself worthy.

"Besides, he had a piano of his own by this time. Big Bang had moved into Little Bang's apartment—what was it?—three years before, and Big B had boosted a piano for Little B to play. Don't ask me how this was done, but he did it. Big Bang never understood this love for Liberace, but he loved Little Bang. If Little Bang wanted a piano, Big Bang would get it for him."

Lee paused to pick up Mercutio and bring the dog up to his face. "We all know that kind of love, don't we, *mi caro.*" Mercutio responded with a series of rapid, wet licks to Lee's face.

"Last month the museum sponsored a contest for pianists to play in the style of Liberace. A 'Play-a-Like,' I believe it was called. The winner was to receive a thousand dollars, and, more than that, a standing engagement to perform a tribute to Liberace. Three times a week! On the very rhinestone piano played by Liberace! Do you see how this was everything Little Bang could have ever asked for in life?"

Emily shifted in her seat, uneasy. She held no fond memories of musical competitions. She took a deep breath and thought of Little Bang, in Liberace's overflowing cape, spraying business cards in the air, and the triangular photo of a piano player in the corner of a magazine. "Tony Sherbé," she said.

"Tony Sherbé!" Lee spat the name out. "Tony Sherbé is one of those dogs—no, not like you, my Mercutio, not like you—a jackal!—who comes around sniffing at the bones of animals who have died. This man sneered at Liberace; he had never seen him play. Possibly he had never even heard of him before the contest. Tony Sherbé was a second-rate graduate of a second-rate music school who was desperate for a job.

"But he was charming, and he had good teeth, and he had cunning. Weeks before the competition, he would spend hours at the museum, finding out who had the power and when they were coming in, and then, arranging to be there just at that moment. He learned the names of the judges, their occupations, their favorite wines. It was shameless. He flirted openly with the older women; he suggestively held the gaze of the susceptible men. *Faugh!* He licked the faces of all of them!

"Little Bang watched this all from behind his mop and pail. Tony never considered him a threat—he was less than a nothing, he was a janitor—and so Tony would even confide in Little B. He had this need to boast. 'Let me tell you something, *amigo*,' he told Little B, one day out by the dumpsters. 'I'm gonna wipe up this competition. Watch me. I can play better with one arm in a cast than that old queer ever did.'

"Little Bang may have wanted to help him into that arm cast, but he never let on. He stopped himself, because he knew he had to save it for the contest. Ah! The look Tony Sherbé had on his face when he found out Little Bang was one of his competitors!" Lee laughed softly, little puffs of soundless air.

"Big Bang and I were there that day. When all the participants came up onto the stage to be introduced and the janitor walked up, well! Tony lost that gleaming smile. There was shock on his face, and dismay, and finally, murderous rage. He felt betrayed. It was too delicious."

Lee produced from nowhere a small biscuit that he placed directly into Mercutio's waiting mouth. "Of course, the pleasure we got from seeing the smugness slip off his face didn't last long. It wasn't Little Bang's fault. He was brilliant, there was no question. I've never heard him play better. He captured something about Liberace's style that none of the others had: the quickness, the lightness, but also the precision and the grandeur. If you had closed your eyes you would have believed Liberace was in the room once more. Everyone felt it; the audience was on their feet the moment he stood up from the piano.

"Little Bang had the soul, he had the passion, but, unfortunately, Tony Sherbé had the sequined vest." Lee frowned at the spray of biscuit Mercutio had left on the cushion. "He sprang onto the stage with his shiny costume and insistently white teeth and we knew all was lost. Notes were slurred, notes were missed, but all was forgiven with a shake of his bobbling blond head. Little Bang never had a chance."

Lee leaned in toward Emily, who was herself leaning forward. "To lose to Tony Sherbé is painful enough. But we had underestimated the extent of his malice. Two days after being installed, he whispers intimately into the ear of the director of the museum, a sadly beguiled dowager by the name of Sylvia Stopplewhite, and the next day, Little Bang is relieved of his duties. Effective immediately, no explanation given. Just like that."

Lee snapped his fingers, and the sound cracked uncomfortably in Emily's ear. She realized she had been holding her breath. "Is that true?" she asked.

"As true as anything is," Lee replied. He nodded to the accordion at Emily's feet. "And what about you? Are you a musician as well? Do you play?"

Emily stared at the accordion for a long time. She didn't know whether it was the tea or the story, but her body had relaxed. She felt a certain vibration, a humming, emanating from her chest and spreading out to her arms and hands, which was not unpleasant. When Lee asked his question again, softly, Emily looked at him and, in answer, snapped the clasps on the case and opened it.

The Rossetti seemed to be the only thing that hadn't gotten road-beaten during the trip. It was as bright and shiny as when she had first pulled it out of the box all those years ago. There were no scratch marks, no scuffs, not one chip on the keyboard. The leather straps were a little darker but nothing else had changed. It still gleamed.

"It's been a long time," she said finally.

"Try it," said Lee.

As pristine as it may have looked on the outside, Emily knew the inside was an entirely different matter. After all these years, the tuning would be awry. The wax holding the reeds would have deteriorated, the reeds misaligned. Even the bellows might have disintegrated. *Nothing lasts forever,* she thought. Still, she grabbed the accordion and hoisted it onto her lap. It weighed nothing now; lifting toddlers in and out of car seats and up two flights of stairs had given her back and arms a new perspective.

Slipping on the straps, Emily had the sensation of watching herself again, but this time, she saw a younger version suiting up. The back straps must have loosened, because she knew she wasn't a petite fourteen-year-old girl and yet they fit her perfectly. The accordion was warm against her body. It was literally pressing on her heart, and she felt it there. Her shoulders squared, her arms bowed, her right fingers stroked the white keys, then drew back instinctively into position.

One snap, two snaps, and the bellows were released. They appeared intact. She pulled back her left arm and took the deepest breath she had taken in six months. With a sweet exhale, her arm pressed in, her fingers pressed down, and a crystalline C-chord sailed out. Up the scale, down the scale, it had not lost its tuning. There was no wheezing, no sticking of the bellows. She tried a slow arpeggio up the keyboard, and to her amazement, her fingers remembered the way.

She looked up. Lee was holding Mercutio in his arms, gently rubbing his tummy. "Why don't you play something for us?" he asked. Mercutio cocked an ear expectantly.

Emily shook her head sadly, but her fingers were already twitching. *Yes, yes, we can,* they insisted. Her brain wheeled backward in time, lifetimes ago, searching, searching. . . . She could. She could try. If she could just remember the beginning of a song. . . . Somewhere far back in her mind she heard Mr. Wojcik entreating her: "The beginning is most important, *ptaszku,* it sets the mood! It prepares the listener for the delicacy that is to come."

Shut up, thought Emily, plucking out his voice and tossing it into the void. *I'm not doing this for you.*

She pressed in and down. The opening chords to "Come Back to Sorrento" soared out. She had opened a door, and there it was before her, the long-lost world of chords and notes that had been silently waiting for her return. Emily started slowly, finding her way back into the music, but it was all there. All of it. Her fingers ran ahead, happy to be back; she grew expansive with every pull and press of the bellows. But the music was different than she had ever played it before. The notes hitched, elongated, took their own time getting to the melody, rather than holding fast to the beat. She was feeling the duskier tones to the music. She knew grief now, and anger, intimately, and it colored her playing.

Emily closed her eyes. Playing the accordion always had a hypnotic, timeless quality to it, and now she realized how similar it was to the late-night sensation of rocking her children to sleep. Especially with Georgia, when there was none of the anxiety and uncertainty she had with Walt. Back and forth in the rocking chair, back and forth, Georgia pressed against her chest, in the darkness, in the quiet of night. *There's only you and me in the world. You and me. Safe.*

Emily began trembling; she felt her arms wobble. She took in a fierce breath and concentrated on the notes, the pumping, the pushing of buttons and keys. She could hide within the music, let it wash over her, let herself be rocked by it. She was the one being held; there was a hollow in the music, and she was nestling down into it. *You and me. Let's stay like this forever.*

Lee was singing. Emily didn't know how long he had been accompanying her; his dark baritone had become so quietly entwined with her playing that she only gradually became aware of it. It wasn't until the final chorus that he burst out in full voice:

Ma non mi fuggir,
Non dar mi piu tormento,
Torna a Surriento
Non farmi morir!

Emily let the last notes linger and fade away. She was winded and breathing heavily. Something had stirred within her. Something had awakened. She looked up at Lee. His eyes were bright.

"I understand," he whispered. "I understand."

He leaned over and wiped Emily's cheek with his thumb, and it glistened when he pulled it away. "Thank you," she whispered, though she wasn't sure what for.

Lee smiled at her. His face was glowing. "You must play. It's what you were meant to do." He stood up suddenly, depositing a startled Mercutio to the ground. "Come with me." He began scanning the walls, pulling one mask off, then another.

"Come with you?" asked Emily.

"To where I work." Lee held up a simple white mask with arched black eyebrows and a single teardrop encrusted with diamanté falling from its left eye. "Perfect," he said, throwing the mask to Emily. "And I have the suit to match."

Emily fingered the papier-mâché mask. "Where do you work?"

Lee grabbed a leather mask that was lying on the dining room table and pulled it on with one practiced move. It covered the top of his head and most of his face, leaving his mouth free. He thrust his head forward, twisted his arms upward in one grand flourish, and leered merrily at Emily.

"The Venetian," he said grandly.

OWEN
OUTSIDE VENICE
EARLIER

It was twelve fifteen. Owen had shredded his entire croissant. He stood up, creating a little buttery snowdrift on the floor by the bench. Emily was nowhere in sight.

The two gondoliers stationed at the loading dock eyed him warily as he walked along the railing of the canals toward them. Perhaps he was moving too fast, or lurching. The gondoliers, one male, one female, shared a glance; Owen recognized it immediately. It was a mental, unspoken coin flip: Who was going to deal with the disturbed-looking tourist?

The man must have lost. He took a step toward Owen. This faux-Venetian was middle-aged, dark-haired, and slightly rotund at the waist, his striped torso the exact shape as those little figures Walt played with at home, the ones that wobbled but didn't fall down.

Buongiorno, my friend, *come stai?* he shouted from the platform, waving one arm like an orator.

Please, I, I'm looking for my wife, Owen said. He tried to speak discreetly, but the man insisted on playing to the crowd.

Ah, is that not what we are all looking for? said the gondolier, waving his arms broadly, looping his hands in the air, and looking, for all the world, like he was playing a game of charades. What about these *donne belle*? he offered, fluttered his fingers toward a couple of thick-ankled housewives, who clucked appreciatively. *Molto belle*, eh?

Owen's hands gripped the rail. *I'm not looking for a wife, I'm looking for my wife. This is not an amusement. And flapping your arms in the air doesn't make you more Italian.* Owen clenched his teeth and jutted out his lower jaw. I have a wife, he said slowly. She's missing.

The gondolier cupped one hand to his ear and fanned himself with the other.

So sorry, *signore*, I cannot 'ear you.

Owen shouted, My WIFE! She's MISSING! This is an EMERGENCY! Owen threw his arms forward, matching the man gesticulation for gesticulation. I WANT to know if you've SEEN her! She is SUPPOSED to be at the GONDOLAS. HELP ME!

The silence was immediate. The gondolier flinched, the Mediterranean swagger drained from his face. An aria from an incoming gondola was cut off mid-*Mio*. The only sound Owen heard was the feet of the housewives thudding quickly onto their waiting boat—thud-thud, thud-thud. *I've done it now,* thought Owen, breathing heavily, suffused with anticipation. *I've uttered the words. This is when she appears, wraithlike, a slim branch of wild olive held in her hand, hellebore twined in her hair—*

Owen's gondolier took a small step toward the railing, hat in his hand. His voice raised an octave, lost all of its rolling *r*'s and musical lilts; sounded, in fact, decidedly south of Manhattan in dialect:

Didja check the gondolas outside?

Hot.

White.

Multitudinous.

Vast.

Owen leaned his hands heavily on the marble balustrade and closed his eyes. The relatively quiet refuge of the indoor canals had beguiled him;

he had forgotten what outside was really like. The space had increased twelvefold, was, in fact, limitless. People were swarming everywhere, not only in the resort, but beyond the resort, coming from other hotels, advancing on walkways, up escalators, extruding from vehicles, stepping on and off gondolas. It was a seething anthill.

One. Two. Three. It wasn't until he reached ten breaths that he felt safe enough to relax his eyes. *White stone. Tiles. Marble—travertine perhaps?* A small cigarette butt flattened into the angle where the floor met the railing. A single drop of sweat splashed onto the tile and beaded on the polished surface. Twenty seconds later it whitened, then disappeared.

Another few inches up, the balusters came into view, but they opened out to the chaos beyond so he jerked his head up, squinting at the sky instead. Pale blue. A bleached, quiet blue. Not as pretty as the painted sky inside, but it had its own charm. The sun wasn't blinding; there were even some darker clouds knitting together overhead. Wind brushed against his face.

Slowly, by degrees, Owen lowered his eyes, allowing himself to focus on the upper strata of objects in his vision. *Spires. Tower.* THE VENETIAN, in gold lettering. A screen—sequined acrobats were leaping and contorting silently on a huge video projection. Closer still, on pedestals—statues. From one column, a griffin pawed at the air. On another, a warrior posed with his spear, standing on some kind of reptile (was that the Doge? The protector of Venice? Owen could recall no mythic lizard-conquering Greco-Roman hero).

Archways. Windows. Buildings, reflecting sunlight. *Streetlights, striped awnings,* and—*and here we go*—*people,* people walking, next to and across the streets, which were filled with cars huddling, waiting for the light to change and then crossing slowly in front of him, jostling like herded cows, buses and vans and long limousines and taxis and—

A blue Volvo station wagon.

It was there, beyond the gondolas, beyond the courtyard, passing by the hotel; it was the Volvo, Emily's Volvo, he was sure of it, moving at a crawl, like she was looking for parking, looking to pull over, it was after work and he had his briefcase and she had the kids in the backseat and he would jump in and they would stop by Reza's on the way home and pick up some Middle Eastern—falafel and garlicky chicken with thin, warm loaves of pita, it was too hot to cook—

The car was passing.

He was stumbling down the steps and across the courtyard into the thick of the crowd which had seemed impenetrable before but now miraculously opened in front of him, he had found the secret passageway, there was space where before there was only mass and he dashed into the gaps, ran until his breath tore in his chest and he was on the sidewalk. Men in baseball caps thwacked their candy-colored girlie pamphlets at him as he ran past, scarlet lips and heaving breasts smacking against their palms, but Owen had eyes only for one woman.

The Volvo was four cars ahead of him and one lane over, about to turn left. It was covered in dirt. He couldn't see the driver but he recognized the vehicle. There was the missing back-door handle, its absence gaping like an open wound, like an accusation, on the side of the car. Owen tried to close the distance but the hotel didn't want its guests leaving that easily. The sidewalk curved away from the road, started veering back to the Venetian. He jumped the concrete barricade and ran onto the street, dashing between idling autos. The Volvo was the last to turn and he was running right behind it, gaining ground, and the cadence of his furiously pounding heart was not *I-found-you-I-found-you,* but *forgive-me-forgive-me-forgive-me.*

The car was too fast. Down Buccaneer Boulevard it raced, him loping after it like a wounded giraffe. Stop! he yelled, waving his arms. Emily! Stop! But that effort cost him the use of his legs. He just couldn't run any more, and stood panting in the middle of the street.

The car seemed to slow down, but in the next instant it sped off again, tires squealing; it couldn't get away from him fast enough. The Volvo rocked wildly from side to side before veering straight toward a row of wooden street benches and an enormous concrete planter.

It happened very quickly. Owen reached out with his arms, fingers spread as if he could grab onto the back end of the car. Disregarding the curb, the Volvo clipped two of the benches and with a sickening crunch plowed directly into the planter. Air bags bloomed white.

The sky had gotten so dark. Time moved very, very slowly. To Owen, it was as if he were always stepping toward the Volvo, always stepping toward a tragedy about to be revealed. How much misery could one car contain? It was cursed—the Volvo of Atreus. It wasn't cursed. He was.

The driver-side door swung open. Owen stopped. For an agonizing moment nothing happened, and then what looked like a lumpy carpet of red, white, and blue ruffles spilled out onto the ground. Immediately after, a giant man with a thick mustache staggered out of the passenger side. Owen blinked twice. What was next, a troupe of clowns?

Using the body of the car as support, the large man made his way around to the other side. He was covered in white powder. There was an old scar running down his cheek and a new gash on the side of his head. He dropped to his knees in front of the ruffled mass.

Baaang! the man moaned. He gathered up the ruffles, and like magic Owen could suddenly see the form of a person beneath the fabric. The giant man pawed through the ruffles, exposing a small bald head that looked like an egg in a fluffy patriotic nest.

The egg howled, Aii! Watch what you're doing with the cape! It's completely hand-stitched! And the bigger man yelled, Fuck the cape! He cradled the small one and said, *Mijo*, are you all right? And the small one said weakly, Why did you grab the wheel, *pendejo*?

The big man pushed down the cape gently, but the smaller one still screamed. Even from where he stood Owen could tell the little man's head was resting at a strange angle. The little man groaned and said, Why did you . . . *Aii* . . . Don't let me . . . bleed on the fabric . . . And with that the small man gasped and collapsed.

Little Bang! Little Bang! the big man begged, rocking the little man. As Owen approached, he could see security men behind the trees, speaking into walkie-talkies.

Please, Owen said. The big man stopped rocking. He turned his head toward Owen with eyes so unseeing that Owen couldn't continue. *Yes, that must be what I look like. That's sorrow. That's exactly it.*

Sirens began in the distance. Little Bang grunted to life. Without opening his eyes, he hissed to the big one, What the fuck are you waiting for? Go.

The big one's eyes widened. Bang! he said, unbelieving. Bang. He pressed Little Bang close to his body, releasing another cry of pain.

Aii. You ox. Go.

The big one got to his feet, still cradling Little Bang. He completely ignored Owen, who might as well have been a ghost. He began moving away from the car, Little Bang wrapped around him like a toddler, his head lolling on Big Bang's shoulder. The costumes! Get the costumes! Little Bang tried to shout, but he was fading.

The big one shook his head and started limping down the street. Wait! said Owen, but the man did not slow. Owen ran behind. Please!

Little Bang opened his eyes and said, What the fuck do you want with us? and Owen asked, Where did you get the car? and Little Bang screamed, Take that motherfucking car! It's a piece of shit!

The woman who was driving it—?

I killed her! Little Bang screamed, in both triumph and pain. From nowhere he brandished a candelabra, swinging it over his head. With this! I bashed her head in! he said, laughing maniacally.

The big one picked up the pace, limping quickly away. Half a block later, he turned a corner, and the two disappeared.

And then it started to rain.

Jove's tears. That's what filled the sky. *Il larme di Giov.* It was the Roman term for rain. Owen had always preferred the Greek expression: Zeus is raining. He found it more poetic; the image of the Sky Father raining down, not tears but his whole self, his essence pouring from the sky in benediction. The crops are saved. Zeus is raining.

But not today. This was not benediction slashing down in sheets, this was Fury. This was Grief. This was Emmie, bludgeoned to death by a candelabra in some parking lot. Today, Jove was definitely, utterly, weeping.

Owen was standing in the empty forecourt of the Venetian hotel, drenched. Most everyone else had already run inside to escape the rain. A few sodden tourists in shorts and T-shirts remained, huddled together under the balcony of the hotel. They laughed and pointed at the sky from their refuge, wringing the water from their wet clothes. They waved at Owen, gesturing for him to join them, but he knew it was pointless, and indeed, in the next moment the wind had winkled them out again, whipping the rain onto their bodies and sending them shrieking indoors for safety.

The canal waters were rising. By the docks, a lone gondolier, hatless, was lashing a bucking gondola to a pole. A large man in a navy windbreaker huddled beneath an open blue canopy by the boarding ramp, shaking his head in disbelief and shouting into a walkie-talkie. Suddenly, the wind crippled one of the canopy's spindly metal legs. The man underneath ducked and the whole tent went skittering across the marble in a tangled heap. It zipped past Owen and expired at the edge of the canal, a wretched sea creature washed up onto the shore.

The man with the walkie-talkie made no move to retrieve the canopy, and if he saw Owen, he gave no sign of it. Instead, he stared at the sky, looking this way and that, as if he were trying to locate the source of a leak. *You won't find it, my friend,* thought Owen. *There's no stopping this.*

Il larme di Giov. Owen thought of his own tears, the ones that poured ceaselessly on the days after Georgia's death. Those were hazy days, then, the time surrounding the funeral and the hearing, but he remembered his face being continually wet. There seemed to be no end to the tears; too impatient to wait for his waking hours, they leaked from his eyes during sleep. Even with the medication—the medication certainly helped with the pain but it didn't take it away. It was still there, muffled in cotton. And always, the waterworks, as Vee so gently called it. Here comes the waterworks, she would mutter. Kind Vee.

Emily didn't cry. No, that wasn't true, that was unfair. He never *saw* her cry. He remembered the day of the funeral. He was sitting on the bed. The act of putting on his shirt, his pants, his tie and jacket, had almost overwhelmed him. It was as if he had run a marathon. Emily entered the room to fetch him (she was the only one who came into the room). Her eyes were red and puffy, but there was a sharpness peering out from under the swollen lids. It was as if her eyes were so bright they had caused the tissue around them to burn and inflame. The car's here, she said, staring at the lamp by the bed. Emily never faltered. She never wavered. Her gentle hands guided him from car to church steps to pew to car to bed again on that terrible day. Her voice had no warmth in it, but no anger, either. It was low and perfectly, carefully modulated, like she were speaking from a tightrope, or a very high ledge. And never once did she look at him. When she had him undressed and in the safety of his bed, he started to thank her for everything she had done, for her strength and her love and her care, but she turned away quickly, grabbed the dinner tray, and disappeared.

Long-haired Emily. He had lost her long before she drove the Volvo away. *Emily of the Bright Eyes.*

Emmie.

Where were his tears now? While the rest of his body was soaked, his eyes were, unaccountably, dry. Tears were unnecessary now, Owen supposed. The waterworks were supplied. *Jove cries for me.*

He started shivering. *It's time,* he thought. *This is when I should sink to my knees, this is where I shake my fist at the sky and rend my garments and cry out in agony. Cue the lamentations.*

They should have had lamentations, at Georgia's funeral. They should have done as the Greeks had, hired professional mourners, women dressed in black with heavy veils and thick eyebrows, to begin the *ololyge*, to beat the earth. Their cries would be artificial at first, rented, but would (because they were professional, because of the tragic circumstances) transform into genuine wails that would pierce the heavens. Cheeks would be scratched; *Katharsis* could begin.

The actual service was quiet, so, so quiet; even the priest whispered. Owen had no idea what he said. It was a hurried affair, everyone wanted to get it over and done with. And Owen, Owen just yearned for the bed, the bed, the safety of the bed.

He felt that way now, shoes squelching with every step, the rain drowning out all sound save its own. He wanted to lie down. Not in a bed, though. In a gondola. He imagined himself rigid in the Venetian boat, like a dead Norseman out at sea, his belongings piled on either side of him. The canals would overflow, the waves would mount, and he'd be carried down Las Vegas Boulevard, washed away on Jove's tears.

EMILY
THE VENETIAN
EARLIER

"It's the swimming pools." Emily and Lee were watching the first drops of rain darken the concrete outside the loading docks of the Venetian hotel. They were in the alley on the steps to the service entrance, looking up at the roiling, soot-colored clouds amassing above them.

Lee squinted at the sky and continued. "It's the pools and fountains and artificial lakes and God knows how many birdbaths out here. Do you know the amount of water that flows out of our sprinklers and down our toilets? Astronomical. I've read about it. It's actually changing the weather. Las Vegas is re-creating its own climate, God help it."

Lee swiped his card at the metal door and ushered Emily inside. She felt like she was trick-or-treating, peering through the Pierrot mask, her oversize white tunic billowing around her. Take away the shiny black buttons running down the front and the ruffled collar and she could have been a Halloween ghost, floating down the white cinderblock hallway, begging for candy.

Emily followed Lee down the corridor. Her feet, clad in black dancer slippers stuffed with tissue, made no noise on the concrete floor. Here, everything was institutional and clean. Nothing hung on the walls but emergency evacuation maps and mandatory employee notices encased in Plexiglas.

"I've always wanted to visit here," she told Lee.

"Believe me, this isn't the Venetian's best side."

Emily went to sweep the hair away from her neck, but her hand met only the stiffly starched ruffles of the collar. Back at Lee's apartment, after showering, she had stared at herself in the mirror, at the sodden mass of tangled hair, matted and twisting like underbrush. She opened the door to the bathroom, towel-clad. "Cut it off," she called to Lee. He already had the shears in his hand.

They stopped in front of a station marked SECURITY in somber blue. A slim black man stood before them in a navy jacket with the Venetian's lion insignia pawing at his breast pocket. He had an ID card hung around his neck and a walkie-talkie in hand. "Where's Maggie?" he asked. Below his insignia a small badge announced his name in gold lettering: JOSEPH SULLIVAN.

"Where's the lute player?" Joseph asked Lee. "The lute-ist?" Joseph tossed the walkie-talkie up and down, spinning it in the air. Emily thought he seemed too young to be a guard. He barely filled out the jacket.

"Sick," replied Lee. "Luckily, we have a replacement." With one swift move, he swept Emily's mask onto the top of her head. "Emmie from Vietnam."

Emily drew in her breath, but Joe wasn't even looking at her face. "That's not a lute," he said, staring at the accordion case.

"Even better," Lee promised. "Just wait."

"Weird weather," Joseph said.

"Weird," echoed Lee.

Joseph spoke into the walkie-talkie. "Performers coming out," he said. They walked through a series of hallways to a plain door with a 4 stenciled onto it. Joseph swiped his ID into a security reader. "Emmie, huh?" he said. "I thought you were a dude." He laughed and disappeared through the door.

Emily glimpsed herself reflected off the glass of a fire safety display. She did look like a boy. In fact, with no makeup on and her hair cut short, she bore a striking resemblance to Walt. The cheekbones, the flattened bridge of the nose, the delicate shell of an ear . . .

"Mask on," Lee said. She shoved her face over her face.

Almost immediately Joseph reappeared, holding open the door. "Come on in," he said. Emily glimpsed the arch of a building and a cobblestone street on the other side, the glow of lamplight.

Lee took a deep breath and lowered his leering mask. He tilted his head toward Emily, displaying the large bump protruding from his leather forehead. "Rub it," he said, "for luck." Emily reached out and touched the bump. It was soft and smooth. "Let's go," Lee whispered, offering his arm. She took it, and together, they strode out into the past.

They were standing in Old World Venice, and it was exactly as she'd hoped it would be. The metal door they had stepped through disappeared into the facade of a redbricked villa. In the same way, all the modern storefronts and the chattering tourists milling around Emily seemed to fade away, leaving behind only the cobblestones, the warmly welcoming streetlamps, the graceful porticos and balconies and gently rippling waterways of impossible Mediterranean blue.

She was only dimly aware of photos being snapped. In her periphery, Lee was extending his arms, bowing his body, striking a pose. Lee was waggling his head, Lee was squeezing a woman by the shoulders. Lee was thrusting dollars into a small leather pouch that hung from his belt. No one paid attention to her, not with the bright Harlequino capering at her side. She was largely invisible to them, as they were to her. Every so often she felt her elbow being lifted, and in this way they made their way down the street.

Emily stared up at the sky, a serene blue muted by clouds tinged with gold. It was so tranquil. There was a small red balloon in the distance, floating up to the sky. She couldn't take her eyes off it. It was supposed to get smaller and smaller and finally disappear, but it never did.

Instead, it stayed, pushing against a wispy cloud, never diminishing, unable to escape. Its white cord slowly undulated in the air.

"Go," Emily whispered. "Go."

She felt a tugging at her accordion. They had reached a small circular platform with a railing. She pulled away from Lee, who was trying to take her case. Lee bowed in apology and extended his arm. She stepped onto the platform, knelt down, and unsnapped the latches on the case. She thought she could hear the distant rumbling of thunder, but the heavens were still blue. She looked at Lee.

"Play," said Lee.

THE PEOPLE THERE THAT DAY WOULD NEVER FORGET HEARING THE MUSIC.

THEY WOULD REMEMBER IT SOUNDING, AT FIRST, SO EXOTIC, SO CAPTIVATING—

AND THEN IT WOULD SEEP IN, AND IT WAS COLD. REAL COLD.

SHIPS THAT HAD LONG SINCE SAILED—

IT WAS THE MUSIC OF EVERY SWEET LOSS THEY HAD EVER SUSTAINED.

—BRIDGES BURNED—

—DEAD PETS—

—LOST YOUTH—

—OR LOST LOVE—

—THE MUSIC PIERCED THEIR HEARTS LIKE A GLISTENING SHARD OF ICE: COLD, HARD, AND BEAUTIFUL.

IT WAS UNBEARABLE.

WITHIN MINUTES, THE ENTIRE 500,000 SQUARE FEET OF THE GRAND CANAL SHOPPING COMPLEX WAS SILENT.

EMILY PLAYED FOR AN HOUR, WITHOUT STOPPING.

NOBODY MOVED.

SHE DIDN'T EVEN NOTICE.

THERE WAS ONLY ONE PERSON SHE WAS PLAYING FOR.

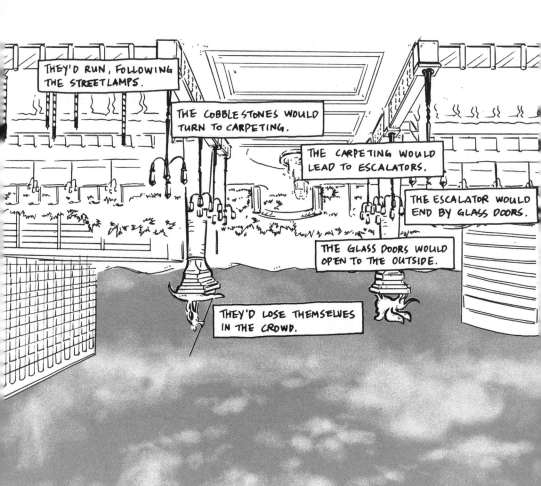

THEY'D RUN, FOLLOWING THE STREETLAMPS.

THE COBBLESTONES WOULD TURN TO CARPETING.

THE CARPETING WOULD LEAD TO ESCALATORS.

THE ESCALATOR WOULD END BY GLASS DOORS.

THE GLASS DOORS WOULD OPEN TO THE OUTSIDE.

THEY'D LOSE THEMSELVES IN THE CROWD.

AND SHE'D BE FREE.

MULTIPLE LIGHTNING STRIKES WERE REPORTED, INCLUDING TWO UPON THE VENETIAN HOTEL ALONE, ONE STRIKING THE CLOCK TOWER AND THE OTHER STRIKING THE HOTEL ITSELF.

THE SECOND-FLOOR SHOPPING PLAZA AND GONDOLA CANALS WERE EVACUATED TO THE CASINO LEVEL, WHERE, DUE TO STRUCTURAL INGENUITY, THE GAMBLERS WERE PERFECTLY SAFE FROM ANY KIND OF ATTACK, EITHER NATURAL OR MAN-MADE.

EVACUEES WERE EACH GIVEN FIFTY DOLLARS' WORTH OF CHIPS FOR THEIR INCONVENIENCE AND ADVISED TO SETTLE IN FOR THE DURATION OF THE STORM.

THE GRAND CANAL WAS DESERTED.

EXCEPT FOR TWO.

—They were on the bridge. Owen led Emily there, directly from the shadowed alcove where they had been hiding during the chaos of the evacuation. He guided her gently, like she was a sleepwalker he didn't want to waken. She had followed, yielding without words. Her fingers had no weight.

I found you, he whispered in her ear, but he knew better than to embrace her; he knew, instinctively, that he must only lightly hold her hands. It was delicate. To hold Emily more closely might mean to lose her. At the same time, he wouldn't take his eyes away. She might vanish. At any moment the oversize white clown costume she was wearing might slide to the floor, revealing that it was all a magician's trick, that she wasn't really there at all. He couldn't take that chance.

They were on the bridge. The sirens had stopped. That which was going to fall seemed to have fallen. The people had left, and other people had not yet arrived.

Look. Venice, he said. She was silent.

Walter's fine, he said. He's with Vee.

Emily's eyes were focused downward, but Owen could tell she wasn't seeing the blue water beneath them.

I know about the pills, he said.

She wasn't seeing anything at all.

Emmie? he said. He wanted her to look at him. He wanted to see her bright eyes.

Emmie, I love you so much.

Perhaps that was why he was on the bridge. He was proposing. He was proposing that she come back.

Emily began shivering.

Come home.

Emily's head shook slightly, more a tremble than a shake.

Let me take care of you. I want to take care of you.

She shook her head, more definitively this time. Owen took a step closer.

You're right, he said. Let's not go back. Let's stay.

A flash, and Owen saw it: a life, a new life, this place, they could stay here, perhaps not exactly here but somewhere near, another city within a city, a place domed, contained and secure, safe.

We could live here, he said.

She would not stop trembling. Owen grabbed her shoulders.

We can be safe here, he said. Together. Our family. No driving. No cars. No curse.

She looked at him, then, Emily of the Bright Eyes.

No.

Her eyes burned.

No, she said louder. She threw out her arms, pushing his arms away, and then she was beating her fists hard against him, striking him on the chest, again and again, like she wanted entry.

It wasn't the curse, she said. It was you. It was you. It was you.

Owen welcomed each blow, never falling but bowing down so she could strike at his head, if she wished. But now, Emily was sobbing, loud and fast, and now he could hold her, she was truly back, and he lifted her up like he would have held little Georgia, she seemed to weigh no more than that, and he carried her easily to the steps leading down to the water, and there was a gondola, waiting, a white gondola with gold trim and gold leaves adorning its prow. He stepped into the boat, setting her down gently, and then he sank down beside her, cradling her, and they set off—

PART 3

"When I woke up, she was gone."

That's how the story ended, as I remember it being told. A piece of sky had fallen from the ceiling into their gondola and knocked my hapless father out. When he came to on a gurney on the side of the canal, there was no one beside him. The paramedics told him he was the only one they had found in the gondola. She had disappeared again.

It was something like that. All these decades later, I know the story blow-by-blow but only as family history, events seen from the wrong end of the telescope, far away and indistinct. The years have eroded the details. Or maybe they were never there. Perhaps my father passed along his past intentionally vague; generality gives hard facts the sweetness and inevitability of fairy tales.

I didn't ask for many details when I lived with him. You'd have thought I would have been more curious, back then; human nature demands we chew on all the grisly details of a catastrophe. It's never enough to know that there was a hurricane that caused fatalities—we want the body count, the gore, the pain. How many died? How many injured? In what ways? Were there drownings? People crushed by falling houses? What about that woman who got decapitated by a falling street sign? And tell again about the baby *that was swept away in the rains but found, miraculously, three days later, coated in mud by a drainage ditch, unhurt. Give us more.*

Only I didn't want more, back then. I had no appetite for it. Parsing the past was a dicey affair: may cause dizziness, depression, and, in some cases, death. It didn't seem particularly relevant, or helpful, to delve into specifics.

When I woke up, she was gone. How much more do you need to know?

WALTER

CHRYSTOSTOM

I don't call Chrysto for almost a week. Partly it's because I don't know when to call, I work during the day and I know he does, too, and at night my father's been up and around more so by the time I can call I don't know if it's too late to call so I don't call and I put it off 'til the next day, and partly it's because I don't know what to say, but mostly, mostly if I'm being perfectly honest, mostly it's fear. I can't get those images of Icarus out of my head: the boy with his faulty wings heading straight for the sun, loving his freedom, making the mistake of wanting more; lost at sea.

But eventually, desire trumps fear. I know I have to either call or throw away the business card. There's this invisible expiration date stamped all over the card: *Offer good for one week only.* After that, no guarantees. It's now or never.

I pull out my cell phone Monday morning. It's really early, but I don't know when he goes to work, so I risk it. I'm out on the balcony, punching in numbers slowly, like I've never used a phone before.

It rings. And rings. And rings. Finally, a click, and a guy on the other end of the phone says, "Yes?" and I hear the barb at the end of the word. That's when I start to feel the awful pull of gravity. The actual plunge begins the exact nanosecond after I blurt out, "It's Walter," and the voice on the other end says, "Who?"

I freeze. The dark sea opens before me.

I'm trying to gather up the syllables necessary to make up my name, but Chrysto saves me with a "Hey! Wal-ter! This is you?"

Damned if those wings didn't work after all.

"Hi," I say, grinning like a mad fool.

"What are you doing?" he asks.

"Nothing."

"Come over."

It's that easy.

Here I am, over. No buzzing in, since the gate to the building's been left ajar and the lock to the outer door is busted. The apartment that Chrysto and Acacia share is at the end of a long corridor on the third floor. The door's cracked open. I'm not sure what to do. Tapping seems too timid; yelling, rude. To grab the knob and go right in seems, well, a little pushy, but knocking would push the door open. . . .

My indecision must be deafening, because a voice calls from inside: "Walter? Come in!"

The room looks large, but that's because it's mostly empty. A couch. A wooden chair. A small table, with a long white vase on it. That's it. And in the middle of the room, Chrystostom, who's standing absolutely still on a thin mat, unblinking. His dark hair is gathered together into a topknot, and he's got on what looks like a pair of white boxer briefs, but aside from that, nothing. The sunlight shafts in from the window, creating a frame around Chrysto. He's in a room of light within the room, set up for display.

Oddly, it puts me at ease, him half naked and immobile. It's what I'm used to. I take my place on the couch. The azure in his eyes has receded into a muted blue. Even his skin seems to have paled.

I say he's motionless, but that's not entirely true. I don't notice this until I've sat down. He's standing on the balls of his feet, and there's not a twitch of his ankles, not a waver, but because I'm close I can see there's movement. He's shifting his weight from the balls of his big toes to the balls of his second toes, slowly, then onward to the next toe and the next until he's reached the base of his pinkies. Nothing else has moved but this subtle shifting of his feet. He repeats this twice more, back and forth along the balls of his feet, within the space of two minutes.

And then, in a gesture that seems gigantic after so much inaction, Chrysto slowly raises his left leg. His foot comes to rest against his inner right thigh; the rest of his body could have been stone. Still elevated on his right foot, he again repeats the pattern shifting from big toe to pinkie. ON ONE LEG. Once, twice, three times, then the whole thing happens again standing on his other leg. There's never a bobble, not so much as a tiny sway.

It's crazy. It's impossible. But he does it. If he had lifted both feet off the ground and just floated, I wouldn't have been surprised.

Finally, his right foot glides slowly back down to the floor, but just for a moment, and then suddenly, with a snap, he kicks off it and is upside down, on his fingertips. He wheels his body around to face me, lifts one hand to give a quick, silly wave, and then pushes off to land, feetfirst, back on the ground.

Chrysto's laughing, and so am I. I'm amazed, and grateful. I feel like I should throw coins.

"Hello, my friend," he says, pulling me in for a quick kiss on each cheek and a happy shake of my shoulders. He's not even winded. "I am finished. Some water?"

I follow him as he pads into the kitchenette, pulling the band from his hair and shaking it free. In motion, he becomes smaller. The hard rock of his muscles melt into something younger, more fluid.

"That was, that was amazing," I stammer. "How do you do that?"

He hands me a small bottle of water and shrugs. "Many years of practice. Since I was boy."

"Is it, like, yoga?" I ask.

Chrysto scoffs. "Yoga! No, not like yoga. Older."

His hand goes to his throat, and for the first time I notice the necklace he's wearing, a small white stone hanging from a thin silver chain that he fingers.

"Yoga's pretty old," I say.

He looks at me as if he'd like to pat me on the head.

"You bring the book?" he asks.

I take the sketchbook I've promised out from under my arm and slowly offer it up. I notice how scratched the cover is, how the binding is beginning to fray. "I don't know why you want to see it," I say, but he's already grabbed the book and has hopped backward onto the couch, legs folded under him. He opens it with one hand and pats the cushion next to him with the other.

There's a certain tang his body gives off: salt and citrus. Sitting next to him, I try to breathe slowly, to keep my eyes open and not look like I'm inhaling big greedy gulps of him. His head is bent over the book but I get the feeling that he's still somehow watching me, or watching me watch him.

Chrysto flips through the pages backward so he's seeing the most recent drawings first. He grunts appreciatively as he views himself in pencil and pen, running his finger across the page. "Yes," he repeats over and over. "Yes."

He turns a page. "This is Acacia! Exactly." She's in her dying swan pose. More pages of Chrysto, hands and shoulders and muscled arms. Chrysto spreads his own arm out in front of him and clenches and unclenches his hand. "Is perfect. Exactly." The hair on his arm is quite dark, but in the pictures his arms are white and smooth. Where could all the hair have gone?

He laughs with delight. "You are excellent, yes?" I smile without meaning to, and he smiles back. He goes quiet for a moment, then raises a finger toward me. "You must do more, Walter. This is important."

He bends back to the book, flipping several pages. "Your mother?" he asks. He's pointing at the drawing of the question mark woman, the one with the long hair who ran out of Viva Las Vegas! "The cheek, the jaw, these are the same." I hadn't noticed that before. He traces the outline of the face on the page with his finger, then brings his hand to my face. I flinch, and hate myself for it.

Chrysto lets his fingers linger in the air before bringing them back down to the page.

"You see?" he says.

"I . . . I don't know who that is," I tell him. "I just drew her. I don't have a mother."

Chrysto's eyes open wide. "Ahh!" he says, turning his body toward mine. "This is me also! I am orphan! No parents. They die. Big explosion, boom! Terrorist. I was very small. You also?"

I try explaining that this is not the case, but I'm having difficulty coming up with words, even syllables are hard, because at this moment Chrysto has placed his hand on my cheek. This time I don't flinch. He doesn't pat my face but instead cups the side with his palm and leaves it there.

European, I think. It must be a European thing. I will move to Europe.

He looks sadly into my eyes, his eyes glistening with shared sorrow. "We are same, yes?"

"Yes," I breathe.

Keys jingle in the lock, and the door opens. "Chrysto—" Acacia begins. She is holding a small bag of groceries. She stops when she sees me.

"'Kash," Chrysto calls out, "look who is here." I can still feel the warmth of his fingers after he has slid them away from my face.

"Ah," Acacia says. "Walter." She says my name like I'm a gymnast. Her lips spread out into a thin smile, but her eyes do not twinkle. They shift back and forth between me and Chrysto.

"Acacia," Chrysto says, eyes shining, "Walter, he is like us, he is orphan."

I shake my head to restart my brain. "No, no," I say, "I'm not an orphan. I live with my father."

Chrysto looks puzzled. Acacia looks puzzled. Finally, she speaks. "Oh, you are trying to kill his father?" she asks Chrysto pleasantly, and disappears into the kitchen.

Chrysto's eyes harden.

"It was my fault," I call out to Acacia, "I wasn't clear." I can hear the sound of groceries being taken out of the bag, but she doesn't respond.

Chrysto has recovered and is waving the black sketchbook over his head. "Acacia!" he calls. "Walter is artist! Great artist! Come look!" There's no answer. "'Kash!" he yells louder. "He has drawn picture of you, exactly! Come!"

There is another moment, and then Acacia appears from the kitchen, clenching a jar of pickled asparagus spears. "Stavros from Athens, very famous painter, many times I sit in his studio." Her shoulders are set back, her feet planted wide apart. "Hans Leipzig, number two artist in Germany, has made paintings of me. One of them, in Berlin National Gallery. More pictures of me, I do not need to see."

Chrysto mutters something in Greek, and judging by the way his teeth drag along his lower lip, I know it's not a compliment. Much shouting follows, none of it in English. Lots of hand gestures. It's all kind of scary and very European. Maybe I don't want to live there after all. I don't hear my name invoked, but several times the jar of asparagus spears is thrust in my direction.

It ends with Acacia storming into the bedroom. "Get ready for work!" she shouts from behind the slammed door.

Chrysto angrily pulls on a pair of jeans and grabs a shirt from the back of the couch. He flips a hand in the direction she has parted, dismissing her. "Walter," he says, grabbing my shoulder and squeezing it, "come. There is still time for eating."

"Bitch," Chrysto says brightly. "My sister, I love her, but she is sometimes bitch."

Chrysto drips the last of the honey into his thick yogurt. We're seated at a small table in front of a Greek café four blocks from where he lives. There's a small white cup of muddy coffee next to his bowl. I've got a cold lemon–poppy seed muffin on my plate, even though I can't stand lemon–poppy seed muffins.

"She thinks she is *mana mou*, my mother, but she is not," he continues. "Very unhappy, Acacia. Does not like this . . . Las Vegas. The *choiros* who stare at her. Also, she"—Chrysto waggles his fist, thumb extended, in front of his mouth—"too much."

"Ohhh." I nod my head, like this explains everything. "How did you end up in Vegas?"

He points the honeyed teaspoon in my direction. "Maybe ... to find you," he says, and smiles. I can't tell whether he's joking or not. He puts the spoon in his mouth and draws it out slowly, thinking. "There is something I am searching for ..." he begins, but breaks off. A shadow darkens our table. It's the waiter, who places the check down. He looks supremely uninterested in us, but Chrysto glowers until he goes away.

"Some things I cannot say. Here. I could be killed." He leans forward, conspiratorially, then suddenly cries out. I think for a moment he's been shot.

"My wallet. I have forgotten it. Idiot!"

"It's no problem," I tell him, and pull out my own. He looks at me, pained, but I shake my head and draw the check toward me.

He takes a last sip of his coffee. "I am happy, Walter. I am so happy to have a friend."

I'm happy, too.

Chrysto leans forward. "One day soon, I will tell you everything. My story. Fantastic." He mimes scribbling on a page. "You know ... writer? Person who writes? I am looking for this."

"I write," I blurt out. "I mean, I can write. I have written ... stuff."

Chrysto grabs both my hands. "You are artist and writer both! Excellent!" He looks me directly in the eyes and pulls me closer. "What have you done with this talent?"

I mumble the truth because I can't think of a lie. "I, uh, I did a comic. You know comics?" The school once ran a series of strips I did, the adventures of Jerry Jackrabbit, the school mascot. The strips usually ended with Jerry being run over by some vehicle, or having his eyes explode from some cosmetics lab experiment. As soon as the teacher sponsor got around to reading the paper she pulled it. That's pretty much the extent of my literary career.

Chrysto frowns and crinkles his forehead, either because he doesn't know what I'm talking about or because he does. "Hmm," he murmurs distantly. He places both hands on the table, like he's made a decision.

"You are young. I am young. Together—" He clasps his hands together, then spreads them wide; I half expect a dove to magically appear.

"What?" I ask. "Together, what?"

He smiles at me, that dimpled, wolfish smile that sails like a thunderbolt straight into my heart. "Everything, Walter. Everything."

And he did tell me many things, little nuggets of information like honeyed nuts that he'd feed me by hand, and I'd lap them up, happy little love-starved puppy that I was. I became privy to some of the tricks he and Acacia employed, like how they managed to get up unnoticed onto the pedestals at Venice Venice. There were doors high up on the wall, next to the pedestals, and when the gondoliers commanded attention by banging their oars and singing on their march to the docks, Chrysto and Acacia would slip into place. He showed me the special powder they had smuggled all the way over from Greece, a white dust ground from the river rocks of Taygetos Mountain, and how, by mixing it with spring water, a clay could be made that was smeared on the body like a second skin, creating the look of statues without any cracks or imperfections. Chrysto even let me in on some of his training, though I could not begin to learn even the easiest exercises; I was too old, too rigid in my joints and tendons, even at the age of seventeen. He had been refining his body since the age of four. There were the exercises he did to slow the pulse down, to calm the breath, to deaden the eyes. He described the horrible and sometimes fatal rituals they practiced, where they would place the young boys in slim wooden boxes, like caskets, and lower them into narrow cracks in the earth, to see how long they could remain perfectly still, and how some would scream the first night and others would emerge three days later, fresh as if they had just stepped out of a bath. Chrysto boasted that he had control of every minute muscle in his body, even many of the involuntary ones, and how he used them to control his breath, his nerves, and his heart.

Chrysto divulged many secrets; I later appropriated some of them in my work. But he didn't tell me the most important thing. Not until it was too late.

HOW SHALL THEY LIVE, SO UTTERLY ALONE?

THE GODS HAVE AN ANSWER.

Throw the bones of your mother behind you...

THEY THREW THE STONES BEHIND
THEM—

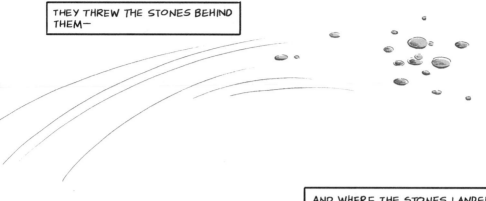

AND WHERE THE STONES LANDED—

—LIFE BEGAN.

WE ARE THOSE STONES.

THE SONS OF DEUKALION AND THE DAUGHTERS OF PYRRHA.

THE PETRIDES.

THE CHILDREN OF STONE

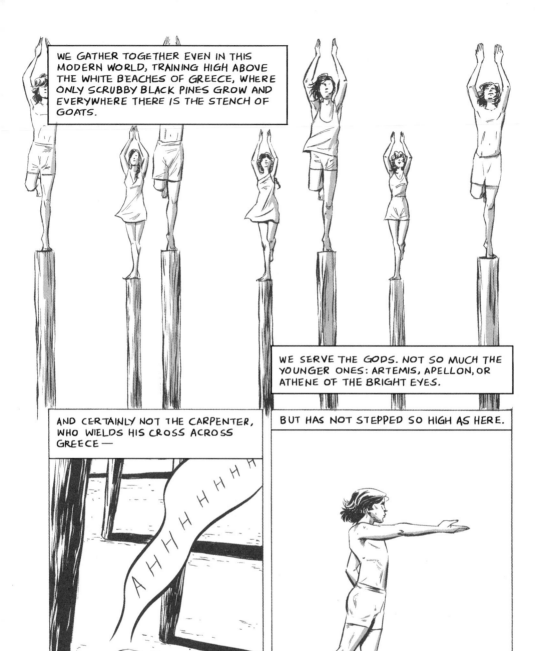

WE GATHER TOGETHER EVEN IN THIS MODERN WORLD, TRAINING HIGH ABOVE THE WHITE BEACHES OF GREECE, WHERE ONLY SCRUBBY BLACK PINES GROW AND EVERYWHERE THERE IS THE STENCH OF GOATS.

WE SERVE THE GODS. NOT SO MUCH THE YOUNGER ONES: ARTEMIS, APELLON, OR ATHENE OF THE BRIGHT EYES.

AND CERTAINLY NOT THE CARPENTER, WHO WIELDS HIS CROSS ACROSS GREECE—

BUT HAS NOT STEPPED SO HIGH AS HERE.

AHHHHHHH

NO, IN THESE REMOTE AREAS THE OLDEST ONE STILL LIVES: METER TAYGETOS, KYBELE.

EVERY SPRING THE PRIESTESS VISITS THE SACRED CAVE. SHE BRINGS WITH HER THE STONE KNIFE AND THE BASKET CONTAINING THE MYSTERIES.

TWELVE NOVITIATES WILL BE CHOSEN TO LINE THE PATH OF HER PROCESSION.

WE WILL BE THE STONES THE PRIESTESS AWAKENS AT MIDNIGHT.

THE DAY BEFORE, OUR HAIR IS CUT OFF AS AN OFFERING, AND OUR BODIES SHAVEN, EVERY PART.

WE ARE CARRIED TO OUR PLACE ALONG THE ROUTE, RIGID AND SILENT AS STATUES, TO LIGHT THE SACRED WAY WHEN EVENING FALLS.

THE NEXT MORNING, THE WHITE CLAY IS SMEARED ON OUR BODIES.

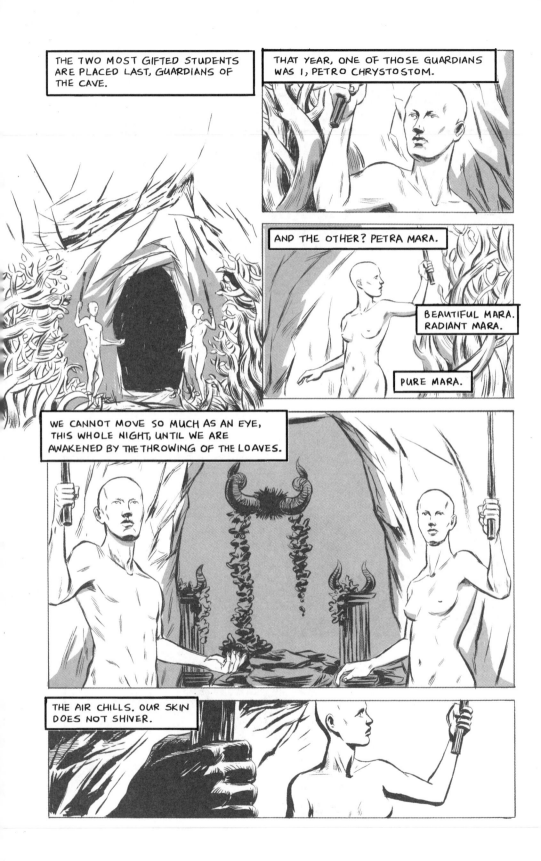

THE TWO MOST GIFTED STUDENTS ARE PLACED LAST, GUARDIANS OF THE CAVE.

THAT YEAR, ONE OF THOSE GUARDIANS WAS I, PETRO CHRYSTOSTOM.

AND THE OTHER? PETRA MARA.

BEAUTIFUL MARA. RADIANT MARA.

PURE MARA.

WE CANNOT MOVE SO MUCH AS AN EYE, THIS WHOLE NIGHT, UNTIL WE ARE AWAKENED BY THE THROWING OF THE LOAVES.

THE AIR CHILLS. OUR SKIN DOES NOT SHIVER.

I CANNOT SEE MARA, THOUGH SHE IS ONLY A BREATH AWAY.

SHE HAS PLEDGED HER LOVE TO ME.

I IMAGINE EMERGING FROM THIS CLAY, AND THIS NIGHT, A MAN.

DAMIANO, THE CARETAKER, COME TO LIGHT THE TORCHES. A MAN WITHOUT MANHOOD.

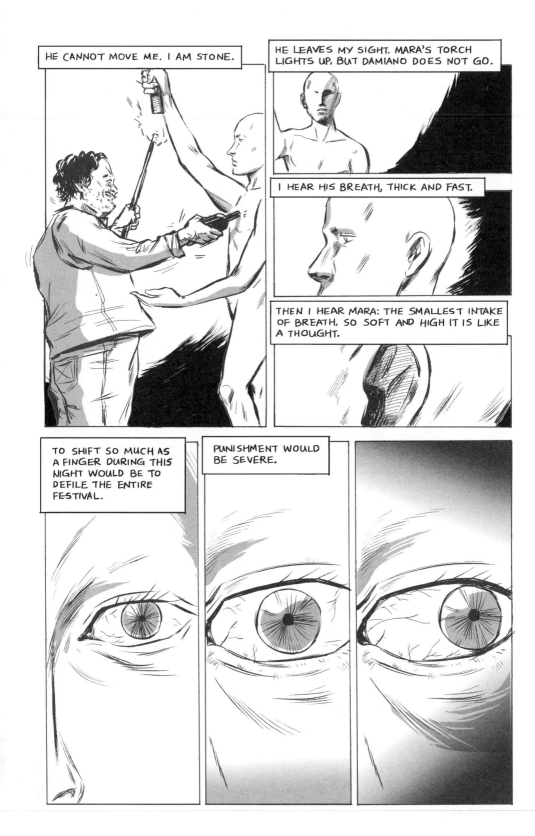

CHRYSTO, NO!

NO...

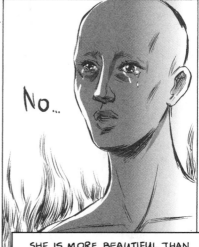

SHE IS MORE BEAUTIFUL THAN EVER. I AM NOT SORRY FOR WHAT I HAVE DONE.

THE WOODS ARE ON FIRE. THEY WILL BE HERE SOON.

WE LEAVE THE PATH. BRANCHES WHIP US AS WE PASS.

CHRYSTO?

WHAT HAVE YOU DONE, YOU FOOLS?

ACACIA, MY SISTER. SHE HAS BROUGHT CLOTHES.

FOLLOW ME. AND KEEP UP.

SHE KNOWS THE MOUNTAIN WELL.

WE RUN THE ENTIRE NIGHT. OUR FEET ARE BLOODIED BY THE SHARP—STONED, NETTLED GROUND.

AT ONE POINT I REALIZE MARA IS NO LONGER WITH US.

I DO NOT KNOW WHEN THIS HAPPENED.

MARA!

MARA!

SHUT UP, OR WE WILL BOTH BE KILLED!

THERE ARE SHRIEKS IN THE AIR, AND SHOUTS, AND THEN, ONLY THE SOUNDS OF NIGHT.

MARAAAAAA...

I REMEMBER THE SOUND MARA MADE AT THE CAVE, THAT LITTLE PUFF OF AIR.

I WONDER IF SHE WILL BE SO SILENT WHEN THE ROCKS ARE PILED UPON HER?

SHE WAS BEAUTIFUL.

SO BEAUTIFUL.

WALTER & CHRYSTO
ROMA

An alarm goes off in the dark. Not mine, someone else's; mine is high and whiny, this one grumbles. No, it's not an alarm, it's something else. It's the doorbell. It's the air conditioner breaking down. Can it be a goat? No, it's my cell phone, glowing and vibrating on the coffee table, and in the stillness of the night it sounds as loud as a slot announcing *Jackpot!*

I plunge down off the couch, scrambling to pick it up. I know who it is, because there's no one else it could be, no one else I want it to be.

"Hello?" I whisper, blinking my eyes into focus.

"Walter, I need your help." His voice sounds rough and strained. He's been crying. "Help me to find her."

"What? Who? Acacia?" I ask, shaking the sleep out of my head.

"No," groans Chrysto. "Not Acacia. Mara. She is here."

At first I think he's saying "Mother," but then I remember the girl from the cave in Greece. "She's here?" I whisper. I feel my way to the sliding glass doors and step out onto the balcony. What was she doing in Las Vegas?

"Not her. Her image."

His story rushes out of him, lurching and stalling, punctuated by heavy sighs and swigs from a bottle. It involves Mara and an American sculptor, who had come up the mountain the winter before the whole lost-in-the-woods disaster and picked her to pose for him.

"Why would someone go all the way to Greece just for a model?"

"Please, Walter, do not be so thick," Chrysto says. "It is done this way, always. For many centuries, sculptors, painters, those of highest artistic quality, have come to us. The Petrides of the Mountain, we are known. Our training makes for us to give the excellent posing, the . . . inspiration. Is easy to understand, yes?"

I think of Apollo, high atop the crowds at the Venice Venice shopping plaza.

"Yes," I say.

"But this is not important," groans Chrysto. "This artist, he has come on commission to make a statue. He tells of this to Mara while she sits and he builds her body small, in clay. Mara whispers this to Acacia that night, but Acacia"—he spits out her name—"she does not tell me! She keeps this from me all these years. Only now she tells me!"

I don't know if I'm still sleepy or just naturally dense. "Tells you . . ."

Chrysto shouts so loud I'm afraid my father will wake up. "Las Vegas! He was making statue for hotel in Las Vegas!" His voice falters then, shrinking down to a piteous mewing. "She is somewhere here, Walter. I must find her. What can I do? You must help me. You understand this city. Find with me this statue."

Honestly, I don't see how finding it would make any difference. Who knows? Maybe the sculptor was a modern artist and he's elongated all of Mara's limbs or put a giant hole in her torso. Or more likely she's somewhere attached to a slot machine, with a Wheel of Fortune spinning inside her belly. How would finding that help?

"Walter." Chrysto's voice rings darkly in my ear. "For so long, I cannot sleep, I cannot eat, I always am weeping and thinking, thinking only of Mara, of what I have done and what has happened to her. I must see her again, to finish with it. Everything will change, my life will go on, better, when I find this statue. You understand?"

The soft, pleading tone in his voice vibrates inside me. Of course I understand. I know what it's like to go looking for pieces of your past, no matter how pointless. And even though I don't have a great track record with finding lost women, locating one who's fixed in one place should be a lot easier.

"When do you want to meet?" I ask.

Two days later, it's getting on toward evening, but the path of my day isn't narrowing down to sleep, like usual. It starts off the same: I've changed out of my work clothes, peeled back the plastic of my father's dinner, checked the Night cup with its evening's meds. But now, in this alternative universe, instead of dismantling the couch and burrowing in, I'm going OUT, out into the bright night, which spreads before me, open and unexplored.

I'm on a mission.

We meet in the concrete alleyway outside of Venice Venice. Chrysto's just finished work, and he's his usual high-energy self, not a trace of desperation or anxiety to be found. He pulls me in for a quick kiss on each cheek, and I notice a streak of clay on his neck, just under the right ear, a spot he must have missed. I resist the urge to wipe it away, to take my finger and swipe a little U on the V of his neck muscle.

"Where to, Walter?"

I point out that only the newer, more expensive casinos would be able to afford a commissioned statue, and that maybe we should start looking in one of those places. It just makes sense. I suggest Roma, the newly renovated Caesar's Palace, which is definitely high-end and has a boatload of statues.

Chrysto squeezes my shoulders appreciatively, blasts me with all the blue of those Mediterranean eyes. "Hey, I think my luck is changed already," he says. I smile goofily back. I'm a head taller than he is but I can nestle easily right in the palm of his smooth, long-fingered hand.

Being on the Strip with someone else makes all the difference. I'm not just pushing past crowds and through them and into them, I'm one of them. Well, not really one of them, I'd never want to be one of them, but it's not just me. I'm part of a pack. A pack of two.

It's clear who the alpha male is. Chrysto pulls me through the crowds, always a little ahead but then suddenly right next to me, tugging my arm this way or that or touching my shoulder to direct attention toward some hidden statuary. I follow, jerked by an invisible thread that keeps me within a body or two of him. I'm learning to navigate in his wake, to make my way through the crowds. The air smells of exhaust and cigarettes, but there's something else, too, a sweaty muskiness, absolutely masculine. The heat coming off my skin mingles with the heat in the air, my molecules mixing with everyone else's molecules until we're all covered with this thin membrane of animal warmth that binds us together until the next sanitized blast of air-conditioning blows it apart.

We arrive at Roma. It's huge. I can't imagine that the real city could be much bigger. Gigantic lobbies, multiple casinos, four swimming pools, two temple gardens, forecourts, after-courts, tennis courts, and a mini Colosseum. We stride through room after room, me spotting statues and Chrysto dismissing them. He barely looks at the figures but can point out all their flaws. This Jupiter is too dull, that Venus is lacking in grace; none of them impress him in the least. "This is no muse, this is a cow," he says of an unfortunate nymph kneeling by a marble fountain.

I moo coquettishly.

"These statues were never alive," Chrysto says with disgust.

"Isn't that the fault of the artist?" I ask.

Chrysto shrugs. "One who sits is equally to blame. One must give the spark for the fire. There must be something for to capture, some emotion, or the artist is looking at . . . plate of fruit. Model must give something of himself, but also, to hold back. This is the true art."

We reach the atrium, where there's a statue I know I've seen before in books. It looms over us: three naked figures, a large man and two youths who are being attacked by a giant snake. The serpent curls around their legs and arms; its open mouth is about to sink into the man's side. I point it out. "Can't complain about this one," I say.

Chrysto scans the statue impatiently. "Yes, yes, of course it is amazing. But, it is only copy. The original stone, the paint, the clay, this contains life that is not translating to copies. You come to Greece, you will see statues that Petrides have posed for. These statues look to be only pausing." Chrysto gives the figure in the middle one more flicker of attention. "This man, he was without doubt a son of Deukalion. Is obvious."

Copy or no, there is something different about the man in the middle. Besides the fact that he's proportionally larger, his body contorts in a way that feels more . . . tortured than the other two. It's hard to look away from the agony. It's like the pain was etched into the marble.

"Hey, Walter." Chrysto's voice slices into my right ear, low and flat. He's standing close behind me. "Why do you all the time look at the men's bodies?"

I feel my face burn. "Whaa?" I say, and stammer something utterly incoherent, but it doesn't matter because Chrysto has already walked away.

We scope out the rest of the casino, mostly in silence. There's nowhere else to go. We're back at the main concourse, outside the Gorgon's Lair Vodka Bar. Chrysto's distracted, withdrawn, carrying on some kind of discussion in his head while his eyes dart back and forth. I've got my own dialogue going on, too. I tell myself that Chrysto's frustrated, that he's thinking of all the places we haven't gotten into, the hotel floors and the private gambling rooms, and that he's not blaming me for a wasted night and he's not bored with my company and looking for a way to ditch me. I wonder what I've done wrong, and I'm afraid of doing it again.

The Gorgon's Lair has drawn back its black velvet curtains, revealing two life-size papier-mâché partygoers, real drinks in their frozen hands, who greet the living couples that glide past them and disappear into the darkness. I'd suggest going in to check the place out but there's no way I'd ever be allowed in. The bar has velvet ropes barring folks like me from wandering in. The Medusa at the doorway, the one with a leather minidress and the bleached, ironed hair, has already given me the stony once-over and curled her glossy, gelatin-injected lip at me. If I were close enough she'd hiss.

Chrysto's eyes are gleaming. His head bounces to the beat of the music. Suddenly he turns to me and pats me on the chest. "Walter. Stay here. Please." Without waiting for an answer, he vaults over the velvet rope to the host stand. The pounding music blocks out his words. Medusa bends her head toward Chrysto but he does not turn into stone. Instead, she is the one transfixed, riveted into place by his breezy banter, the toss of his dark curls, the full-wattage smile he flashes at her. His hand cups her bare shoulder as he pulls her in, whispering in her ear. The hand disappears from view, takes a brief trip down her bony shoulder blade, and then travels back to the top, where it warms and inspires.

My own shoulder has never felt so lonely.

Another laugh, and he's gotten by. I can only guess that he's of age, but it wouldn't matter anyway. Chrysto passes the ropes and disappears into the blackness. He doesn't look back. Medusa smiles and twirls her snakes. I walk four steps away and park myself against a marble column, loyal dog.

Ten minutes pass. I wonder how long I should wait. And what am I waiting for anyway? "Why do you look all the time at the men's bodies?" His eyes get harder every time I replay it, his lip curls upward with disgust. He's disgusted by me, by my mutant head and skinny body and puppy eyes. He's hiding in there until I leave.

I need an offering, to prove my worth. "Two strawberry daiquiris," I recklessly tell the counter girl at the Nectar of the Gods frozen drink stand across the concourse. I brace myself for an ID challenge, but she doesn't even look at me. The drinks are served in plastic vessels shaped like the *Venus de Milo*. There are Day-Glo pink straws poking out like a severed artery from the opening at her neck.

I take the ladies back to my post. At the nightclub, there's now a new gorgon occupying the host stand: a chiseled black guy with bleached dreads erupting from the top of his head. Maybe blond hair is a prerequisite for working there. He does quite a professional job of ignoring my very existence. I suck furiously on my straw.

Chrysto is never coming out. He's probably found his Mara: her statue was posed by the women's restroom and he kissed it and she sprang to life and they're now on the dance floor, boogying down to a techno version of "Lady Marmalade." Or, the statue wasn't there at all, but that blond Medusa has snaked her way into his heart and become his new, living Mara, and they've slipped out the back door already, on their way to her apartment, where she can shimmy out of that tight dress and they can begin their shiny new life of fabulousness, while I stand here holding two sweating red *Venus de Milos*.

"Walter." My ear prickles with the sound of his voice. Chrysto's at my side, and I fight the urge to cry by sucking down some drink, only it's too fast and I choke on my drink and a little strawberry daiquiri splooshes out of my mouth and down my chin. Chrysto laughs and gently bats at my face, wiping it away. He examines the red slush on his fingers, then sucks them thoughtfully. "Good," he says.

I offer him a *Venus* and he grabs the torso just under her stumpy arm. "Excellent," he says.

Chrysto's grinning again. The clouds have parted. All is right with the world.

I raise my *Venus*. "Daughter of Pyrrha?"

He takes a sip. "Undoubtedly. Do not look at me this way, it is true!"

"Any luck?" I ask.

He waves away the Gorgon's Lair. "Nothing. This place is . . . disgusting. Nothing real." And then he's pushing his drink against my chest. "You are real, my friend. Thank you for helping me to look." His breath has that fiery, sweet, undiluted smell of ouzo.

He looks into my eyes one second longer than I can bear. Something has passed between us. "Hey, Walter," he says, that wolfish smile slowly spreading across his face, "come to my house. I wish to show you something. Yes?"

Time slows down briefly as I try to have a reasonable thought. I fail. "Sure," I say immediately.

"Good." Chrysto lifts his *Venus* and drains her in one long swallow. He shakes his head furiously and breathes deeply, to ward off the brain freeze. She's no longer red. He tosses her in the trash bin behind us. "Let's go."

I follow him out, holding on to my drink, sipping it for as long as I can. I want to make it last.

The apartment building Chrysto and Acacia live in houses a lot of performers who work on the Strip, most of them foreign. Chrysto gives me the rundown on nationalities as we pass each of their doors: on his floor there are three Czech aerialists, two Canadian gymnasts, a French production manager, and four tiny Thai contortionists. We stop in front of an apartment that, for the moment, is vacant. For some reason Chrysto has a key. "So not to bother my sister," he tells me as he unlocks the door. The light from the hallway juts sharply into the room, stabbing into the softer glow of the street spilling through the living room window.

Chrysto flicks on the entryway light, pulls out the key, and rushes through the room without pausing. "I need to piss," he calls out, and disappears into the bathroom.

The room looks exactly the same as Chrysto's, down to the furniture and paintings on the wall, only this one faces the street instead of the alley. I swing my backpack onto the couch and wander to the window. There's nothing much to see but I'm looking awfully hard all the same. I need to be doing something as I try not to listen to the sound of Chrysto peeing, which goes on forever. The buildings run pretty close to one another. It's not much nicer than my neighborhood, but stupidly I find it somehow magical, with the amber light of the streetlamps making the concrete all orange and the terra-cotta buildings glow.

The peeing stops. Listening for the bathroom door makes my legs tingle. It's late at night and I'm alone in a cheaply furnished apartment with a guy. I've watched enough late-night TV to know how this could go down. Lights are lowered, the soft jazz saxophone music starts playing. Champagne is poured, sometimes in a bathtub with lots of candles. Or, I could have completely misjudged the situation, as I've done all night, and he's really about to bring out a photo album of Greek landmarks to share with me. I have no idea.

The bathroom door clicks open.

What happens next happens fast. I look back into the room as Chrysto turns on the overhead light. He's got no shoes or socks on—"Are you ready, Walter?"—and before I can answer he's peeling his shirt off over his head and three quick blinks later he's pulling off his pants and Holy Zeus he's not wearing underwear. Holy Zeus. I'm paralyzed. Chrysto stands before me, naked, fully illuminated. No clay, no fig leaf, just unabashed body. He grins and extends his arms. "What are you waiting for?"

I'm waiting for a sign that I'm not going to fall into some kind of seizure. After a few long moments I finally remember the mechanics of breathing and gulp in some air. This makes my gaping mouth close, which is probably a more attractive look for me. I reach for the buttons of my shirt, my fingers pressing tight to my chest so I won't tremble so much.

"The book," Chrysto says, smiling. "Go get your book." He has to nod his head toward the backpack on the couch before I understand what he's saying. Confused, I go to the couch and pull the sketchbook out of my bag. I turn and hold it out for him, but he's retreated to the middle of the room. "How do you want me?" he says. An agonizing pause, and then a synapse finally takes a slow leap across the barren wasteland that is my brain.

He wants me to draw him.

"Oh," I say. I tell myself I'm relieved, but that twist in my gut thinks otherwise. How do I want him? It's a loaded question. I just shrug.

"Come on. Give me a feeling," Chrysto says.

"Confused?"

Chrysto laughs. "All right," he says, settling onto the floor. He folds into himself, twists his limbs into a posture of bewilderment, head cocked to one side. His face mimics what he must see in my own. This makes me laugh. I can feel my body relax. Well, most of it, anyway. His pose hides nothing. I sit on the couch and pull out my pen, grateful that the book covers my lap. Though he's the naked man here, I'm the one feeling exposed.

"Now you shall see, Walter," Chrysto says, "what a Petrides can offer to an artist." One hand is pushing back his hair, mid-sweep. The other is suspended by the side of his mouth, a fingertip pulling gently at his lower lip. He's definitely looking perplexed. But not more than I am.

"I'm not an artist," I mumble, looking down at a blank page. The pen feels heavy in my hand, unwieldy.

"Perhaps, not yet," Chrysto says. "Let me help you."

"I've sketched you before," I point out.

"It is not the same. This is only for you. The connection between artist and subject must be very close, very intimate," he says, drawing out the last word. Though he hasn't moved, his voice draws him nearer.

I look up. "Why are you doing this?"

He stares at me with those wide-set eyes, unblinking. "I am tired of old artists and their old artist hands. You are new, Walter. I am new." He watches me watching him, making me look down to the pad. My pen hovers over the page, awaiting orders.

"I like you," Chrysto says.

When I look back up at him, I read something in his steady eyes, reflected back from the blue. There's uncertainty there, and it's not just the pose; it's like he's trying to make up his mind about something. This time I don't drop my gaze. I want to stay in those eyes. I want them to look at me forever.

"Draw, Walter."

They're what I sketch first. I draw them big on the page: those eyes that will never look away from me. Pupils, irises, heavy lids, and dark, dark lashes. Thick, expressive eyebrows and the bridge of an exquisite nose. When I finally lift my pen, many minutes later, those eyes stare up at me, bright and questioning, but the questions they're asking are my own.

I turn the pad around and hold it up for Chrysto, so he can look at himself looking at himself. I like it. For once, my hand has set down exactly what my eyes have seen. Chrysto allows himself a break and smiles. I think he's pleased, too. "See, Walter? No need to look at other statues. Not when you have me."

Other statues. I think of the giant stone man grappling with a snake in the atrium of Roma, and Chrysto's darkened mood there. Was this some sort of professional rivalry? Was he jealous of a statue? I look at this chiseled man, so willing to put himself on display for my benefit.

The gods are needy.

"Why are you smiling?" Chrysto asks.

"Hey, don't move," I say, turning the page over. "I'm not done with you yet."

I still have those eyes. I've pinned them up in every crumbling apartment I've ever squatted in, and when I didn't have a permanent residence I carried the drawing, carefully folded, in whatever sketchbook I was using at the time. Only my beloved black canvas backpack came close to staying with me as long, and I don't remember when that finally burst its last seam (safety pins can only do so much). Years later, when Dark Eye Press published my "Steal Wool" series (a modern-day Jason and the Argonauts story, set in Iraq), movie-option money rained down like manna from the heavens. With it I bought myself a tiny home in a once-derelict, then-gentrified, now-derelict-again neighborhood in Los Angeles. It was more space than I could have ever imagined owning. I set up my studio (a studio!) in what was once the nursery, peeling all the faded duck and lamb appliqués off the wall but keeping the puffy painted clouds floating on the blue ceiling.

The first thing I hung up in my new study, above my desk, was the creased sketch of Chrystostom's eyes, finally framed. I look at them often, and they look at me. They're staring at me now as I type this. Those eyes are my talisman, a reminder of that electrifying moment when potential, inspiration, and desire first fused in me; they're a command made manifest: "Draw, Walter."

WALTER & CHRYSTO
APARTMENT

"Be heroic."

"That is not a feeling."

"All right. Brave. Be brave."

"That is not an emotion, brave."

"Yes, you can feel brave. 'I am feeling brave.' "

"All right, Walter, but this is very boring, brave."

It's our fourth night in the apartment. This whole week has become one wheeling, vampiric odyssey: meeting after work—searching hotels for Mara—back to the empty apartment—posing and drawing late into the morning.

I can't even remember what happens during the day.

Chrysto takes one last swig of Heineken and puts the bottle down. Alcohol doesn't seem to affect his posing in the least. Along the wall a small battalion of green bottles line up, awaiting orders. Take-out containers litter the floor—Chrysto, it turns out, is very fond of Chinese. He supplies the poses, I supply the food—a small price to pay for a private art studio.

All of his clothes are piled up in the corner. Chrysto pulls himself up in front of me, throwing his shoulders back and puffing up his chest.

His fists and jaw are clenched. He looks out, chin lifted, a Greek hero scanning the horizon for the oncoming hordes. I see a fleet of Aegean ships advancing in his eyes. The next moment he drops his head toward me, and he's just Chrysto, one eyebrow raised. "Is this what you wanted?" the eyebrow asks.

"Beautiful," I whisper. "Classic." I scamper around him, studying him from all angles. My head buzzes with possibilities. "Wait!" I say, and run into the kitchen. I return with a broom. "Hold this."

"What am I, the brave janitor?"

I take his fist in my hand and pry open his fingers. Close them on the broom handle. Cup his bent elbow and guide it upward so the broom is angled in front of him—a spear, or sword. His muscles feel like rock, but his skin is so soft. Every time my fingers touch his body, I feel this shimmer of electricity pass from him to me. The small thatch of dark hair curling up from the cleft of his chest is so wiry, so resilient I can't imagine how it could have been hidden, even under layers of clay. Of course, there's also an area that I don't touch, but that doesn't mean I haven't glanced over in that direction from time to time. It's there, hooded, impressive but uninterested. If only my own equipment were so nonchalant.

More adjustments. At first I found it awkward, touching him. I tried to make chit chat. Did he need a break? Was it ever boring? Did his shoulders ever get sore?

"Walter," he said finally, "this is what I believe. To participate in Art brings you close to the gods. That boy who became for Michelangelo his *David*? You do not know his name, but he lives forever. So shut up. I am fine."

Now I appreciate the silence. It feels natural, but special. I finish manipulating Chrysto. He freezes in the position, and I watch the blue fade from his eyes. The human becomes the object. My object.

My pen strokes the page. Out of the white, a form appears, teased out with lines and shadows, saturated with ink and desire.

I twist open two beer bottles, listening for that satisfying hiss of effervescence, as Chrysto looks over my work. He nods his head and grunts appreciatively.

"I'm getting better, right?" I ask.

He shrugs, but his smile tells a different story.

We lean back on the couch, emptying our bottles. The cool bitterness of the beer, now that I've gotten used to the taste, feels like a sweet reward. Sometimes Chrysto will pull on his pants, but tonight he just lounges unclothed. He seems even younger naked and unposed. On the couch, our bodies equalize in size; our heads are close together, staring up at the same brown water stain on the ceiling. We're breathing the same air; our thoughts occupy the same space above our heads.

"Walter," Chrysto says sleepily, "why must you go back? It is too late. Stay here tonight."

I've imagined him saying just those words. I've imagined, in explicit detail, what could happen afterward. Sometimes I imagine it two or three times a day. Once, quickly, I imagined it in the employee bathroom at Viva Las Vegas! I'll probably be imagining it when I get home. But I know his question is not the invitation I want it to be.

"I have to get home."

"What if I don't drive you?" This has been one of my favorite parts of the ritual, the nightly drive home on Chrysto's motorbike, our bodies working together to navigate the streets, leaning into the swerve, into his back.

"I'll get a cab home," I say. What he doesn't know is that I do take a cab home—every night, after he drops me off at the Plaza, where he thinks I live.

"No. Better to go in the morning."

"I have to work."

Chrysto pushes me playfully. "Ah, what is this work? Telling the history of a make-believe city?"

I push him back, doing a lame imitation of his curving, honey-coated drawl of an accent. "Ah, what is this work? Posing for drunk tourists in a make-believe city?"

"Hey, Walter? Bite me." Chrysto tips back his beer and drains it, pleased with the newfound insult I've recently taught him. He clasps the bottle to his chest. "You know what I am going to do, after I find my Mara?"

"What?" I say. It's more a challenge than a question.

"After I find her, then—*ppsht!*—out of this stupid town."

I start to throw a "Shut up" at him, but the playfulness has leaked out of the words, stranded them in my throat. I'm left sounding like a small balloon quietly deflating.

Chrysto continues, staring up at the ceiling. "This is not the place for me. Nothing real here. You know where I go? Los Angeles."

I don't move at all, but my heart is pounding so fast I swear I can feel it pulsing underneath my shirt. "What are you going to do in Los Angeles?" I manage to toss off.

Chrysto sits up, animated. "Many things always happening there, Walter. Movies! Movies—better than paintings, Walter. Movies last long time. Not just your body, your face, but your life is captured— forever! Plus credit."

It sounds crazy, like he's just decided he wants to sprout wings and fly. "You mean, a movie about you?"

"Of course. Why not?"

I mumble into my beer all my worldly knowledge of how things don't work that way in Los Angeles.

"Why not?" Chrysto repeats. "My life is very good story. Would make great movie, I have been told this."

"Who told you this?" I ask quickly, but Chrysto doesn't seem to hear.

"Los Angeles. Yes," he says, as if he's just convinced himself.

I hunch down deeper in the couch. I'm a stone. He seems to float above, untethered. "Well, what about Acacia?" I ask. "Does she want to go?"

Chrysto shrugs. "Who knows what Acacia will do? She all the time wants to return to Greece; maybe she will go back."

"You'd go to L.A. alone?" I can't imagine anything more frightening.

"Is not a problem," Chrysto pronounces airily. He stares down at me for a long moment. "Maybe you come, too."

It's my turn to stare. "Me?" I squeak.

"Why not? You can drive us."

"But, I . . . I don't have a driver's license."

"So you will get one! For me, this is a problem. But you, you are American citizen, this is your right."

I try to say something, but all that comes out is a kind of half burble/half laugh. "I can't—"

"Of course you can! Come on, Walter, we go together! You help me write this movie. I give you story, you put down the words."

"Chrysto, you're crazy! I don't know anything about writing movies—"

"So you learn! Is no problem. Hey, I come here from Greece with my sister: no visa, no passport, no money. I make it happen. There is no problems, only solutions."

Chrysto is perched on the arm of the couch now, a beautiful naked gargoyle, ready to pounce. My arms are wrapped around the couch cushion, clutching it like I'm about to go under. "Chrysto," I say, "I can't. My dad, I have to take care of my dad."

Chrysto kneels down on the cushion next to mine. "Hey, who is the father and who is the child? This is your life. What will you do with it?"

That sounds so much like a sneaker commercial I almost laugh. He misinterprets my smile and returns it. "Yes, Walter, yes!"

"No, Chrysto, no." I shake my head. "I can't. Really. I can't."

Chrysto will have none of it. He stands above me in all his unclothed glory. I imagine wings unfolding. "Look at you. So scared. This is not an execution I am offering to you, Walter, this is life!"

He pushes down on the cushion I'm holding and shakes it. "Why all the time 'can't'?" He darts his hand under and pokes me in the side. I giggle and try to squirm away, but he's got me pinned. "Can't! Can't! Can't!" he repeats, laughing and poking me. "Say yes!"

"Stop, Chrysto, stop!" I shriek, laughing, tortured and turned on at the same time, but he keeps on tickling until I can't find my breath. "Stop!" I gasp.

And he does stop, not because of my pleas but because at that moment there is a pounding on the door, followed by Acacia standing in the entrance, keys in hand.

Chrysto doesn't even try to cover himself up, but the moment he sits on the couch I throw my cushion on him. He hugs it sullenly as Acacia stares at him. She's wearing a long yellow silk robe with dark purple, pointy flowers swirling on it. Her arms are folded in front of her chest.

"What?" Chrysto says finally.

"Get dressed," she says in a low voice.

Chrysto throws the cushion aside and stands up. He swaggers over to his clothes in the corner. "Come on, Walter," he says, grabbing at his pants. "I'll drive you home."

"You cannot drive," Acacia sneers. "You are drunk!"

Chrysto half turns his head toward me as he bends over to pull on his pants. "*Tchss.* Look who is talking," he says under his breath.

In four quick strides she is on him, striking him on the back of the head three times—forehand, backhand, forehand. The third slap topples him, but in the next moment Chrysto springs up, eyes blazing, fist held high, and just as quickly backs away and throws himself insolently on the couch. He looks casually at his fingers. "I don't care," he says under his breath, bored. "You drive him."

Acacia keeps staring at him, even as she talks to me. "Pick up your things, Walter," she says. "You come with me."

If I were expecting some kind of explanation from Acacia, I'd be disappointed. She doesn't say a word the entire ride back. Being on a motorbike with her is much more terrifying than with Chrysto. She goes faster around corners, she's lighter, and there's nowhere I'd dare hold on to. I grab the bar behind the seat and pray.

I didn't say good-bye. Chrysto didn't even look at me as I left.

At the Plaza, Acacia stops her Vespa. "Where now?" she asks.

"This is it," I say, pointing to the hotel.

"Walter." Acacia takes off her helmet, turns, and gives me her patented withering stare. "My brother may be idiot, but I am not. I see your shoes, your clothes. You do not live at Plaza Hotel."

I swallow hard. "Just drop me here."

Acacia stares at me, supremely doubtful. She gives a long, hard sigh, and even without the cigarette I can imagine the smoke curling out of her mouth. She cocks her head sharply to the side. "Do as you will. Get off."

I slide off the seat. "Thanks," I say.

Acacia exhales again and I take that to mean I'm dismissed. I'm almost to the revolving doors when I hear her call me. She gestures for me impatiently.

I walk back really slow.

"Listen," she says, when I finally sidle up next to her. "My brother, he is not the same . . . as you."

I feel my face getting hot. "What do you mean? What do you mean by that?"

Acacia stares at me for a long moment, but there is nothing that can be read on her face. When she finally speaks it's clipped and cold. "So. You stay away from him. Is better. Okay?"

"No," I say. "Not okay."

Again, the half-lidded glare. "You are big fool."

And with that, she delicately straps on her helmet, guns the Vespa once, and speeds away.

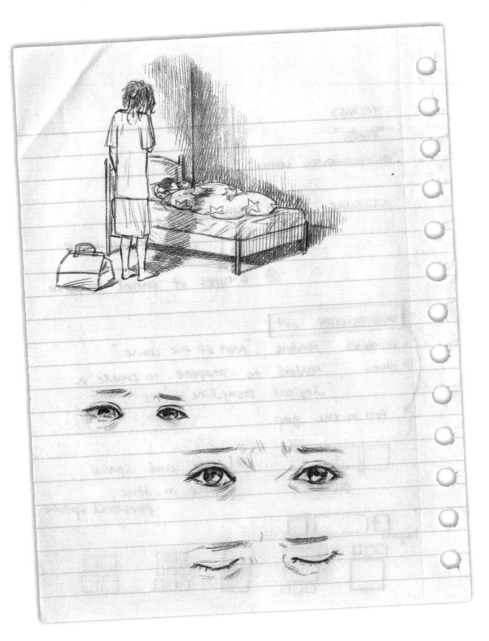

Sketch #3: A pretty early drawing.

The Weeping Madonna—now with customizable sorrow!

WALTER
VIVA LAS VEGAS!

My cell phone is one of those cheap disposables you get at liquor stores and gas stations, the ones favored by drug dealers and terrorists everywhere. No games, no music, no Internet connection. Bare-bones calls and text. I bought it three years ago, after my father left the LV Med Center with those new pills that gave him the awful side effects. It was Elantrazine; no, the one before that, Rellexor. Vertigo, nausea, and a fluttering heart. We didn't want to take any chances, so I got the disposable and taped my number to the telephone at home. I threw it in my backpack and it's lain there, dormant, until just this month, when I've roused it from slumber into active service.

It's never been as silent as it is now. I'm staring at this piece of plastic clenched in my hand, hoping if I squeeze it hard enough it will produce sound once more. Speak, damn it, speak!

An entire day and night and day, and no word from Chrysto. It's been the longest two days of my life. No invitations to hotel adventures, no art classes. I've called him twice (oh so very casually) and I've texted a few times, equally casual:

《 Hey. anything up tonight? Seen any statues lately ?? :) 》

Ugh. I've been reduced to smiley faces. I need an intervention.

No answer.

Work drags on, endless. Every tour of duty through Las Vegas history, desert oasis to gift shop, is another eon my phone's not ringing. I have it hooked onto my belt, under my vest, and check it, on average, three times per tour: once in the MegaResort room, again during the video, and a final time when the last guest has cranked through the exit turnstile. I'm waiting for my last tour to start. I turn the phone off, then on, to make sure it works. I know it's got juice; I replaced the batteries at lunch. I turn it off again, then on.

Kenny sidles up. "Hey, Walter, expecting a call? Got a hot date lined up?"

"Fuck you," I say.

Finally, Yrma gives the go-ahead. Only three people are waiting for me: Midwestern housewives, squeezed lumpily into HARD ROCK CAFÉ T-shirts.

"LadiesandgentlemenwelcometoVivaLasVegas," I mutter, and push in.

I give my guests the opening speech about the meadow and Rafael and blah blah blah, and then just let them free-range. I'm blaming Acacia for Chrysto's disappearance. Maybe she's gotten to him, persuaded him to stay away. I don't understand why she hates me. I was once her hero. Maybe it has something to do with ethnic purity, or maybe she's told him I'm a sham. But what I'm really afraid of is that she's pointed out to him what should have been obvious about me and now he's uncomfortable. He's repulsed. Aren't Greeks supposed to understand things like that? Didn't they practically invent it?

I'm alone in the room with mechanical Rafael and the snake. My guests have wandered off. I find them in the last room, staring at the diorama with arms folded across their chests. I've skipped my entire spiel. Shit. If Kenny found out I'd be ratted out to management for sure. "Just let me know if you have any questions," I say lamely. The women stare at me with puckered mouths. I quickly lead them to the video room.

In the cover of darkness I contemplate my next move. I could hang out by his apartment building. Or watch the alley where he leaves from work. Standard stalker procedure. Maybe it wasn't Acacia at all, maybe he's pissed I didn't want to go with him to Los Angeles. I'm useless to him.

My stomach hurts.

The "Las Vegas Today" music is thundering in my ears when the call comes. I don't even hear the ringing, but there's a tiny, insistent vibration at my side. I claw at my waist, wrenching the phone off the belt while vaulting past the turnstiles. Lumpy 1, 2, and 3 can find their own way out. I run to a corner of the lobby and punch the "talk" button. Press the phone against my ear.

"Hello?" I say breathlessly.

"Walt," my father says, "come home."

When I arrive at the apartment my father's on the couch, but barely. He's facedown on the edge, one arm wrapped around his head, the other dangling over the side, phone in hand. I can't see his face but his breathing is shallow and fast. The rest of him is absolutely rigid.

I squat close to his head. "Dizziness?" I ask quietly. He gives the tiniest nod.

The anti-vertigo medication's in the medicine cabinet. I push a pill in between his clenched lips and he swallows it dry. We wait. I hadn't noticed how much weight he's lost. He's out of his robe and into clothes, jeans and a baggy T-shirt. His hair is greasy and too long. I should have cut it weeks ago.

Finally, his body relaxes. He's able to turn himself over and lets out a small sound.

"What happened?" I ask.

He gestures toward the kitchen table. There is a jumble of clean, wrinkled T-shirts, underwear, socks, and a couple of my work shirts dumped on the table, a few half folded.

"I did the whites," he mumbles.

I feel the back of my neck getting red. All around the apartment are the signs of my neglect: dishes crusting over in the sink, a clump of my dirty clothes skulking by the side of the television, bills spilling out from their spot at the corner table. "I was going to do whites tonight," I say.

My father exhales and gives a slight shake of the head, meaning, What does laundry matter? Meaning I'm not mad at you, meaning cut yourself a break.

Dad's sitting hunched at the table, sipping a glass of water and watching me fold laundry. "Your mother," he says out of nowhere. "You fold clothes like her."

I roll my eyes.

"No, really, she'd smooth the shirts down, just like that." He saws his flattened hand in the air to demonstrate. "She also folded the underwear in thirds. Where'd you learn that?" He's witnessing a miracle.

"It's how you fold underwear," I reply. Really, that's how they come in the package.

My father continues. "When I brought the laundry up I was thinking about your mother. I think it was the smell, you know, when it comes out of the dryer, is it the bleach?"

"Softener."

"Softener. That's the smell. And she would come up from the basement with a basket of laundry, this was when you were just a baby, and there'd be your little socks, just like mine, but so tiny! And she'd hold out one of your socks and say, 'Can you believe a foot could fit in here?'"

I'm not sure where this conversation is going. It could be a sign that he's getting better, or it could go south very, very fast.

He grabs a pair of my briefs from the table. "—and I remember when your underwear used to be so small. Now look how big it is—"

"Could we not talk about my underwear?"

"—look how big you are!" My father's eyes boggle, like he's just seen a magic trick. "You're so tall! Grown up! How could I not have noticed?"

"How 'bout a bucket of chicken tonight?" I ask quickly, but he's already retreated to somewhere in the back of his mind. He slumps in his chair, staring at the corner of the table. I'm thinking, his brain's about to capsize, but after a minute it seems to steady itself. He looks up, blinks twice, slowly brings the water glass to his lips, and takes a sip.

"The laundry used to be much whiter," he says.

"We've got a shitty washing machine," I say.

"No, bleach. Bleach," he says. "That's where that comes in."

I can't eat fast enough. This is our usual triumphant, welcome-home-back-from-the-dead meal—take-out fried chicken with little white tubs of sides. I'm plowing through it. There's a pile of bones on my plastic plate, and I'm grabbing for more. More chicken. More coleslaw. More mushy baked beans. I scrape the Styrofoam bowls frantically with my hard plastic spoon, and little white flecks melt on my tongue along with the last bits of scooped-up brown sauce and soggy cabbage strips. I'm not even hungry.

I look up, mid-gnaw, to find my father staring at me. His hands are folded in front of him, a half-eaten drumstick and a biscuit on his plate. He looks concerned.

"What?" I say, a strip of chicken tendon dangling from my lower lip.

"Everything all right?" he asks.

"Yeah, sure," I say, grabbing another biscuit. "Why?"

He gives a smile and a little shrug, but there are a lot of unasked questions hovering in his eyes.

"Everything's cool," I tell him, before shoving the biscuit in my mouth.

"Your leg's shaking," he points out. I look down. It's quivering beneath me like an idling motor.

I push my heel down on the floor. "Sorry," I say.

He pulls at his beard for a minute and then says, "Do you have to . . . go somewhere?" He says this very carefully.

"No. No," I say, resisting the urge to look at my black backpack on the couch.

He nods. "Oh." He stares off to the side for a bit, then comes back, remembering. "I saw the letter."

I have no idea what he's talking about.

"It was open on the counter," he adds, but my brain's not focusing right. "Las Vegas University," he says, and it finally clicks.

"Oh yeah," I say, "I got accepted."

He leans forward and grabs my hand with his big mitt. "That's great, Walt! Congratulations!"

I shrug. "Lobotomized lab rats get accepted into LVU."

"Still . . ." he says, trailing off. He grabs at another thought. "Anywhere else?"

"It's the only place I applied."

He adjusts his glasses. "Why?"

I shrug again. A flick of my eyes takes in the entirety of our apartment, of our world here. My dad's eyes flicker back in comprehension. He looks away, drags the tines of his fork across his plate.

"College is very important," he says, almost to himself. I take another swig of Coke, wishing it were something stronger.

He stops his fork and asks, hesitantly, "You're done with high school, right?"

"Yeah. Early."

"Graduation?" He looks alarmed. He's afraid he's missed it.

"Next month, but don't worry about it. It's no big deal." I wasn't even planning on going.

He pulls at his beard again. "You're all right, yeah?"

"Yeah," I say, deflecting his question with a don't-be-crazy smile. I start to clear the table. My father continues to mess with his beard, staring at me, trying to work out something in his head.

"You're so different," he says finally. "I look at you and . . . in some ways, I don't know who you are."

He pauses, and when he looks back at me, his eyes are the most clear they've been all day.

"That's a good thing," he says.

So here we are. He's sitting on a kitchen chair, facing the television. His hair is still wet from the shower and lies flat against the back of his neck. One of our old white sheets is wrapped around his body; he's a va-nilla sundae with a head on top. His eyes are closed; the lines on his forehead and by his mouth have relaxed. He might as well be lounging by the tide pool at Mandalay Bay, listening to the waves. I've got the scis-sors poised in the air.

We've done this a million times before.

I started cutting my father's hair four years ago, around the time he stopped leaving the house. I was fourteen. I remember coming home from school to find him hacking away at his bangs—"Just getting it out of my eyes"—and doing a spectacularly bad job of it. I grabbed the scis-sors from his shaking hand and proceeded to do a slightly less spectacu-larly bad job, but one that at least didn't involve bloodshed. The end result was a hairstyle that suggested a show poodle that had been chased around the dog pound one too many times.

We kept trying. I'd get out magazines and lay them out on the kitchen table. They'd be open to those ads of men shaving, stroking their smooth faces in the bathroom mirror, or the ones with fathers lounging around in their underwear, sipping mugs of coffee. Their hair was smooth, per-fectly shaped. And then I'd wade in, hacking away at the tangled wavy mess that was my father's head, using these men as a guide. I'd cut off any tufts of hair that I found sticking out, snipped away at any noncon-forming curls. Huge swaths of hair would be mown down to try and make it flip this way or that, but in the end his hair was too resistant to structure. The top of his head became an origami project gone hay-wire.

"It's perfect," he'd say.

Things have improved since then. I don't go for any particular look now; I just try to tame the beast. Snip snip snip; little pieces of him flutter to the floor as he becomes himself again. It takes no time at all. I mean, he's not going to win any prizes, but he doesn't look homeless, either.

I step back, viewing him from a bit of a distance. His hair's more gray, but the head is familiar. Snip snip snip. I'm shaping him, fashioning him into a father I remember.

"How's it looking?" I ask, holding up the toaster in front of his face. We've never gotten around to getting a hand mirror.

He opens his eyes and stares at the elongated, fun-house head in the chrome side of the toaster.

"It's perfect," he says.

I lurch awake. I'm sitting on the couch. It's dark. The television glow is the one light on. Some guy in a pink polo shirt is selling a new pill that's going to add vigor and excitement to your married life. He's in a daisy field, for some reason.

The TV clock flashes red: it's past midnight. Beside me, my father sleeps. He's back in his robe, but at least it's clean now. His head tilts back against the couch; his hands are clasped in front of him. He looks 200 percent better with his hair cut, even though his beard still needs a trim. Time enough for that tomorrow.

The apartment is quiet. The room seems settled now, at peace. Back to its old self. On the screen, a white-haired couple sits on their couch, talking to me and my snoring father. They're holding hands. It's the best time of their lives, they say. They've never been so satisfied, or so in love. They walk along the beach, and a phone number flashes on the bottom of the screen.

It's time to nudge my dad awake and help him to bed, but I can't move. Can inertia be inherited? I'm transfixed by the letters pulsating on the screen: GET THE MAGIC BACK! it says.

When I first hear the buzz, I think it's accompanying the flashing words. I've forgotten what the sound is, again. Finally I see the glow coming from my open bag. Even then, I'm slow. I drag the backpack over and fish it out. The tiny screen tells me there's a new text message. It's Chrysto's number. Chrysto called. The blood rushes into my head and I fumble for the right button. Words come up, glowing orange in the dark:

≪ i found her ≫

WALTER & CHRYSTO
VENICE VENICE

We're outside on a covered bridge overlooking the street, shadowed by the jutting red clock tower. The lampposts below have just switched on; in this last hour of the day it's just a glow, a faint promise of excitement to come. On the other side of the bridge, past the escalators and the wax museum, is a gold-and-marble mecca of luxury known as Venice Venice. It's the only place in Las Vegas I've ever been specifically prohibited from entering.

It's the one place Chrysto wants to go.

"She has been here all along! Can you believe it?"

He gives no explanation of where he's been, no apology for unanswered calls. There isn't time for that; Chrysto's a body in motion. Bouncing, rocking, doing mini push-ups off the railing, he's shot past his usual stillness straight to hyper. He's got words, and breath, only for his big discovery.

Mara's in Venice Venice. Some friend of his spotted a statue of a woman in one of those exclusive high-roller rooms. Chrysto couldn't have seen it, since hotel employees aren't permitted on site during off hours. Lucky for him, this friend isn't an employee of the casino. This friend called the statue "extraordinary." This friend thought it could be her.

And who, exactly, was this friend? I get no answer.

"I know it will be her, Walter. Believe me."

I do believe him. That's the problem. He's found his precious Mara, and it wasn't even on my watch. Our mission's done. Over.

Chrysto taps my arm. "Come on."

But I can be a statue, too. "I can't go in there, remember? And you're not supposed to, either."

Chrysto shrugs and takes my arm, but I'm not moving anywhere.

"Why doesn't your friend go with you?" I ask. I try to toss that off as a light remark, helpful even, but as soon as it leaves my lips I know it's hardened into something sulky and cheap. I'm afraid he'll take me at my word, turn around and walk away, but he doesn't.

"Walter." Chrysto grabs me gently by the back of the neck and brings my head close to his. He looks directly in my eyes. "I don't want to go with this friend. I want to go with you. I need you there."

Damn. I want to stand my ground, I want to be the voice of reason, but there's no withstanding the full wattage of Chrysto's eyes. They can melt marble. He adds a smile to it, and against direct orders my face reflects it back. The mutiny's complete. My disobedient heart leaps out of my chest and begs to play fetch.

Chrysto practically sprints across the bridge, hand firmly clapped on my shoulder. We go through the revolving doors together. I wait for the alarms to go off and the SWAT teams to bust through. Nothing. I guess no one recognizes Chrysto out of makeup, and I've been camouflaged by the flock of Chinese tourists scurrying before us. We're in.

We walk down the Great Hall, past the columns and the bright frescoes. I keep my head down, trying not to look for security cameras. The familiar floral scent brings me back to my weekly visits with the deities on high, back when they were frozen and unattainable and a whole lot less trouble.

"How are we going to get into that room?" I whisper.

"It is a room, we enter it," Chrysto says. Spoken like a true god.

We reach the casino floor, cut through the Pachinko machines, pass the roulette tables, go around the Wheel. Of. Fortune! slots. We ignore the raised green felt altars inviting worshippers to their particular denomination: Caribbean; Pai Gow; Let It Ride. There's a frenzy of activity. The casino's never sounded so loud, but it doesn't matter because Chrysto's not saying anything. He strides through, loose but intent, a jungle cat on the prowl through the underbrush.

Finally, we reach the Race and Sports booking lounge. Next to it, up two steps, is a room without doors, obscured by large, frosted-glass panels—it's open and forbidding at the same time. This is not an entry for the casual-minded.

Chrysto gives me a look. "Ready?"

"For what?" I ask. "For what?" That old feeling of dread spreads out like a rash behind my neck and prickles down my arms.

Chrysto answers with only a smile. One that shows his teeth. The next moment he's gone, sliding into silhouette behind the translucent wall.

The first thing you notice when you enter the room is how utterly quiet it is. No piped-in music, no bells, no chatter. Every molecule of distraction has been sucked away. Four men hunch over a curved table, their hands in silent, terse communion with the dealer standing on the other side, whose own hands are in constant motion, soundlessly dispensing cards and revealing them and sweeping them away, as flowing and effortless as a bird in flight. There's a bar at the far end, small but well-stocked, with a bartender, equally small, who fades into the rows of liquor bottles. A cocktail waitress glides a few steps toward us. Behind the dealer stands a rectangular man in a drab olive suit, a man whose stillness is an activity in itself. A small black cord curls out from under his collar and whispers in his ear.

I look to Chrysto, but his eyes are fixed on the far corner of the room, where two leather armchairs sit unoccupied next to a round marble table, behind which stands—

Her.

It has to be.

She's beautiful, even from here.

The statue's white and glowing, like a full moon. A naked figure made of marble, delicate and whisper-fragile, Mara's graceful arms stretch toward the sky, her gaze pierces the heavens, like she's inviting, or entreating, some reckless god above. The smoothness of her torso gradually twists into the trunk of a laurel tree that she's trying to burst from, that she's slowly becoming. Her hair twines and spreads downward to her shoulder like a forest canopy.

I'm expecting tears—for Chrysto to throw himself on the ground, weeping for his newfound love, but he's not even looking at her. His eyes sweep the rest of the room casually. He nods his approval, a pleasant smile fixed on his face.

"Hey, Walter," he murmurs, turning toward me. His face stays pleasant, but his words are fast and low. "Do this favor for me, okay? I need for you to get Acacia. Now, please. Go now."

Chrysto gives me two friendly pats on the chest and turns away without waiting for an answer. He's back in motion, nodding at the man in the olive suit, dancing right up to the cocktail waitress, exchanging words with her while switching sides without so much as a break in movement. It's like he's at his Greek tavern, high-fiving all the patrons, but this time his walk seems looser, his legs more wobbly and less in control. He heads straight for the bar, staggering slightly, and I could swear he's drunk, but all the time he's getting closer and closer to the statue. Without seeming to mean to he suddenly stands in front of it and looks up as if he's just run into a close friend.

"Here you are," he says, a little too loudly. His fingers stroke the side of her smooth face, which is turned away, yearning for escape. The cocktail waitress hovers uncertainly nearby. The man in the olive suit hasn't made a move, but mouths something into the air. The gamblers couldn't give a damn, continue with their finger dance.

Chrysto gives me a flash of his eyes, warning me of some storm about to break, but I can't leave, not just yet. Next to the frosted glass, I watch him clasp his hand firmly around Mara's neck.

"Hey!" he yells to the gamblers. His voice is thick, giddy. "How is the luck in this room? Bad, yes?"

Still holding her neck, Chrysto pulls and rocks the statue forward, base and all. He catches her by the throat with the other hand and pushes backward, his own body swaying in counterbalance like they're about to step together and twirl across the room.

"Your luck can never be good, not with this one!" Chrysto yells over his shoulder. "She never forgives, she only brings curses!" He spits out something in Greek and then he's got both hands on the back of her head and is pitching her forward, fast, and down Mara crashes, her head hitting the marble table, decapitating her at once. The left arm breaks at the elbow, the other is still reaching out, not up but toward me, begging for help. "Bitch," Chrysto says. He grabs Mara's head by one of her tresses, still attached, and she stares up, wide-eyed, a lovely Medusa slain by mad, mad Perseus.

Already security has entered the room, four huge men in blue blazers who pass me to form a wall blocking Chrysto from sight. The man in the olive suit has taken three steps forward to protect his gamblers, but they've already turned back to their game: they've seen this kind of thing before; they know how it turns out.

Chrysto's holding Mara's head high in the air, about to smash it down. One guard grabs Chrysto's wrist—"Let it go, sir"—before yanking down the arm in one swift motion. The action is accompanied by a sharp cracking sound, and one of them must be holding Chrysto's mouth shut because I can only hear a distant, muffled cry. And immediately afterward the blue wall of blazers is crashing over Chrysto, the men put their collective weight onto him, slowly but implacably forcing him onto the ground, with only the smallest of grunts coming from an invisible Chrysto, and then there's a sudden crackle of electricity and a few muted thumps on the soft carpet and the last thing I hear before I run out of the room is one gambler cackling to the other: "Hey, twenty-one. The kid did something right."

I sprint to the apartment, trying to convince myself that I'm running for help and not running away. I'm feeling failure even as my finger presses on Chrysto's apartment number. Sure enough, no one answers. Acacia's gone. I have no idea what to do. I shouldn't have left Chrysto, I think, I should have stayed with him. I was afraid.

≪ A not home ≫

I punch out the text, even though I'm sure he's in no position to read it.

≪ r u all right? ≫

I tear out a page from my sketchbook and quickly write a note to Acacia, leaving her my cell number, and wedge it in a corner of the intercom box. I start back, though I'm sure I can't even get near Venice Venice again. German shepherds are probably sniffing me out at this very moment. I look at my reflection in the tinted-glass window of the 7th Heaven Quik Mart on the corner. That's the face of a Wanted Man. Cowardly accomplice to the destruction of a priceless artifact.

Acacia's in the store.

I think it's her. She's in the liquor aisle, staring at a bottle of vodka, so that's like her, but under the fluorescent lights, she could be Acacia's mother, she looks so much older. The bottle in her hand weighs her whole body down—she hunches. Her eyes are hidden behind sunglasses, but the rest of her face looks puckered, worn down, six days shy of a good rest. It's like she's not quite fully inflated. Acacia the Elder grabs the bottle by the neck and walks away, out of sight.

I run into the store and scan the aisles: one, two, three. But she's already at the front, waiting in line at the checkout counter. Acacia's steel-rod posture is back, her unlined face lifted and cocked to the side as she gives the clerk that little cat's purr of a smile. She's completely revived. The dark silk scarf around her shoulders has stopped looking crone-like and become fashionable again.

Acacia's eyes narrow, then pop open wide when she sees me. She drags me out of the store. "What? What has happened?" she asks.

I garble out some words, and for a moment, her face looks like it's going to collapse again, but instantly she snaps her head back, looking up at the sky. "Idiot!" she fumes, followed by a roiling stream of Greek. Acacia fumbles in her bag for her cigarettes and lights one. Her hand is trembling.

"Bitch," she mutters, echoing Chrysto.

"I thought he loved her."

Acacia lets out a blast of smoke, halfway between a grunt and a laugh. "That whore? He doomed her. She could not keep her hands off him." She takes a thoughtful drag on her cigarette. "I should never have told him about the statue," she says, almost to herself.

"Why did he break it?" I ask.

The usually minimalistic Acacia erupts, all slashing hands and thrusting chin. "He has traveled halfway around the world for this fucking statue! He thinks it is her curse to him, for what he did to her. I tell him, stop making this dream for yourself! She is most definitely dead, I tell him, this bad luck, you have baked it yourself; stuff it in your mouth and be done with it."

Her words sound angry but she's slipping a hand underneath her sunglasses and wiping her eyes. "Idiot," she repeats.

She takes one fierce drag on her cigarette and throws it to the ground. "I must go to him," she says abruptly. She strides away, then quickly returns, thrusting the paper bag with the vodka at my chest. "Why don't you listen to me?" she asks, shaking her head. "Stay away."

She sounds almost sorrowful. "Go home."

WALTER & CHRYSTO

The cages have all been sprung at Chrysto and Acacia's building—every unit is wide open. As I approach the doorways I hear the muted sounds of life within: television, radio, a murmur of French conversation, and, from every apartment, the constant hum of portable fans working over-time. Everyone's on display. There's the gymnast Chrysto pointed out earlier, eating breakfast; a woman on a couch fanning herself with a magazine; a muscled acrobat sweating over his ironing. I pass the door-way of the four Thai girls, who are sprawled on the carpet in front of the television, watching cartoons. Their chins are propped up by their hands, their legs are curved behind, and their tiny feet tap on their heads in unison.

Acacia's standing in the doorway in a simple white sundress. Her short hair is wet against her neck. When she sees me, she doesn't move; her face doesn't change expression, either. Then her eyes latch onto the bottle of vodka I'm returning. Apparently that's the key to entry because a small smile curls on her mouth. Her hand crinkles the brown bag as she takes the bottle.

"It should never be so hot," she tells me.

Chrysto calls out from inside, "'Kash, we live in the desert, re-member?"

Acacia shrugs, unimpressed with the information.

"The central air, *phtt*, broken," Chrysto yells out.

"Yes, more of your good luck," she shouts behind her, and precedes me into the room. "Look, your *boyfriend* has brought you flowers."

It's hot in the apartment. The ceiling fan rattles above at top speed, fast but ineffective. A rusted box fan spins the hot air around the room. The shades are all drawn, so Chrysto's in shadow on the couch. "Acacia is becoming too soft," he says as I approach. "She forgets summers we lived on rocks of Taygetos, so close to sun."

"There was an ocean at our feet, idiot," she mutters, disappearing into the kitchen.

Chrysto reaches for the lamp by the couch, clicks it on.

"Christ, Chrysto."

He's in boxer shorts, hair tied up on top of his head. His good hand waves away my stare. "Two places they broke it: here, and here," Chrysto says cheerfully, pointing to general areas on his right arm, which is in a cast, shoulder to wrist, supported by a sling. On his face, a dark cloud of purple blotches over his left eyebrow; it has an angry red center with a distinct crescent shape; I can imagine the tip of a shoe easily carving out that space. A large pad of white gauze follows the bottom curve of his rib cage and disappears into the waistband of his shorts; it's stained by antiseptic, or leakage, or both.

"It is nothing, Walter, do not cry." My friend leans forward and with the barest of winces takes my wilting daisies. Under his breath, he tells me, "Already I am making my body to heal. Very soon, all better." He falls back against the cushions, calling out, "'Kash, bring something for the flowers."

Acacia is already by the couch with a green vase, sloshing water as she swings it over to the coffee table. She lazily snatches the bouquet away from Chrysto and plunks it, plastic and all, into the vase, all the while continuing a conversation they haven't been having. "Yes, good luck they smash your arm to pieces. Or else now you would be on plane to Greece."

She addresses me, turning her back to Chrysto. "When I see him, I scream loud. Ohhh!" Acacia holds her hands up in front of her face and shakes them in mock horror. "I say, this boy work for you, he is not so good in the head, and you treat him like this? I yell, is American brutality! Is oppression!" She lowers her arms and smiles slyly, clearly enjoying this retelling. "I frighten them. 'No charges, take him home.'" She reaches up and grabs my chin in her hand. I feel the points of her nails press into my skin. "Not to worry. Poor Walter."

Chrysto mutters darkly behind her, "Why don't you go to work?"

Acacia turns to him, smiling her sweetest smile. "Yes, who else is going to work? Who else will pay the bills now, hmm? You? Of course not. Me, always me." She says this last part in my direction. Clearly she's speaking English for my benefit.

"Come, Walter," she says, swiping her bag from the small counter. "You have brought your flowers. Now, out."

But she knows I'm not going anywhere. She doesn't even wait a beat before swaggering to the door. "Keep him here," she says over her shoulder. "If they see him anywhere, anywhere on that street, they will grab him and *phtt,* out he goes from United States."

"How am I moving from this couch?" Chrysto says. "Tell me this."

Acacia mutters something filthy in Greek and with one last baleful glare, sails out, slamming the door behind her.

Silence. I feel the heat collecting on my skin. The door's only been closed for a minute and the room has already warmed.

"Walter," Chrysto says softly, "why do you stare at the floor? Do I look so terrible?"

I concentrate really, really hard on the corner of the sofa. "I shouldn't have left. You."

"No, of course you should have, I asked you to. You did . . . perfect."

He's the mangled one, and he's cheering me up.

"I found Acacia," I say.

"Yes. Exactly!" Misery lifts, ever so slightly. Chrysto looks to the door where Acacia has left, and sneers. "I allow her to have this moment of victory, but what she says? Not so true. They already decide to let me go before she comes in to scream and make embarrassment."

"Why?"

Chrysto waves his hand vaguely. "This friend I have, he spends much money in this casino. He talks to hotel, everything is okay."

"So he got you out?" Misery descends again.

Chrysto speaks softly. "Yes, but now he is very angry with me. I think maybe, I not see him anymore." Chrysto sighs sadly. "But, you are here, my good, good friend. I am happy to see you."

These words should lighten my heart, but instead I feel sick. I ask him why he went crazy, why he did what he did. "They could have killed you."

Chrysto smiles back at me. "No, no, it is good, Walter. My luck is my own, now. I feel this inside of me."

"How can Mara bring you bad luck?"

He shakes his head. "It was not her. It was her memory. Her memory stick in me, like, like a . . . splinter. Now, splinter gone. I am free!"

I point out that he can't get off the couch.

"Is not so bad. Really. Soon, I will be one hundred percent. And then—" He shoots his good hand into the air—a rocket in flight.

"You go?" I say quietly.

"No," he says with great excitement. "WE go."

I draw in an exasperated breath, but Chrysto presses on. "Come on, Walter, say good-bye to Las Vegas, with all the fat tourists and bad food."

"There are fat tourists in Los Angeles," I say. "Giant ones."

Chrysto shakes his head. "Only beautiful people out there. The fat ones, *phtt*! They are invisible."

"Who told you that?" I ask.

"Please, Walter, make company for me. I need you."

"What would I do in Los Angeles?" I ask.

Chrysto shoots back: "What you doing here?" He beckons me closer and pulls me onto the couch. "I have plan—"

"Movies?" says skeptical me.

Chrysto brushes aside that idea. "Maybe later. No, this is perfect plan. Exercise! Exercise training. Very big in L.A. I set up studio, I train stars, I make videos. Big business! You—you help in studio, make phone calls, all these things. This is perfect, no?"

It would work. I see the business in my head. He's got the charisma, he's got the training, if anyone were special enough to pull this off, it'd be Chrysto. But it still doesn't mean I can leave.

"Go with Acacia."

"Enough! Enough with Acacia!" he thunders. "I am tired of Acacia! Listen, Walter. Listen to me. Family is important, yes? But one day, we must leave family. We must become who we are. This you will never know until you leave. You must come. Come with me. Be free, my friend. Be with me."

He stares at me with those crystalline blue eyes that glow even in the shadowed room. I feel sweat trickling down the side of my body. Time's ticking away and there's no decision I can make.

I stare at the floor again.

Chrysto pats my face and lifts it up. "That's okay, Walter," he says softly. "No problem." Which makes it all worse. He's ten inches away from me and already he's gone. Already I see him in the distance, flying away while I watch from my tower of bricks. I've got no wings; my father's been too busy sleeping to make them for me.

"Walter, do not look so sad. Come, let us do some drawing, okay? Give us some light."

I trudge over to the window. Sunlight slashes in through the blinds I twist open, and the room is instantly bright again. When I turn, Chrysto is attempting to get up. He looks golden, gashes and all.

"Hey, I can be wounded warrior for you," he says, trying to stand with only the use of his legs and one arm. I run over and offer my shoulder. He's glistening with perspiration; from the heat, or effort, or both.

It's an attractive misting, like he's just risen from his poolside deck chair. I, on the other hand, sweat like a pig.

"Help me," Chrysto asks, and it's only then that I realize he's trying to take off his underwear.

I start to protest but he insists. "Why not?" he says. "Pull down."

He's got beads of sweat around his navel, on the hair below, which tousles its way downward. How can his skin be so tan when he spends all his time indoors? I kneel before him, tugging his shorts down to his ankles, and there's a musk coming off him that almost makes me dizzy. The hair on the back of my neck starts to tingle. I guide his feet out of the shorts. His boxers are still warm; I have to resist a totally pervy desire to take a big, luxuriant whiff.

Chrysto looks down at me. "Walter, you look like you have soaked in bath. Take off your shirt, yes?"

I haven't undressed in front of someone not related to me since I was in sixth-grade gym. Mine is not a body meant for display. I'm too embarrassed. I can't.

And then I do.

Chrysto doesn't laugh, or wrinkle his nose at my sunken chest and scrawny arms. Instead, he strokes the top of my shoulder with his finger. "Your skin, Walter, so soft," he murmurs, almost in disbelief. "So nice." He cups my face with his hand. I almost explode, right there.

Chrysto pushes me away and with a loud yelp, flops back onto the couch. He takes a few breaths to recover himself, then looks at me.

"All right, what shall we draw? Give me a feeling."

I walk slowly to my bag; I'm so hard each step chafes. I fish out my pad and pen and stand there, staring at my notebook. A word enters my head: it fills my entire brain; it crowds out any other thought.

"What is it?"

My mouth is dry, the word sounds like a parched grunt, or a moan.

"Lust."

"What?" Either he can't hear me or doesn't know what the word means.

"Lust, lust!" I stammer loudly. "You know...love..." But I don't know how to go on. I just swallow.

Chrysto's eyes widen just a fraction, comprehension brightening the blue. "Oh, Walter," he says softly, with a smile as welcoming as a warm pool, "with you, that one is easy, very easy."

He's on the couch, reclined, and Holy Zeus, there it is, there's no denying his feelings on this point, it rises up in front of me, insistent and proud. Chrysto holds out his good hand to me, and my own hand springs up to meet it, and in no time at all my own deity is sprung as well, not as awe-inspiring as his, but every bit as sturdy.

I have to be careful where I touch, and there's not a lot of movement, but it's enough. By the gods, it's more than enough.

WALTER
VOLVO

I can't believe he took me back, but there he was, waiting for me by the car at three thirty sharp. We're sitting in the front seat now, awkward, like it's a first date, me in my jeans and pitted-out tee, him in his wrinkled gray suit and fat tie. I think he's the only teacher left in the country who still wears a tie.

"Stahl." Mr. Handy says my name so quietly, it might have been a sigh. He coughs and starts again. "Behind the Wheel's over, you know that, right? I don't teach it this late in the year."

I nod. The school secretary's already filled me in: it's unheard of, him even considering giving me a second chance. Extraordinary. She'd never seen Mr. Handy make an exception. I'm counting on it. How else am I going to learn to fulfill my role as designated driver?

I'm going to California. Me and Chrysto, as soon as we can. I've just come from his apartment; I've left him lightly dozing on the couch, sticky with me. There's probably some of him still on my body, I probably reek of him, but I don't care. It suits me fine. I'm funkalicious.

"You know what?" I say, grabbing the steering wheel firmly. "I was thinking of maybe knocking this out in maybe two lessons."

Mr. Handy straightens out and raises a bushy eyebrow. "You haven't even started a car, Stahl. Highly unlikely. Highly unlikely." He sniffs. I can feel him thinking it out. He taps his clipboard with his pencil, all business.

"Let's see what you remember."

"Mirror. Mirror. Mirror. Ignition. Brake. Gas." I point out each quickly, but the drill sergeant in Mr. Handy has been replaced by a fussy old man who spends way too much time checking off each item on his clipboard. I need him to go faster. I'm already flying down the road in a red convertible, Chrysto in the passenger seat, hair billowing in the wind. We're wearing shades. We're cool.

Chrysto's sleeping on the couch. This morning I was there, too, my head resting gently on Chrysto's thigh. The sun, and the sex, settled over on us a sleepiness, a heavy contentment, but rising up at the same time were these little smiles, like bubbles of happiness, effervescent. I wiped a puddle of myself off my chest and started humming "California, Here I Come." Couldn't make him understand why I was laughing.

"Key in the ignition."

Mr. Handy holds out the keys. My hands leave their sanctuary at ten and two. I make my adjustments. Grab the keys. They jangle in my fingers.

My body's humming, ready for movement. All I have to do is bring this car along with me. I take a deep breath. Chrysto's face floats in front of me. "What are you waiting for?" he asks, with that freaking confidence, that dimpled smile.

I have tasted that smile.

Key in the ignition.

Lock. Acc. On. Start.

The car roars to life.

Of course, it all goes downhill from there.

WALTER
EVERYWHERE

It's my first flying dream. Well, not flying, exactly; my flying is more like
bouncing, as if the ground were made of trampolines. I'm running on
the street, fast, and then suddenly up I go, up past buildings in a blurred
rush, legs still pumping, high in the air, moving forward but suspended
at the same time, and just as I get used to the height I sink back down,
slowly losing altitude until I touch Earth again, still running. I get in a
few strides and then up I go again, rising maybe as high as the Wynn
Hotel but lower than the Stratosphere, but it's hard to tell because I'm
in a Las Vegas that doesn't look like Las Vegas. There are no flashing
lights and MegaResorts, at least none that I can see. I think, oh, I can
find my way out when I'm in the air, I'll get my bearings, but when I'm in
the air there's nothing I see that I recognize, just mile after mile of indus-
trial buildings and run-down apartments. And then a few strides later I
lift up into the sky again and see something sparkling and bright and
blue up ahead and I think, oh, there's the Strip, I know where I am, and I
do an amazing leap, kind of curving and twisting, finding just the right
current to carry me farther, and it lands me on a cliff in front of the blue
I saw, only it isn't lights, it's water, there's a huge ocean below me, waves
crashing, louder than a casino on Saturday night. And next to me is

someone I know to be my mother, only she looks like Acacia, Acacia without the accent and the smirk, and I shout to her over the waves, this must be California, and she says (without yelling, I hear her just fine), she says, no, this is Chicago, don't you remember it? and I think, oh, I must have gone north instead of west, and then she says, California's just on the other side of the water, can you get there? and although I can't see the other end I don't want to disappoint so I say, yeah, I think so, but inside I'm not so sure, and then Acacia/Mother says, don't get wet or it won't work. And I back up away from the cliff so I can get a good running start and my mother says, it's time, it's time! and away I sprint, feet digging hard into dirt all the way to the edge and I push off, up into the air I soar, up over the water into the blinding sun—

I wake up wet, with the taste of salt on my lips. Even the sofa mattress is soaked. I close my eyes. I want to know if I made it. I think I must have. It was the best leap I've ever done.

"Green, Stahl. Green means go."

I understand the rules of driving, the physics of it. If I could drive my own body on the streets it'd be no problem. But this giant metal coffin I'm steering? Who knows where it's gonna go?

"Slow. Hand over hand."

Love can make you brave, but love can't buffer you from an oncoming truck. I think of that, and my father's curse. It's not the kind of thought you're supposed to have while trying to merge with traffic on I-15. I'm under the protection of Apollo, I think, gripping the steering wheel. He's not going to let anything happen to me. Not while I'm designated driver.

"Lean back, Stahl," barks Mr. Handy, "you're not going to get there any quicker."

Three lessons done, and not a single death. Me, Mr. Handy, and the car, all intact. Sure, he still jerks on the steering wheel from time to time, but he's been doing that less and less with each outing. And the barking's toned down, somewhat. Maybe I'm getting somewhere after all.

Sitting in the car in the school parking lot, Mr. Handy usually details my near-fatal errors for the day, and then dismisses me with a curt "All right, you can go." But today he's not giving me the usual heave-ho. Instead, he's silent, squinting at the glove compartment like it's giving off glare.

"At the DMV you need a car to take the test," he says finally. "You have a car?"

I shake my head. That's one of the biggest holes in our plan: lack of wheels. Chrysto doesn't think it's going to be a problem. "There are cars everywhere," he says. "We will get one." When I ask him how we're going to pay for it he waves the question away. My job is to get the license. He'll work on getting the car. Chrysto's getting impatient. He wants to be off, westward bound. He doesn't understand why I can't just take the test and be done with it. "Because I'd like us to live," I told him.

Mr. Handy's frown deepens. "Look, Stahl," he says, not looking at me, "when you're ready to take the test—and I'm not saying you're ready—I can drive you over there. If you want."

He clears his throat and continues squinting. It's only three seconds later that I realize he's making an offer.

"Oh," I stammer. "I mean, thanks."

He nods and turns my way, still squinting, and his face raises up into a smile, a quick one, up and down, like a curtain.

"Thanks," I repeat.

Mr. Handy takes one long suck of his teeth and smacks his lips.

"All right," he says, "you can go."

≪ where r u? should I come over? ≫

No word from Chrysto, after two texts and one voice message. I was hoping to stop by before Acacia got home. I've already seen him this morning before rushing off to work. I see him as often as I can: after Acacia leaves for Venice Venice; when I get off work, late at night when Acacia's in bed; I'll even trek over there during my lunch break. I'll take the bus from Fremont Street to the monorail at the Stratosphere and then walk the six blocks just to say hello before running back. I can't help it. I need the fix.

This morning he was restless, uncomfortable, roaming from bed to table to couch without settling down anywhere. His face was, amazingly, almost healed, but his arm was still in a sling. With the other hand he picked at the bandage at his side like it was itching.

"What are you doing?" I asked.

"Off! Off!" he shouted, grabbing the gauze and tearing it away from his body in one move. The tape ripping off from his skin made him shout with pain, and he flung himself on the bed, panting with exertion and irritation.

"For someone so good at standing still you're pretty caffeinated," I told him.

He ran his hand over his head and grabbed a handful of black, spiraled curls. "For body to be still, mind must be still. For mind to be still, you must know absolutely you are in right place. I am losing this feeling!" He jumped up, anguished, and prowled around the room, hand batting the air. "I am not here, I am not there, I am nowhere!"

I almost knocked over a lamp getting to him. "You're exactly where you should be," I said. My hands did their own prowling. Ten minutes later, I left him on the bed, arm over his eyes, still enough.

Where is he now?

I look at my phone again, and there's some weird message flashing on the screen. I'm out of minutes. Shit. Three years, and I've used up all my time in just a few weeks. This disposable phone is ready to be disposed of. It's dead.

He could be calling me right now. Calling me and getting no answer.

I try not to panic. I fight the urge to take a taxi and race to his apartment. Go back home, I tell myself. Call Chrystostom's phone from there, not to bother him, just to tell him that my phone's not working. Maybe arrange for a get-together later on tonight. And, if I don't get him, I could stay in and spend some time with my father.

Or I could buy a new phone.

The 202 lumbers toward my destination. On each corner, a new adversary climbs aboard, intent on slowing down time itself: hordes of geriatrics; inept baby-stroller wranglers; bike wielders; gargantuan folk puffing up each step. They manage to snare our bus in every red light we come across.

To avoid watching this parade of disabilities, I pull out my sketchbook. Poor, neglected sketchbook. Truth is, there's not been much drawing lately. Our late-night sketch sessions in the unoccupied apartment (aka the Love Den) have produced more stimulation than art. Even now, when I open to a new white page, it's difficult to draw him. I know him with my hands now, with my mouth, not my pen. His image has been magnified in my mind, too large to contain on paper.

His eyes, though, I can still draw. The ones I watch watching me.

He likes me naked.

"Walter," he said to me last night, lying on the floor of the Love Den. "Never be ashamed of this body. Your skin is so soft, so smooth."

I scoff. I tell him I'd rather be muscled, hard like a rock, like him.

"But you have something everyone desires. You are young. Remember this, Walter. It is precious. It is power."

"Yeah, well, you're young, too," I said, running my hand down the impossibly taut line separating his stomach muscles.

"Of course I am," Chrysto says, revealing that wolfish smile from beneath his curling, luscious upper lip. "We are lucky, are we not?"

I'm at the Stop-N-Save by my house, picking up groceries. There are some staples we desperately need, like toilet paper instead of the Kleenex we've been using the past week. And since I'll be home early, I'll make my dad a home-cooked meal. I'll pick up spaghetti, some sauce, bread, maybe something sweet. He likes something sweet.

The Stop-N-Save also sells disposable phones.

I haven't seen much of my dad, but there've been signs of activity: tea mug on the table, TV on in the living room, exploded meal in the microwave. Trouble is, I'm rushing to get out the door in the mornings or stumbling in late at night, so we haven't had a lot of face-to-face time. I tell him I'm going to work, or out with friends, and he seems to buy the explanations.

I pop an extra box of Nabisco into the cart.

The disposable phones are on display by the checkout line.

My wallet's a little bulimic these days, spitting out cash as soon as I put some in. It's the bottles of beer and ouzo, the take-out food, the occasional taxi ride from my apartment to Chrysto's—it's adding up. Plus I've had to cut some hours at work to take my driving lessons. My salary's tinier than ever.

Food for my father, or a new phone. Get the food, of course, I think, but my hand's still holding the phone. I can't let go. It's like I'm waiting for it to ring. It's only when someone behind me asks, "Are you in line?" that I throw the phone back in the bin and shove my cart forward.

I rush out of the Stop-N-Save, but my steps get slower and slower the closer I get to home. I think of my father, sitting up at the kitchen table, waiting for me. What will he do when I leave? I tell myself that he's on an upswing, and the truth of it is, he *is* better. He's spending more and more time out of his room and on the couch; his appetite has returned. Maybe he's coming all the way back this time. It'll be like four years ago. He'll be able to leave the house. He'll be able to live alone. It'll all work out.

No use thinking about it now. Time enough to figure it all out when I pass the test. Just get the license.

All the same, when I push the front door open I'm relieved to see he's not on the couch. I peek into his room—he's asleep. If I'm lucky, I'll get ahold of Chrysto, make the spaghetti, plate it up, and be gone before my father wakes up.

Just as I reach for the phone it rings. The readout says BLOCKED CALLER, which has become synonymous with one person—Chrystostom. I'm so relieved he's called that I don't wonder how he got my home phone number.

"Hey," I say breathlessly, "I was just about to call you."

"Hello?" says the voice on the other end.

It's a woman's voice.

"I'm sorry," she continues, "I'm looking for Walt Stahl. Is he there?"

The prickling on the back of my neck. No one calls me Walt but my father. "This is he," I say.

"Are you, is your father Owen Stahl?" There's a slight tremor to her voice, but she lays down each word deliberately. Her voice is warm.

I nod in answer, and it's only four fast heartbeats later that I realize she can't hear a nod. I swallow to get some moisture back in my mouth. "Yes, it is, I mean, he is. My father."

There's a commotion on the other end of the line, and a muffled "Oh my God!" and then the only thing I hear on the phone is my own fast breathing. In out, in out, in out.

Finally, there's a scraping sound, a hand being taken from the receiver. She's back. "Could you, could you hold a moment, Walt?" she asks delicately. I nod again, but no reply's necessary, since she's already muffled the phone.

I'm perfectly still. Does that mean I'm exactly in the right place? I wonder. The only things I feel are my eyes, which have become two little reservoirs, filling up.

All this time I've been trying to figure out what my mother looked like, I never considered what she might sound like.

She'd sound like this.

There's an intake of breath on the other end of the line, a raspy, ragged breath: "Hello?" This is not my mother's voice. Her voice has been replaced on the line by someone who sounds like Mr. Handy, only wheezier. There's another strangulated breath.

"Hello?" I say.

"Is this Walt?" the person rasps.

"Yes," I reply.

Another wheeze. "This is Vee. Your grandmother. I'd like to meet you."

WALTER & VEE

I'm approaching forgotten territory. No monorail stops here. Even the bus passes by three blocks away. This hotel was one of the big casinos in its day, but now, as the colossal resorts have migrated north, it's been left dangling at the bottom, isolated and obsolete, the tailbone of the Strip. Where it once towered, it now hunkers down, unloved, marking time until the wrecking ball makes its way up the street.

When I finally make up my mind to push through the revolving doors, I'm surprised to find a light crowd. Its faded reputation must still have a little glow, like stars that keep twinkling years after they've actually died. There are a few shabby suits checking in, a couple of overheated families sitting on their luggage, and a backpacking German couple looking lost as they stare at the dim gallery of celebrity photos lining the wall.

I'm five minutes early, but instead of heading to the elevators I linger at the photo wall. Black-and-white pictures and color ones so washed out they may as well be black and white. I know most of these old dinosaurs—the same faded grins line the Wall of Fame at Viva—but still, I take my time, read each name off the little gold placards like I'm studying for a test. Liberace and his mirrored piano await me at the end of the row. His eyebrow raises in my direction; he taunts me with those dark, glittering eyes and that open mouth. What are you waiting for? he asks, that devil-may-care, diamond-encrusted hand sweeping the air. Directing me upward.

The elevator has no mirror or wallpaper. It smells, as the whole building does, of stale cigarettes and slightly rancid cooking oil. The glowing green light overhead patterns itself into digits, until it flashes mine. Ding.

The hallway on the sixth floor is dim and badly lit. The carpets and wallpaper have darkened into the same shade of dirty mauve. I pass a room service cart jutting out into the hall, abandoned. On the floor next to it is a white tablecloth with a dark red stain wadded against the wall.

There's not a sound.

Step by step by step by step. The hallway goes on forever. When I'm five rooms shy of my destination it occurs to me I should have brought something: flowers, candy, an offering. A black rooster ready for sacrifice. Maybe a bulb of garlic or a crucifix. I don't know. I wish I knew what I was getting into. I wish I could remember. Anything.

I'm here. My fingers touch the door. I can almost feel it breathing.

Tap. Tap.

The door opens almost immediately, but only a crack. A woman's face (not Vietnamese, not my mother) appears, quickly followed by her fingers, arms, torso, and then, ta-da, she's squeezed her entire self out on the other side of the door. Her wide hips are a surprise following such a skinny face. I throw her image into the black void that is my memory but nothing illuminates. She's no one I think I should know.

"Walter." Her smile is warm but rapid, like she's being fast-forwarded. She's older than her voice on the phone but not old enough to be Vee; maybe she's in her sixties. Her hair is straw-colored, gathered into one long braid that drapes over her shoulder. "We talked on the phone. My name's Jenny."

Jenny's wearing clothes that she'd roast in outside, a long denim skirt and a long-sleeved plaid blouse with a matching bow, plus a dark purple velour sweat jacket embroidered with LAS VEGAS that she's got wrapped over her shoulders like a shawl. She gives a little shiver for my benefit and pulls the sweat jacket tighter, fussing with it at her breastbone. Jenny's got nervous fingers.

"They keep the hotel so cold, we're not used to it," she says. "I had to go buy this downstairs." She blinks rapidly, then gives another quick smile. It might be a tic. "Vee's very—well, she's very excited to see you."

Jenny adjusts her glasses, then leans in closer, whispering: "Please be careful. She's not—"

"Jenny!" a voice growls from inside. "Bring him in here!"

The voice doesn't have much force behind it, but it carries.

Jenny opens the door and steps aside.

If there was going to be any flash of recognition, any long-locked memories jarred open, it would be now. I'm ready for my mind to crack apart. But all I see is an old person I don't recognize in a wheelchair by the window. It's hard to even tell the gender of who's staring at me behind those thick glasses. White hair cropped short and a body hunched into a shapeless cotton shirt, shrouded by the same purple sweat jacket Jenny's wearing.

She doesn't look anything like me, I think, before I remember that she wouldn't. Stupid.

There's no one else with her.

I stop in the middle of the room because it's the closest I want to get to the legendary Vee right now. She's ancient, as wrinkled as one of those dried apple dolls. People that old don't last long out here, I think. Out here they're laid out to bake and eventually fossilize and are mixed into the concrete to repair roads. Vee's been eroded by age, but you can tell by the way she grips her chair, chin thrust out, that what's left is pure steel.

Jenny warned me to be careful. For Vee, or of her?

She says nothing. Neither of us moves. I fight the urge to look around the room, to check and see if there's someone else here, hiding in the bathroom, maybe. Waiting.

Jenny can't tolerate the silence. "We arrived just a day ago," she chirps from behind me. "We're here with a church group. I know it must seem strange for a church group to be meeting down here, but it wasn't any more strange than for us to be joining them." Her smile comes and goes like a flickering light.

"Jenny!" Vee looks like she's waving a bony good-bye, but her trembling hand is really beckoning. She looks, for a moment, frightened. "Turn me around!" she demands, without taking her eyes off me. "Turn me around, Jenny!"

Jenny's there in an instant. She wheels Vee toward the window, away from me. Vee's hand claws upward and Jenny bends down to meet it. A loud, ragged gasp. "He's got a lot of her," Vee whispers hoarsely, as if I'm in the next room and not four feet away. "The eyes. The face. Her."

I wonder if this is the time Her is going to be showing herself, but Vee is already circling her arm about, demanding to be turned around again. Her face is wet, glistening eyes magnified by her glasses, but she stares at me defiantly, daring me to notice. Her mouth turns down like a bulldog's as she looks me over from head to toe. My shoes have never felt so shabby. She moistens her thin, quavering lips and smacks them shut. "There's a lot of him, too," she sniffs.

Jenny's perched by Vee's right side, her hand gently resting on Vee's shoulder. "That's fine. That's just fine," she says, about nothing in particular.

"I said I would never set foot in Las Vegas," Vee says, addressing me for the first time. "I meant it."

Jenny squeezes Vee's shoulder. "Well, it's lucky you're in a wheelchair, then, isn't it," she says brightly. Vee flicks Jenny's hand away, and it flies up, hovers uncertainly above Vee, and lands on the side of Jenny's still-beaming face.

"You ever wonder about me?" Vee says.

I shake my head.

"Why not?"

"I thought you were dead," I say.

Jenny's mouth forms an alarmed O but Vee cackle-coughs. "Not yet, not yet," she rasps. Her eyes narrow. "It'll happen soon enough."

Jenny flutters around Vee, all denials, but Vee cuts her off. "Jenny," she croaks, swinging her head to the side, "go down to the gift store."

"But I was just there, Vee—"

"Go again."

"I don't need anything."

Vee rumbles quietly, "Buy another thimble, Jen."

Jenny's hand touches down once more on Vee's shoulder, and Vee meets it, briefly, with her own. "All right, then," Jenny says.

The door snicks closed. I'm alone in the room with Vee. This is the time, I think. The curtains part, my mother steps out. Camera close-ups. Studio audience applause.

"You look exactly the same," Vee declares.

"That's not likely," I say softly.

"Manners," she says. Then: "You remember me at all?"

I shake my head.

Vee snorts weakly. "You didn't just lie in a coma those first five years, you know," she tells me. "You were old enough to remember something. Come here." I step next to her chair and she jabs a finger, surprisingly hard, into a faint crescent-shaped scar, pale on the fleshy part of my thumb. "Canning jar—in the basement," she says. She presses it again, as if it is the button that will release this and other memories.

It doesn't. There is no time with her that registers with me, even after she runs down her list of heroics—the ice bath to cool the fever that stayed for days, the slow rocking and the quick back pats to lull me to sleep—none of these catch on any part of my consciousness. She evokes no feeling in me. She smells of age, and sourness.

Vee finishes her trip down memory lane. I just stand there. I've got nothing to add. She glares at me, clearly disappointed. The silence congeals around us.

And then, suddenly, she breaks it.

"What about your mother?"

Here we come to it. That one question: a surge strong enough to pull me up and over the cliff.

"What about her?" I say slowly.

"You remember anything?"

I shake my head.

"Why not?"

I look at the floor. "I don't even know what she looks like."

"What? Don't you have any pictures of her?"

I shake my head again, and this sets off a palsy in Vee. Her lips are pressed together tight but her body trembles. She balls her hands into fists. She looks like she's about to explode.

"So that's how he wants it," she says tightly. "It's square one with you. Maybe that's better."

"It's not," I say thickly.

She shrugs. "Too late now."

And that's when I know it; there's no one else here, no one about to pull back the curtains and reveal herself, at last. This has been a complete waste of time. I want to get out. I want to find Chrysto and hide in the Love Den. I want to go home.

"Is there something you want to know?" Vee asks.

Her question feels like a slap. She's deliberately withholding information. She wants me to beg for it. I hate her.

I shake my head.

"Well, then, I'm here to square up some things." She adjusts her glasses, all business. "You're going to be eighteen in a few days, that right?"

I nod, surprised that she remembers, that anyone remembers.

Slowly, Vee pulls out a manila folder hidden by her side. She lays it on her lap, unopened. It's got my name on it, written dark in Magic Marker. "First off. Jenny's getting the house. She's been there ten years, it's as much hers as anyone's. And it's not like you've got any attachment to it."

I don't know what she's talking about. Why is she bringing up houses?

"There are a few things in it, though, you might want to take a look at. Things Jenny's got no use for, but you might. Might not. After that, the rest is yours, when I'm gone. Not much, but it's something. You have a banking account?"

There's a gap here, something missing. I feel the sharp edges of it without allowing myself to see it entire.

"It's for you, you understand? Not your father. He wants to cut himself off, that's his business. But my money is my business and I'm leaving it to you."

"Why?" I ask.

Vee frowns and blinks three times. "You're family, Walt," she says flatly. "That's what family does."

"But what about—" But I can't continue. My mouth is tight, about to begin a question I don't know how to finish. She looks at me, taking in all my agitation without reflecting any of it back.

"What about what?" she asks.

I take a deep breath, force the air out sharply. "My mother."

"What about her?"

I stare at her straight on.

"Something you want to know?" asks Vee.

"Jesus!" I want to strangle her. "Do you know what happened to her?"

Vee looks at me like I'm crazy. "Of course I know what happened to her. I buried her myself, didn't I?"

There's actual pain. Physical. Sharp. Vee looks at me, indifferent. Irritated. Like it was the stupidest question in the world.

I finally find my voice, crouching way way down at the back of my throat. "You could have, you could have told us, you know."

"What?" she says, like she can't understand what I'm saying.

I jerk forward. "You. Could. Have. Told. Us!" I shout, shoving each word into her face.

Vee doesn't flinch. Her lips are tight, her eyes cold and unblinking, reptilian. She looks right back, but she's staring through me, she's somewhere else. Then she gets her mouth moving, and when she finally speaks, her words are low and measured.

"Boy. Don't lay this at my door." She flicks out her tongue and dabs it over her lips. "Ask your father. Let him tell you the facts."

Then she focuses in on me, gives me her half-lidded gaze, strong enough to petrify. "He's the one who brought her body home. And you were there when he did it."

The world freezes.

Vee continues, cold, unstoppable. "They found her in the bathroom of the Liberace Museum. Of all places. She drove down there—Lord knows why—in one shot, no stopping. Just like her. Drove to this god-damned city, went straight into the goddamned museum, took out your father's goddamned pills and swallowed them all. I got the call that day. Sent your father down to bring my baby girl home."

Her neck muscles constrict and release as she swallows down noth-ing. Her eyes are as dry as the Vegas sands.

"Anything else you want to know?"

~ Though the time has come for us to part, you always will remain within my heart ~

AT THIRTY-EIGHT, I CAN SEE THE RAGGED EDGES OF THE TALE, PULL ON ITS THREADS, BUT WHAT EIGHTEEN-YEAR-OLD FACT-CHECKS THE FUNDAMENTAL TRUTHS OF HIS EXISTENCE?

THE EARTH ISN'T REALLY ROUND.

STARING DIRECTLY AT THE SUN DOES YOU NO HARM.

You'll be always near somehow ~

~So please don't shed a tear, say ciao ~

THIS MUCH I DO KNOW, NOW: THERE WAS NO FLOOD. THE VENETIAN HAD CLOSED DOWN FOR RENOVATIONS, NOT FROM ANY ACT OF GODS.

Time

will disappear ~

WE ACTUALLY LIVE ON THE BACK OF TURTLES, PILED ONE ATOP ANOTHER.

AND YES, MY SISTER GEORGIA DIED A LONELY DEATH IN THE BACK SEAT OF THE FAMILY CAR. SHE WAS NOT, IN THE TRADITIONAL SENSE, KILLED IN A CAR ACCIDENT, AS WAS TOLD TO ME.

I WAS RIGHT, IN A WAY. BUT IT HASN'T STOPPED ME FROM TRYING TO PIECE THEM TOGETHER, ALL THESE YEARS LATER, SHARD BY BLOODY SHARD.